P9-CEN-808

# Praise for
# gods in Alabama

"Hip . . . sassy . . . endearing."
—*Atlanta Journal-Constitution*

"Masterfully constructed . . . has more twists and turns than a wiggle worm at the end of a small hook . . . The story intertwines Arlene's present and past—drives the novel to an intense and shocking conclusion."
—*Orlando Sentinel* (FL)

"Jackson writes with a crisp voice and has a flair for language."
—*Washington Post Book World*

"Sure-handed writing and a bawdy sense of humor that never loses its Southern charm . . . a book full of self-deprecating, blue-collar humor that conjures up the modern South."
—*Milwaukee Journal-Sentinel*

"An appealing and confident debut novel, filled with humor and unexpected twists of fate . . . both witty and wise about the tangled relationships among women, mothers and daughters, aunts and cousins—whether they're steel magnolias or down-home sweethearts."
—*New Orleans Times-Picayune*

"Required reading."
—*New York Post*

"Put some Drive-By Truckers on the stereo for this bumpy ride through the dirty South."
—*Entertainment Weekly*

*more . . .*

"A compelling, darkly humorous read that kept me turning the pages."
— Haywood Smith, bestselling author of *The Red Hats Ride Again*

"GODS IN ALABAMA has everything a first (or any) novel should possess but seldom does: an engaging plot, a protagonist whose original voice has you alternately laughing out loud and misting up, and a vividly etched sense of place . . . What really elevates GODS, though, is Joshilyn Jackson's fresh, unpredictable way with words. She writes so creatively that you slow down, because every sentence is a delight of some sort . . . GODS IN ALABAMA leaves readers grateful for the journey and smiling at the redemptive powers of love."
— *Cleveland Plain Dealer*

"A fresh voice."
— *Albany Times Union*

"A compelling first novel that happens to have one of the most striking characters you'll ever encounter . . . Arlene's sassy, guilt-ridden voice never fails to engage or surprise."
— *Virginian-Pilot*

"Forget steel magnolias—meet titanium blossoms in Jackson's debut novel, a potent mix of humor, murder, and a dysfunctional Southern family."
— *Library Journal* (starred review)

"This winning novel is the kind that readers crave: you can't stop turning the pages, but you wish it would never end."
— Christina Schwarz, author of *Drowning Ruth* and *All Is Vanity*

"Scores with Arlene's honest and tongue-in-cheek narration . . . passionate dialogue . . . interesting characters . . . a breezy, fun read . . . one of the best-plotted books I've read recently—a page-turner that succeeds and thrives from strong writing."
— *Florida Times-Union*

"Joshilyn Jackson's story of friendship, murder, love, and betrayal is as rich and mysterious as Spanish moss. A knockout first novel full of astonishing surprises."

—Lolly Winston, author of *Good Grief*

"Cleverly disguised as a leisurely paced Southern novel, this debut rockets to the end, even as the plot turns back on itself, surprising characters and readers alike."

—*Booklist*

"Vibrant, endearingly screwed up, funny and fierce, Arlene gets you on her side . . . a mess on two feet, nonetheless, she's a blessing."

—*The State* (SC)

"The writing in this sometimes hilarious, sometimes heartbreaking book is disarming and fresh; the voices are authentic; and the story has more surprising twists than a patch of kudzu."

—*Birmingham News*

"Read the startling first sentence of GODS IN ALABAMA, then try to put it down."

—Cassandra King, author of *The Sunday Wife*

"A frank, appealing debut . . . Jackson brings levity to familiar themes with a spirited take on the clichés of redneck Southern living: the Wal-Mart culture, the subtle and overt racism, and the indignant religion."

—*Publishers Weekly*

"Wild, salacious, and hard to put down . . . Reading the book is like sitting on your neighbor's porch, drinking lemonade, and listening to all the good gossip . . . a great new voice for Southern literature. Joshilyn Jackson's sweet, sassy, smart Southern voice is one that will resonate for those born and raised below the Mason-Dixon and Yankees alike."

—*Arkansas Democrat-Gazette*

*more . . .*

"Joshilyn Jackson tells the searing tale of a young woman who faces her demons and finds her angels. GODS IN ALABAMA is a courageous debut from a talented new voice."
—Valerie Ann Leff, author of *Better Homes and Husbands*

"An absolute joy to read . . . This debut novel is as Southern as tomato sandwiches, sweet tea, and hot, muggy summers."
—*Anniston Star* (AL)

"I couldn't put this book down. From the first chapter, the plot leaps forward, and it doesn't stop twisting and turning until the last page . . . Funky and cool."
—Melanie Sumner, author of *The School of Beauty and Charm*

"Jackson masterfully combines mystery, humor, dramatic irony, social conscience, and prejudice in a plot that pushes the reader to gobble up every fact and action through the startling end."
—*Decatur Daily* (AL)

"Some books just suck you in from the get-go, and this is one of them . . . Thought-provoking."
—*Jackson Free Press* (MS)

"GODS IN ALABAMA is a roller-coaster of a book that takes the reader on a wild ride, right up until the end!"
—Rosemary Daniell, author of *Fatal Flowers: On Sin, Sex and Suicide in the Deep South; Sleeping with Soldiers;* and *Confessions of a Female Chauvinist*

"This novel has deep shadows and sharp edges. And if you're not careful, it will break your heart."
—*Creative Loafing* (GA)

# gods

# in

# Alabama

JOSHILYN JACKSON

WARNER BOOKS

NEW YORK   BOSTON

If you purchase this book without a cover you should be aware that this book may have been stolen property and reported as "unsold and destroyed" to the publisher. In such case neither the author nor the publisher has received any payment for this "stripped book."

This book is a work of fiction. Names, characters, places, and incidents are the product of the author's imagination or are used fictitiously. Any resemblance to actual events, locales, or persons, living or dead, is coincidental.

Copyright © 2005 by Joshilyn Jackson
Reading Group Guide copyright © 2006 by Warner Books Inc.
"Nothing Says Love Like a Tequila Bottle Upside the Head" copyright © 2006 by Joshilyn Jackson
Excerpt from *Between, Georgia* copyright © 2006 by Joshilyn Jackson

All rights reserved. Except as permitted under the U.S. Copyright Act of 1976, no part of this publication may be reproduced, distributed, or transmitted in any form or by any means, or stored in a database or retrieval system, without the prior written permission of the publisher.

Warner Books
Hachette Book Group USA
1271 Avenue of the Americas
New York, NY 10020

Visit our Web site at www.HachetteBookGroupUSA.com.

Printed in the United States of America

Originally published in hardcover by Warner Books, an imprint of Warner Books, Inc.
First Trade Edition: June 2006
10   9   8   7

Warner Books and the "W" logo are trademarks of Time Warner Inc. or an affiliated company. Used under license by Hachette Book Group USA, which is not affiliated with Time Warner Inc.

The Library of Congress has cataloged the hardcover edition as follows:
Jackson, Joshilyn.
        Gods in Alabama / Joshilyn Jackson.
        p. cm.
        ISBN 0-446-52419-0
        1. Quarterbacks (Football)—Crimes against—Fiction. 2. Interracial dating—Fiction.
3. Women murderers—Fiction. 4. Chicago (Ill.)—Fiction 5. Young women—Fiction.
6. Alabama—Fiction. I. Title.

        PS3610.A3525G63 2005
        813'.6—dc22

                                                                    2004053589

*Cover design by Anne Twomey*

ISBN-13: 978-0-446-69453-7 (pbk.)
ISBN-10: 0-446-69453-3 (pbk.)

For Betty before me and Maisy after

writer that will come out of my generation, and she's also graced with a fine critical eye. Lydia Netzer, Jill James, Jill "~" Patrick, Julie Oestreich, Nancy Meshkoff, and everyone in the In Town Atlanta Writers' Group (especially Crime Fiction writer Fred Willard, Diane Thomas, Bill Osher, Linda Clopton, Anne Webster, Anne Lovett, Skip Connett, Jim Taylor, Jim Harmon, and Barbara Knott) were invaluable in getting this book polished. I learned about character from Dr. Yolanda Reed (and the rest of the crew at Pensacola's Loblolly Theatre) and Ruth Replogle and Dr. Natalie Crohn Schmitt. I could not work without the support I get from my community at PSFUMC.

It's almost a given that a Southern writer needs a savage and spectacularly dysfunctional family, but I am afraid mine has failed me. Every one of them is disappointingly mentally stable and supportive. Scott Winn is my sweetheart and my spine. Betty Jackson always takes my side. Bob Jackson is my hero—to this day my conscience speaks in his voice. For the record, Bobby Jackson is wrong and Julie, Daniel, Erin, and I are right.

Samuel Jackson and Maisy Jane did absolutely nothing to help me write this book. In fact they dragged me away from work at every possible opportunity and made me go look at bugs. I thank God for them.

# ACKNOWLEDGMENTS

A novel is a process, and the only portion of it I understand is the part where you sit down and write it. After that, it turns out there are all these other things that must be done, and quite frankly, they scare the pants off me. In order to do these other parts, you have to be many things that I am not, like savvy and discerning and brave.

I was as gormless and dewy as a bunch of ducklings, and I was lucky enough to imprint Jacques de Spoelberch, my magical agent. He did the parts that I didn't know how to do, and he did them beautifully, and then he walked me over to Caryn Karmatz Rudy at Warner. If you close your eyes and wish for the perfect editor, and if you've been very, very good your whole life, Caryn might appear. If, like me, you haven't been very, very good your whole life, you'll have to get Jacques to go find her.

Many thanks also to hand-holding editorial assistant Emily Griffin. Production editor Penina Sacks pulled a thousand details into a coherent whole, and copy editor Beth Thomas valiantly took on My Tendency to Randomly Capitalize.

I have a crew of readers who alternately jollied and kicked this book along. Lily James is, I promise you, a contender for the best

# gods

## in

# Alabama

# CHAPTER

## 1

THERE ARE GODS in Alabama: Jack Daniel's, high school quarterbacks, trucks, big tits, and also Jesus. I left one back there myself, back in Possett. I kicked it under the kudzu and left it to the roaches.

I made a deal with God two years before I left there. At the time, I thought He made out pretty well. I offered Him a three-for-one-deal: All He had to do was perform a miracle. He fulfilled His end of the bargain, so I kept my three promises faithfully, no matter what the cost. I held our deal as sacred for twelve solid years. But that was before God let Rose Mae Lolley show up on my doorstep, dragging my ghosts and her own considerable baggage with her.

It was the week before summer vacation began, and my uncle Bruster was getting ready to retire. He'd been schlepping the mail up and down Route 19 for thirty years and now, finally, he was going to get a gold watch, a shitty pension, and the federal government's official permission to die. His retirement party was looming, and my aunt Florence was using it as the catalyst for her latest campaign to get me home. She launched these crusades three or four times a year, usually prompted by major holidays or family events.

I had already explained multiple times to Mama that I wasn't coming. I shouldn't have had to explain it at all. I had not gone back to Possett since I graduated from high school in '87. I had stayed in Chicago for nine Christmas vacations, had not come home for nine spring breaks, had faithfully signed up to take or teach classes every summer quarter for ten years. I had avoided weekend fly-downs for the births, graduation ceremonies, and weddings of various cousins and second cousins. I had even claimed exemption from attending the funerals of my asshole grampa and his wife, Saint Granny.

At this point, I figured I had firmly established that I would not be coming home, even if all of Chicago was scheduled to be consumed by the holy flames of a vengeful Old Testament–style Lord. "Thanks for the invite, Mama," I would say, "but I have plans to be burned up in a fire that weekend." Mama, however, could wipe a conversation out of her mind an infinite number of times and come back to the topic fresh as a daisy the next time we spoke.

Burr had his feet propped up on my battered coffee table and was reading a legal thriller he had picked up at the grocery store. In between an early movie and a late supper, we had dropped by my place to intercept Florence's eight o'clock call. Missing it was not an option. I called Aunt Florence every Sunday after church, and every Wednesday night, Flo parked my mother by the phone and dialed my number. I wouldn't put it past Florence to hire a team of redneck ninjas to fly up to Chicago and take me down if she ever got my answering machine.

Florence had not yet mentioned my uncle's retirement to me directly, although she had prepped Mama to ask me if I was coming home for it through six weeks' worth of calls now. With only ten days left before the party, it was time for Aunt Florence to personally enter the fray. Mama was so malleable she was practically an invertebrate, but Florence had giant man hands on the ends of her bony wrists, and she could squeeze me with them till I couldn't get any breath to say no. Even over the phone she could do it.

Burr watched me over the top of his book as I paced the room. I was too nervous about my upcoming martyrdom on the stainless-steel cross of Florence to sit down with him. He was sunk hip deep into my sofa. My apartment was decorated in garage-sale chic, the default decorating choice for every graduate student. The sofa had curlicues of moss-colored velvet running all over its sage-green hide, and it was so deflated and aslant that Burr swore he only ever kissed me the first time because of it. We sat down on it at the same time, and it sucked us down and pressed us up against each other in its sagging middle. He had to kiss me, he claimed, to be polite.

"About how long do you think this is going to take?" Burr asked now. "I'm starving."

I shrugged. "Just the usual Wednesday-night conversation with Mama."

"Okay," said Burr.

"And then I have to have a fight with Aunt Florence about whether or not I'm going down for Uncle Bruster's party."

"In that case," said Burr, and he levered himself out of the depths of the sofa and walked the five steps to my kitchenette. He opened the cabinet and started rummaging around for something to tide himself over.

"It's not going to take that long," I said.

"Sure, baby," he said, and took a pack of peanut-butter crackers back over to the sofa. He sat down with his book but didn't open it for a moment. "Try to keep it under four hours," he said. "I need to talk to you about something at dinner."

I stopped pacing around. "Is it bad?" I asked, nervous because he'd said it in such a serious tone of voice. He could mean he wanted to break up again or he could mean he was going to propose to me. We'd broken up last year over Christmas and both hated it so much that we'd found ourselves drifting back together casually, without even really talking about it. We'd been coasting along easy for a few months now, but Burr would not coast forever. We had to be going somewhere, and if he thought we weren't, then that would be it for him.

I said, "You know I hate that. You have to give me a hint."

Burr grinned at me, and his brown eyes were warm. "Don't panic."

"Okay," I said. I felt something flutter down low in my stomach, excitement or fear, I wasn't sure which, and then the phone rang.

"Dammit," I said. The phone was on a crate full of books at the other end of the ugly sofa. I sat down next to Burr and picked it up. "Hello?"

"Arlene, honey! You remember Clarice?"

Clarice was my first cousin, and we were raised in the same house, practically as sisters. Mama was possibly the only person on earth who could have asked this question sans sarcasm to a

gods in Alabama

daughter who had not been home in almost a decade. Aunt Florence would have gotten a lot of miles out of it, and in fact I couldn't help but wonder if Aunt Florence hadn't somehow planted the question in the fertile minefields of my mother's mind.

It was not unlike the Christmas card Mama had sent me for the last five years. It had a red phone on it, and it said, in bright red curling text, "Daughter! Do you remember that man I introduced you to the day you were born? Why don't you give him a call? I know he never hears from you, and today's his birthday." Open it up and there, in giant candy-striped letters, was a one-word explanation for the terminally stupid: "Jesus," it said. Three exclamation points.

Mama got those abominations from the Baptist Women's League for Plaguing Your Own Children to Death in the Name of the Lord or whatever her service club was called. My aunt Florence was, of course, the president. And my aunt Florence, of course, bought Mama's cards for her, held them out for her to sign, licked the envelopes, got stamps from Uncle Bruster, and mailed them for her. In Florence's eyes, I was on the high road to apostasy because my church was American Baptist, not Southern Baptist.

But all I said was "Obviously I know Clarice, Mama."

"Well, Clarice wants to know if you can drive over to the home and pick up your great-great-aunt Mag on Friday next. Mag needs someone to carry her over to the Quincy's for your uncle Bruster's party."

I said, "Are you seriously telling me that Clarice wants to know if I'll drive fourteen hours down from Chicago, and then go another hour to Vinegar Park, where by the way Clarice lives, and

5

pick up Aunt Mag, who will no doubt piss in my rental car, and then backtrack forty-five minutes to Quincy's?"

"Yes, but please don't say 'piss,' it isn't nice," my mother said, deadly earnest. "Also, Clarice and Bud moved on in to Fruiton. So it's a good forty minutes for her to go get Mag now."

"Oh, well then. Why don't you tell Aunt Florence—I mean Clarice—that I will be sure to go pick up Mag. Right after Aunt Flo drops by hell and picks up the devil."

Burr was jammed deep into the sofa with his book open, but his eyes had stopped moving over the text. He was too busy trying to laugh silently without choking to death on his peanut-butter cracker.

"Arlene, I am not repeating blasphemy," said my mother mildly. "Florence can ask Fat Agnes to get Mag, and you can drive me."

Oh, Aunt Florence was crafty. Asking my mother to have this conversation with me was tantamount to taping a hair-trigger pistol to a kitten's paw. The kitten, quite naturally, shakes its fluffy leg, and bullets go flying everywhere; a few are bound to hit something. I was, after all, talking with my mama about whether or not I would pick up Mag, not whether or not I was coming. A cheap trap worthy of Burr's legal thriller, and I had bounced right into it.

"I can't drive you, Mama," I said gently. Why shoot the messenger? "I won't be there."

"Oh, Arleney," my mother said, sounding vaguely sad. "Aren't you ever coming home for a visit?"

"Not this time, Mama," I said.

Mama made a pensive little noise and then said, in a cheerier voice, "Oh well, I will just look double forward to Christmas, then!" That I hadn't been home for the last nine Christmases was not a factor in Mama's fogbound equations. Before I could even try a quick "Love you, bye" and escape, I heard Aunt Florence's voice barking in the background, and then Mama said, "Here's Aunt Flo's turn!"

I heard the rustle of the phone changing hands, and then Aunt Florence's muffled voice asking Mama to please go check the Bundt cake. There was a brief pause where my mother presumably wafted out of the room, and then Aunt Florence took her hand off the mouthpiece and said in a disarmingly affectionate tone, "Hello, serpent."

"Hi, Aunt Florence," I said.

"Do you know why I am calling you 'serpent,' serpent?"

"I couldn't begin to guess, Aunt Florence," I said.

"I am referencing a Bible verse. Do they have the Bible at that American Baptist church?"

"I believe I may have seen one there once," I said. "No doubt it fled the moment it realized where it was. As I recall, it had a lot of serpents in it, and I am sure I could justly be called many of them."

Burr was still amused. I busted him looking at me, and I gestured at his book. He stifled his grin and turned his eyes virtuously back to the pages.

Aunt Florence, adopting a low and holy voice, intoned, "How like a serpent you have nestled to your bosom is a thankless child."

"That's not the Bible, Aunt Florence. You're misquoting *King Lear.*"

"Do you realize that the women in our service group at church all sit around nattering like biddy hens about what horrors your poor mama—and me—must have inflicted on your head to make her only girl-child flee the state, never to return? Do you realize the vicious things those biddies say about your poor, poor mama? And me?"

"No, Aunt Florence, I didn't realize," I said, but Aunt Florence wasn't listening. She barked on and on into my ear, etc. etc. you-a culpa with breast beating and a side of guilt. Who did I think had put bread in my mouth? Uncle Bruster and his mail route. And now all he wanted was for his family to gather and eat buffet dinner at the Quincy's in his honor. I countered by asking Florence to please pass Bruster the phone so I could tell him how proud of him I was right this second.

Florence wasn't about to give up the phone, not even to her husband. She shifted gears abruptly, dropping her voice to a reverent whisper as she segued into the "Your mama will probably be dead by next year" theme, asking sorrowfully how I would feel if I missed this last chance to see her. I pointed out that she'd used that argument for nine years running and Mama hadn't died yet.

Burr set his book down and reached across me to grab the pad and pencil I kept on the crate by the phone. He scrawled something down on the top page and then tore it off and passed it to me. The note said "Say yes to the trip and let's go eat."

I crumpled it up and bounced it off his chest, sticking my tongue out at him.

"You don't know how bad off she is, Arlene," Florence said. "She's failing bad. She looks like the walking dead. She's been to the hospital to stay twice this year."

"The real hospital?" I said. "Or the place in Deer Park?"

"It's a real hospital," said Florence defensively.

"Real hospitals don't have padded walls in the card room," I countered. Burr uncrumpled the piece of paper and held it up like a sign, pointing to the words one at a time, in order. I shook my head at him and then dropped my head forward to hide behind my long dark hair. "It isn't just that I am not coming. I can't come. I don't have the money to make the trip down right this second."

I peeked up at Burr. He narrowed his eyes at me and touched two fingers to his chin. This was code, lifted from his mock-trial days back in law school. It meant "I am in possession of two contradictory facts." I knew what he was referencing. Fact one: Burr knew that as of last week I had almost three thousand in savings. Fact two: Burr knew I didn't tell lies. Ever. I pointed at him, then touched my chin with one finger, signaling that there was no paradox; one of his facts was off.

Aunt Florence talked about wire transfers and loans and me getting off my butt and taking a part-time job while Burr thought it through. After a moment a light dawned, and he got up and walked towards my front door, looking at me with his eyebrows raised. I braced the phone against my shoulder and clutched my arms around my middle, pantomiming that I was freezing. I realized there was silence on the other end of the line, and I hurried to fill it.

"Aunt Florence, you know I won't take your money—"

"Oh no, just the food off my table and a bed in my house your whole childhood."

Burr reversed direction and went to my kitchenette. I pretended I was even colder, wrapping an imaginary blanket around myself.

"The school pays me a stipend and a housing allowance, plus my tuition," I said into the phone. "It's not like I'm on welfare."

Burr walked the four steps past my kitchenette, back to the doorway into the walk-in closet my Yankee landlord called a bedroom. I mopped imaginary sweat from my brow and threw the invisible blanket off, then fanned myself. He disappeared through the doorway, and I could hear him rummaging around, feet padding on the scuffed hardwood as he searched.

"No," I said into the phone, "I don't think this rates a special collection at church."

But maybe it did. Florence was getting to me a little. She always could. I thought of my uncle Bruster, with his wispy blond tufts combed over his bald spot, his big belly, his broad sloping shoulders. Bruster looked like what would happen if the bear got over on the mountain and they had a baby. He had the Lukey blue eyes, large and powder blue and a little moist-looking, and when I was eleven, he had been my date to the Possett First Baptist Father-Daughter Pancake Brunch. Clarice had been on his other arm, but he had pulled out my chair for me and called me Little Lady all morning.

I heard my closet door squeak open, and then a pause that Florence filled with alternating sentiment and invective. The closet door shut, and Burr came back in the room toting the Computer City bag with my new laptop in it. He pantomimed a whistle, looking impressed, but I didn't believe it. Something else was going on in his head as he stared down at the laptop in its bag. I couldn't tell what he was thinking.

Burr was a good lawyer and an even better poker player. He and I used to play a card game we made up called Five-Card Minor Sexual Favor Stud, but I quit for two reasons. One, it led us too far down a path that could only end in frustration and a whomping great fight. And two, he almost always won.

Burr sat back down and put the bag on the coffee table. He picked up his book again, but he wasn't reading, and he wouldn't meet my eyes.

Eventually, against all odds, Aunt Florence got to the part where she told me she would be praying to God, asking Him to help me not be such a selfish little turd. Then she let me get off the phone. I gave her a vague promise about taking a hard look at my summer course schedule and seeing if I could squeeze in a trip home sometime before fall. Aunt Florence's final skeptical snort was still ringing in my ears as I hung up.

"That's a speedy machine," Burr said casually, indicating the bag. "You really are broke."

"Yup," I said. I had cleaned myself out to buy it. In fact, I bought it to clean myself out.

"Lucky I'm not," said Burr.

"Very lucky, since you're taking me to dinner," I said. I got up, but Burr stayed wedged down in the sofa.

"That's not what I meant," he said. "Lena, remember I said I wanted to talk to you about something at dinner?"

"Yes?" I said, and all at once the flutter was back. I was standing up, already looking down at him. I was wondering if there was room between the sofa and the coffee table for him to slide down onto one knee, or if I should move out from behind the coffee table to give him space.

"I think I better ask you now," he said, and his dark eyes were very serious. Burr had nice eyes, but they were small and square. I never noticed how sweet they were until I got close enough to kiss him. His face wasn't about his eyes. It was about his cheek-bones and his sharply narrow jaw, severe enough to contrast with his wide, soft mouth, with the gorgeous teeth his mama paid eight thousand dollars to straighten. "I'm a little nervous."

"You don't have to be nervous," I said, but I was nervous as all hell.

"Take your aunt Florence out of the equation, and your mama. Take everything out of the equation but you and me. If I said it was important to me, would you take the trip down to Alabama for this party next week?" Burr asked.

I sat down again abruptly. "What?" I said.

"I can pay for the trip."

"I can't let you pay for me to go down and see my family," I said.

"I wouldn't be," he said. "I would be paying for both of us to make the trip."

"I can't let you do that, either," I said.

"Can't or won't?" he said. He was smiling, but I could read him now, and underneath the smile he was angry.

"Won't," I agreed. There is a big, fat downside to never telling a lie.

"Don't worry," Burr said, gesturing at the laptop, still smiling his beautiful, angry smile. "Computer City has a ten-day no-questions return policy." He stood up and stalked around the coffee table away from me. "Because obviously you have no intention of keeping this thing."

"No, of course not," I agreed. And immediately the words "There are gods in Alabama" rolled through my head so powerfully that I thought I was going to say them aloud, but Burr stopped them by speaking again.

"Lena, if you won't take me down and introduce me to your family, we're coming to a dead end."

"But I love you," I said. It came out flat and wrong, though I was remembering how it was with us when we made out on the sofa in the late nights when Burr came over after I'd studied myself sick. I was thinking of how we were together when his huge hands were on me, and we both knew the rules.

His hands were so big, Burr could practically span my waist with them. And he had a jet-rocket metabolism, so his skin was always liquid hot to the touch. His big hands would slide over my body, slipping up or down into forbidden zones. As he touched me, I could see in my mind the flex of the muscles, how the dim light would reflect on the shifting planes of his hands as they moved on me. And I could take my hand and push that big hand away, down off my breasts, onto my waist. Guide it so slowly out from between my legs onto my thigh. His hands always went where mine told them to go, immediately, no matter what. The power of that, the ability or maybe the permission to move something so much stronger than me, left me light-headed and feeling something I couldn't name, but it was close kin to longing. Eventually I would have to shove him away, push him out the door with hasty little kisses, both of us dying of wanting to and not, both of us laughing.

Burr said, "You say that a lot." He was standing by the front door, looking at a point somewhere just over my left shoulder. He sometimes did that when he was ticked off, carry on a fight while peering moodily off at the horizon, as brooding and ugly-beautiful as Heathcliff thinking, "Oh! The moors! The moors!"

I said, "If I didn't love you, I wouldn't say it at all. You know I don't lie."

"There are a lot of things you say you don't do, Lena," he answered. "You don't lie, and you don't fuck, and you don't take your boyfriend home to meet your family. You say you love me, but you have a hundred ways to avoid the truth without ever lying." He pointed at the laptop on the table. "Case in point. Today you tell your aunt that you're broke, and tomorrow you return that and get your money back. And that's what you call telling the truth."

"No, it's what I call not lying. There is a difference, you know. I am not under any obligation to tell anyone everything. I just don't lie, which is more than ninety percent of the freakin' world can say, and anyway, why are we having this fight? Why did you this minute decide I need to take you to my uncle's retirement party? That's not what I thought you were going to ask me."

Burr said, "Maybe it's not what I planned to ask you, either. But Lena, I watched you work your aunt over, and I found myself wondering—not for the first time—how often you work me, to keep me out of the middle of your life."

"First of all, Possett, Alabama, is not the middle of my life. It is not my home. It's the fourth rack of hell. I don't go there myself, let alone want to take you—"

"Look at your phone bill," Burr said.

"And second of all," I went on as if he had not spoken, "I don't see the connection between not having sex with you and taking you to Alabama."

"It's what women do when they fall in love with a man," Burr said. "They have sex with him, or they take him home to meet their family. In point of fact, Lena, most women do both."

"But my family is insane," I said in what I hoped was a reasonable tone. "Why would you want to meet them?"

"Because they're yours," he said matter-of-factly, one hand reaching for the doorknob. "I thought you were mine."

I was instantly furious. It was too good a line, a movie line. People don't get to say smashing things and then walk out in real life. Burr could say crap like that more often than most because of his low-slung basso profundo voice. He could say hyper-dramatic lines that, if I said them, would have whole crowds rolling on the floor, shrieking with laughter and telling me to get over myself. But Burr? He could say "Luke, I am your father," and get away with it.

But not with me.

"Don't you dare try to Rhett Butler your way out the door in the middle of a fight," I said, getting up and coming around the coffee table after him.

He let go of the doorknob and said, "You've never so much as mentioned my name to your folks, but you spend half your free time at my mama's house. You won't be my lover, but you can't keep your hands off me until I'm clinically insane. I'm a twenty-nine-year-old man, Lena. Not some fifteen-year-old kid who says he loves you in the hopes of seeing his first tit."

I said, "It isn't that I don't love you. But I swear before God, you don't want to make this trip. It would be like stepping into a soap opera, except no one is beautiful or rich or interesting. If we went down there, you have to know what it would be like. I mean, come on, Burr, what do you see when you look at us?"

Burr said, "I always saw the best couple going. The question is, what do you see?"

"Same thing," I said. "But that is not what they are going to see down in Possett, Alabama. They'll look at me and see that weird Arlene Fleet who was never any better than she should be, and when they look at you, they'll see that nigger she's fucking."

Burr smiled a little and said, "But I'm not fucking you."

15

"Well, we could maybe get you a T-shirt that says you aren't, but they wouldn't believe it, because why else would I be with you? It can't be that you're smart, or handsome, or interesting, or successful, because you can't be any of those things when you're in Possett, Alabama. You will be much too busy being black. When you're with my family, being black is such a big job, it takes up your entire definition. You don't get to be anything else.

"If I show up home, wanting to bring my black boyfriend to my uncle Bruster's good-ol'-boy retirement party, they're going to take that as personal. Like I got a black boyfriend specifically to use as spit for their soup.

"And maybe then you'll get it in your thick man head that I picked you because you're black and that's a button I can push. I mean, a girl doesn't go home for ten years, you have to guess she has some issues with her family. But that's not why at all. I picked you because you're you, and you're perfect for me, and because I'm so in love with you."

Burr said, "I love you, too, Lena. But I'm done being played."

I said, "What does that mean? You're giving me an ultimatum? 'Fuck me or lose me'? Because that sucks, Burr."

"Don't misunderstand me," he said, his voice rising. "Don't make this about me trying to get over on you. I've never pressured you that way. And yeah, obviously I want to have sex with you, but that's not what I'm saying here. I'm asking you to introduce me to your family. That's all. I'm asking for a commitment, Lena. We've been together two years now."

"On and off," I said.

"Mostly on."

He reached for the doorknob again, and I said, "Don't you dare walk out on me in the middle of a fight." I was so angry, I was practically screaming. "I mean it, don't you do it." He paused for a second, but then he flipped the dead bolt.

The door seemed to catch in the frame, so he gave it an angry shove. It swung open, knocking back a girl who was standing on the other side. She was so close she must have had her ear pressed up against the wood, and the force of Burr's exit spilled her all the way backwards onto her bottom.

"What the—" said Burr, and he stepped over the threshold towards her, already reaching down to help her up. She went scuttling backwards like a panicked crab. He stopped moving, and she bounced back to her feet, scrabbling frantically in her huge macramé purse. She was dressed like one of my students, in tight jeans and a peasant blouse, but I didn't recognize her. Her hand came out of her purse and up, holding a tiny spray can aimed at Burr's face.

"I heard you yelling," she said to me. She was breathing hard, but once on her feet, she seemed more exhilarated than frightened, taking a theatrical *Charlie's Angels* pose with the spray can.

"Whoa," Burr said. He put his hands up. "Calm down."

She didn't take her eyes off him, but she was talking to me. "You go for the soft parts," she said. "And then we run while he's down."

I realized I had put my hands up, too, instinctively. I dropped them and walked over beside Burr. "Are you all right?" I said to her. "It was an accident. We didn't know you were there. What on earth were you doing?"

"Lena, is this one of your students?" said Burr. He angled himself, trying to stay between me and the Mace, which was easy since she had it pointed aggressively at his face. She had her legs apart in a fighter's stance, and both her arms were fully extended, aiming the can like a gun.

"I don't think she's after me, Burr," I said, and because I was so angry, I couldn't help but be amused, watching this tiny girl hold him at bay. "Her problem's with you, looks like."

"I was just leaving," said Burr.

"Bet your ass you are," the girl said.

"He was only trying to help you up," I said to her, but she ignored me and kept the can trained on Burr.

Burr dropped his hands slowly and walked past her, and she turned in a circle, keeping him covered.

"We're not done with this conversation," I called after him.

"I am," he said and went on down the stairs.

I started after him, but the girl turned sideways and then stepped to block me. She whipped her head back and forth, trying to keep an eye on both of us.

"Excuse me," I said, but she ignored me. Burr turned the corner, and the moment he was out of sight, she faced me and dropped her arms, grinning triumphantly. "They're almost all sonsabitches."

At second glance, she was too old to be one of my students. I put her at about thirty. She was my size or maybe even a little shorter. I doubted she could claim five-one in bare feet. Her thick dark hair was cut in an aggressive bob, shorter in the back and angling down into two razor-sharp points on either side of her fiercely pretty face.

"We were only arguing," I said. "Excuse me, I need to catch him." I started after Burr, but she moved into my path, blocking me again. She still clutched the spray can.

She said, "If I had a dime for every time I said those words!"

"Put the Mace away," I said.

"Oh, right." She dropped it into her bag. "What timing, huh? I heard you yelling in there, and I was about to bust this door down and come in after you."

She said the word "you" as if it had a W on the end. It was pure Alabama. I forgot about going after Burr and stared at her, taking in her pointy face and the huge violet-blue eyes gazing out from between the sharp wings of her hair.

"Rose?" I said, but it simply couldn't be. The last time I'd seen Rose Mae Lolley, she'd had waist-length hair and had moved with the slow grace of an underwater ballerina on opium. The Rose Mae I knew and loathed years ago, back in Alabama, would never go leaping around wielding Mace in a Yankee stairwell. And she certainly wouldn't lower herself to speak to me.

But she was nodding and saying, "Can you believe it? I look different, huh? You don't. Not much, anyway. I mean, older, sure. But I knew in a glance I'd found Arlene Fleet. May I come in?"

"I don't think so," I said. I thought for one absurd moment that she had to be here on a mission from Aunt Flo, a tactical maneuver in the perpetual war to bring me home. Before I could stop myself, I found myself asking, "Who sent you? Was it Florence?"

Rose looked puzzled and said, "Florence? Oh! Mrs. Lukey? Clarice's mom? Lord, no, I haven't seen her in a dog's age. How is she doing?"

I boggled at her. "This isn't some sort of old-home week, Rose. I haven't seen you in ten years. I didn't even know if you were alive or dead, and quite frankly, I didn't much care. And now you are standing out in my stairwell, apparently eavesdropping on me and my boyfriend? It's none of your business how my family is. If

Aunt Florence didn't send you as some form of torture, then how the hell did you even find me? What are you doing here? What do you want from me?"

She briefly looked nonplussed, but then she plastered a smile on her face and said, "Okay, Arlene. I guess you never were one for social graces. That's fine. It's kind of a long story, but if you want the short, standing-in-a-stairwell version, I can do that. I got in a fight with my therapist, and now I'm on a spiritual journey. Congratulations, you're my next stop."

I looked at her skeptically. "Is this about the retirement party?"

"No, I don't even know what that means. Surprisingly, everything in the world isn't all about you, Arlene. This is about me. I told you, I am trying to follow a path I've devised for my own spiritual development—"

I held up my hand to stop her talking and said, "If this is some sort of twelve-step thing, making amends or whatever, fine. I forgive you. Now I need to go catch Burr."

"Forgive me for what?" said Rose. We did a little three-step dance in the hallway as I tried to get around her, and she bounced back and forth from foot to foot, hair swinging, to stop me. "Wait, Arlene, one minute. I'm sorry I sounded snippy. I really do need your help. I'm only doing what you're trying to do. Going after the one that got away."

I stopped trying to get around her and eyed her warily. You can take the girl out of Alabama, but how do you stop Alabama from following you over a thousand miles to lay siege to your doorstep? I felt the beginnings of an old anger stirring; God was not supposed to let this happen. It was an unspoken part of the deal. I took a step back towards my open apartment door. "Whatever this is, it can't have anything to do with me," I said.

"But it does, indirectly. See, my therapist said I get crappy men because I go looking for them, not because men are mostly crappy." I took another step back, and she started talking faster, trying to make me hear her out. "She thinks I choose assholes because that's what I think I deserve, blah blah, masochism, blah blah, low self-esteem. You know how shrinks talk."

"No," I said pointedly. "I don't."

Rose looked skeptical. "With your mother? Come on. Anyway, she's wrong. I've been thinking through my romantic history, looking for a guy I picked who wasn't an asshole. If I can find just one, then my shrink is wrong and it isn't me, it's the men. And there is one, I know it. I remember. But I need you to help me find him."

"Find him?" I said. While she was talking, I continued to edge backwards. Rose followed me, step for step but with a longer stride, so she was now much too close to me. I could smell fruit gum on her breath, and her eyes held the fervid light of a convert.

"Yes. I have to find Jim Beverly," she said.

The last syllable had not cleared her lips before I was leaping wildly into my apartment. I slammed the door in her face and then shot the bolt and put the chain on. I couldn't breathe. I had not heard his name spoken aloud in ten years.

Outside, Rose Mae Lolley gave my door three sharp raps. "Arlene?" she called.

I bolted across the room to the boom box that was sitting by the sofa. I dug around in the box of jumbled CDs next to it, looking for something, anything, loud. I came up with the Clash. I had not noticed until I tried to get the CD out of the jewel box and load it into the player how violently my hands were shaking.

All of me was shaking. My teeth were banging together as if I were freezing.

"Arlene? This is ridiculous. I need maybe five minutes of your time," Rose Mae Lolley called, kicking my door once for emphasis. At last I got the CD tray to slide home. I pumped the volume up to about six.

Rose gave the door a good pounding I could hear over "London Calling," so I upped the dial to eight, neighbors be damned. Then I sat on the floor with my arms at my sides, pressing my palms down against the cool hardwood while the first song played out. I wanted to go and look through the peephole, but I was afraid I would see her giant lavender eyeball peering in at me.

I cast about for something to distract myself. I had a stack of freshman world literature papers I needed to grade, but I wasn't in any shape to face the grammar. I also had three books I was reading in tandem, research for my dissertation, but my heart was pounding and I doubted I could concentrate. I felt like going to bed, or maybe crawling under it and never coming back out.

I noticed Burr had left his book behind, facedown on the arm of the sofa. The old cushion had a sinkhole in it where Burr had been. I wedged myself into his warmth and read, forcing myself to concentrate on the words, and not on whatever Alabama drama might be playing itself out in my hallway, or Aunt Florence's demands, or the fact that my boyfriend had just walked out on me, maybe for good this time.

It might have been easier if Burr had left a better book. He liked courtroom dramas, and he was the fastest reader I had ever seen. He ate text like pudding, no chewing, but he still managed to digest it. And these lawyer thrillers, he devoured two or three a weekend. In real life he was a tax attorney who wouldn't touch criminal law, but he loved the books. They ran the gamut from literature to penny dreadfuls. Burr didn't care about the quality. He ate them in bulk. If it had a lawyer protagonist, plot twists, and someone with big tits in jeopardy, he was all for it.

This was one of the bad ones. The prologue alone had a body count of seven. The bad guy had killed five of them. Because he was bad, his reaction was to laugh gleefully and dance in the mayhem. The young DA, backed into a corner and in the wrong place at the wrong time, whacked two people. Self-defense, of course. Because he was good, his reaction was to vomit and think deep thoughts along the lines of "Oh the humanity." Complete crap.

I've personally committed only one murder, but the truth is, it's not that simple. You can't tell whether you're the good guy or the bad guy based on whether you laugh or throw up. The truth is, I did both.

I read for as long as I could stand it before I reached down beside me and hit the pause button on the boom box. My ears rang in the sudden silence. I did not hear anything from the hallway. I threw Burr's book across the room. It smacked into the front door and bounced off to the floor. No reaction. Rose Mae Lolley was gone, for the moment.

I was still shaking. I wanted to pray, but I was too angry with God to concentrate. Ten years, ten years I had been faithful, and now God was breaking the deal.

Before I left Possett, I had promised God I would stop fucking every boy who crossed my path. (Although when actively involved in prayer I used the word "fornicating," as if this would spare God's delicate ears.) Now I was losing Burr over it. The truth was, I had worried that I was losing him for months, but still I had stayed faithful.

I had promised God I would never tell another lie, and I hadn't. Even when lying would make everything easy with Aunt Florence and my family, I had never let a word of untruth cross my lips.

Lastly, I had promised that if He would get me out safe, I would never go back to Possett, Alabama. Not for anything. I wouldn't even look back, lest I turn to salt.

And now God had allowed Possett, Alabama, to show up on my doorstep.

As far as I was concerned, all bets were off.

# CHAPTER

## 2

I WAS FIFTEEN YEARS old when I killed Jim Beverly, right at the end of my sophomore year. There was a dirt road that led to a ring of wooded hills just outside of Possett. It was where all the kids used to go to make out. There was a level place to park at the foot of the one we called Lipsmack Hill. Cars were lined up at the foot of that hill every weekend, full of kids playing feelio boobio and you-show-me-yours-and-I'll-ejaculate-in-my-pants. There was a wooded path you could take up to the top of Lipsmack, away from the cars.

If you saw a white T-shirt hanging on the lowest branch of the sycamore right by the path, you didn't go up there. It was occupied. Traditionally you could claim the hilltop only if one of the people involved was a virgin. The white T-shirt was an announcement.

I was familiar with that hilltop. I had 102 kids in my class at Fruiton High. Fifty-three of them were boys. During the course of my sophomore year, I fucked fifty-two of them, neatly, in order of their sixteenth birthdays. I would have given Bud, the last one, a go, too, if he hadn't been Clarice's boyfriend. Thirty-one of the boys, under the pressure of my hand in their jeans and the threat of hand-in-jeans removal, admitted they were virgins. All thirty-one had a white T-shirt tucked under the driver's seat. Hope and dicks, springing eternal. At any rate, I visited that hilltop over thirty times, so I knew it probably better than anyone.

The woods, mostly scrub and loblolly pine with a few syca-more and oak trees, ended on the hilltop. There was a little grassy clearing where you could spread a blanket and get on with it. The clearing ended in a track of gravel at the lip, and where the hill started its descent on the other side, the heaps began.

"Heaps" was our name for kudzu, a fast-spreading vine that climbed anything it could find and turned it into a shaggy, amorphous mound. The heaps had eaten the woods in the pit at the center of the ring of hills, creeping over the ground, coating the trees. They had formed piles and climbed up themselves when nothing else was offered. In some places they loomed up higher than the hilltops. Roach Country, Clarice called it. Roaches love to nest in kudzu. Clarice would not have been caught dead on top of Lipsmack. The only place she ever went all the way with Bud was in his clean basement rec room, under the pool table. And she didn't even do that until they were engaged, over halfway through senior year.

The night I went up Lipsmack Hill after Jim Beverly, I was fucking a boy named Barry, the last of the fifty-two boys. Barry swore he wasn't a virgin, so we did it in his car. He had a crabbed car, like a wadded-up version of a sedan. And he had endless pale legs, as skinny as a stork's. There wasn't room to get him any-where near in me in the backseat, although we'd twisted around and jammed ourselves up pretty good trying. His knees kept popping up, and his long legs flexed and folded around me, entangling and hampering me.

Finally I lost my temper. I swear, at that age boys should all say they're virgins, even the ones who aren't, so girls won't blame them when they are completely awful at sex. I told him to sit his butt down in the passenger seat, but first to button his shirt because the moon was full and high and we'd be visible once we sat up. Then I pulled my dress back on over my head and climbed into his lap facing him, and bingo, just like that, popped Tab A into Slot B.

I felt like saying "How hard was that," but I didn't want to interfere with his concentration. Barry was going, "Um, um, um," and making desperate lunges upward with his hips. Freakin' liar, he had to be a virgin.

Barry had backed up to the hill, so I had a pretty good view of the path leading to the top of Lipsmack over his shoulder. I saw a freshman girl I did not know to speak to heading up. A few steps behind her, Jim Beverly unfurled a grimy white T-shirt like a flag, and as he passed the low tree branch, he flung it over one-handed. He half jogged to catch his date, stumbling a little, and slung an arm over the girl's shoulder to steady himself. He had a bottle swinging in his other hand. The moon was so high and bright, I could see moonlight glinting off the golden liquid sloshing inside.

Something about watching him drifting drunk up the hill with that girl—it got to me. There I was crouched in the car on top of a moaning boy, a boy who was delirious and lost in me, and up until I saw Jim Beverly, I'd been so relaxed, so in charge of it all. Now I could see myself reaching down to Barry's face with my hands, using my thumbs and calmly digging out his eyes. I could see myself tearing my own face off with my nails. Something, anything, to stop this insane juxtaposition of me, doing this bloodless deed with Barry Watkins, while Jim Beverly walked up Lipsmack Hill with yet another girl.

I must have jerked or tensed, because Barry looked up at me with his mouth open, and came, shocked and blinking. I was barely present, but somehow I managed to be polite. I patted his hair and said something nice to him, kissed him on the mouth. He was a sweet boy, really, the kind with a mother who still gave him home haircuts. His milky skin was as soft as a girl's. I said to him, "You dating someone, Barry?" I knew he wasn't. He shook his head at me. I said, "Well, you will, but you already fucked me, so you don't have a thing to prove with her, do you?"

He looked at me, uncertain of the correct answer but willing to give it. Finally he shook his head. I gave him another quick kiss and did a scan out the window. I saw Bud's old VW Rabbit. Thank God for reliable couples—I knew Clarice would be in it with Bud. I leaned over into the backseat and snatched up my panties and shoved them into my purse. I was running blind now, on complete instinct. I had to get to Jim Beverly and his stupid ass of a date.

I told Barry that Clarice and Bud would give me a ride home. He was too dazed or relieved to stop me, just said, "Okay," and sat there in his buttoned shirt with his pants around his ankles, blinking at me. I clambered off him and hopped out the door.

I'll tell you how sweet he was, though I barely clocked it at the time. I had no intention of going over there and interrupting Bud. Clarice and I were barely speaking at that point, and climbing in the car where she was trying to have a decorous make-out session would definitely not improve my standing in the ratings.

But Barry didn't drive off. I saw him struggling to get his pants up, and then he sat there in the passenger seat of his car watching me. He was watching to make sure I made it safe to Bud's car, the way a boy will watch a girl run up the stairs of her front porch and disappear inside the house. It was almost like he thought this was some sort of real date, instead of the natural result of me walking up behind him as he was playing Centipede in the empty game room at Pizza Hut, cupping his balls, and whispering, "Got a car?" in his ear.

His eyes stayed on me, so I didn't have a choice. I went over to Bud's dirty Rabbit and opened the passenger door and climbed in. As soon as I was in, I saw Barry driving off. Bud and Clarice were wound around each other in the backseat, but completely dressed and sitting up. They broke apart when the door opened. Clarice stared at me wax-eyed for a moment, as if she had been sleeping some sort of sweet, untroubled sleep and I had woken her.

"Arlene?" she said, just surprised, but it took only two more breaths till she was irritated.

Bud gave me his usual bland and brotherly grin and said, "Hey, Arlene."

"What on earth?" said Clarice.

I wasn't thinking right. I said the first thing that came into my head, which happened to accidentally be the truth. "Oh, well, I was fucking Barry Watkins, but I got finished up and came over here."

Bud let out a startled laugh, but Clarice said, "Good Lord,

Arlene." She shook her head at me and turned away to stare out the side window.

Clarice was not aware I had a plan to fuck the entire male half of our sophomore class, much less that I fucked them mostly for her sake. But she knew I was pretty loose and had a locker-room reputation beyond the wildest dreams of most Alabama small-town sluts. I had become legend, at least to the sophomore males. The girls didn't care for me much—now there is a huge under-statement—but they didn't make my life a living hell because I was still at least partially sheltered under the golden umbrella of Clarice's blond goodness and monstrous popularity. In other words, Clarice wouldn't let them outright torture me. She pro-tected me even though sometimes I thought she plain hated me, for reminding her of mess and complications when she liked everything so neat and clean and swept away. But we'd been so close growing up that she couldn't bring herself to cut me dead or ditch me. Then, too, on some level, perhaps she knew she owed me. And after all, how far away from me could she get? We lived in the same room.

"Well, we were kissing, actually," said Clarice primly. "And it was going very well. So thanks for checking on us and all, but you can go now." Even back then Clarice would have been able to talk like she was at a Junior League meeting if a total stranger had walked into the house and taken a crap on the rug.

"Clarice, I need a little help," I said. I couldn't believe how calm I sounded.

Bud was instantly on the alert. "That Barry get cute with you? That Barry hurt you?" Bud took the stance that I was Clarice's cousin, practically a sister. This meant that even though I was a slut and he knew I was a slut, if anyone treated me like a slut in his presence, Bud would beat the living crap out of that person. And Bud was a linebacker who made varsity in his sophomore year. He could beat the crap out of pretty much anyone.

"No, Barry is fine, but . . . Clarice, I need you to take me home. I'm sick or something."

Clarice turned back to look at me. "You don't look sick."

Bud said, "Hey, if Arlene's sick, I'll just run y'all both home. You got curfew in a hour anyway. We can let Arlene go on up to bed and maybe sit out on your porch swing until you got to go in."

Clarice was already nodding in a resigned way when I said, "No, Bud, that's sweet and all, but I need Clarice to take me home. Just Clarice. I need to talk to her."

Now they were both staring at me, but it was Bud who said it. "Arlene, are you, like, in trouble?" Meaning, of course, was I pregnant.

"No, no," I said. "I'm not in trouble, I just have a female girl-thing problem. I'm not in *trouble*, though. I just need to talk to Clarice."

Bud nodded, satisfied. I don't know what he took that to mean. Some mysterious menstrual thing he didn't want to know about, or maybe he thought I had given crabs to Barry Watkins.

Clarice narrowed her eyes at me but didn't object. Bud looked around and said, "There's Clint's car. I'll go roust him and Jeannie. Just about her curfew anyway. I'll see if old Clint wants to shoot some pool at my house. But I need my car back early. Remember, I got Saturday practice."

Clarice said, "I'll pick you up in the morning and stay to watch. I'll pack us a lunch, too, for after. We can picnic."

" 'Kay, sugar," said Bud, untroubled about walking off and

31

leaving her in charge of his car. He was so easygoing and sweet with her. Maybe a tiny part of me was sad he was the one boy in the class I wouldn't go with. He got out and ambled off to ruin the rest of Clint's date.

"I swear to God, Arlene," said Clarice bitterly. "Every time I think you have gone about as stupid-crazy as a person can possibly go, you come up with a way to get worse. And this wasn't just crazy, it was also mean. And rude. And a bunch of other stuff I am too mad to even think of right now." She clambered out of the backseat into the driver's seat. Bud's keys were hanging in the ignition. She started the car.

"Clarice, wait a second, we can't go home yet. I need your help."

Something in my voice stopped her, and she paused with her hand on the gearshift. "This better not be some more of your crap, Arlene. I am so, so sick of your crap."

"It isn't, I swear it, I really do need your help right now. Really bad. But I need you to do what I say and not ask me a bunch of questions. Please help me now, and tomorrow you can ask all the questions you want."

She looked at me for a long moment, suspicious and maybe worried. "What do you need?"

"I need you to drive off now like you're taking me home, but as soon we get around the corner, away from these people, you slow down and let me hop out—"

"Arlene—"

I talked louder to shut her up. "Then I need you to drive home and tell your mama I'm home, too." In our freshman year, Aunt Florence had agreed to let us start dating, as long as we doubled with each other. Clarice and I had immediately started training her parents. We had the same curfew (even though I was techni-cally a year younger, I was in the same grade), so when we got home, one of us would call down the hall, "We're home! Good night!"

We would wait until we heard one of her parents (usually Aunt Florence) give us a sleep-logged "okay" from their room at the end of the hall, and then we would go in to bed. My mother slept in a room that used to belong to Clarice's brother, Wayne, directly in between our room and Aunt Florence's. But most nights Mama was too medicated to hear us come in. She never answered us.

Aunt Florence and Uncle Bruster got used to hearing only one of us at random. That way one of us could stay out longer, and creep in later, after Flo had shifted from her nebulous my-daughter-is-out-in-the-night doze into real sleep.

Clarice was shaking her head at me. "Arlene, if this is some stupid thing like you got rid of Barry and now you want to climb off him and go meet still and yet some other boy, I am going to be—"

"No, it isn't, I swear. I swear. I wouldn't come over here and bother you and Bud like this if I didn't please, please really need you. Please, Clarice, don't ask me any questions, just help me. I so need you to help me now." I was sobbing, tears blinding me as I begged her, and then my throat clogged up so I couldn't speak.

Clarice reached out and touched my hair, soft and uncertain. "I don't think I should, Arlene."

I don't think she'd seen me cry since that one awful night fresh-man year, when I was so hurt, and we lay in each other's arms in my bed like someone's broken toys. She'd taken care of me. She'd helped me then. But that night, I had made her swear, never happened. And Clarice, so serene all the time, universally beloved and calm and pretty, had somehow managed to make it so in her own brain. But I wasn't like her.

She shrugged at me apologetically and started the car up. "I'm taking you home." She couldn't trust me, so I decided I had to trust her.

"Jim Beverly is up on top of Lipsmack with some freshman girl," I said.

She went completely still, and then she said, "Why did you let Bud go? Oh, no, we need Bud."

"No, we don't. Bud can't know anything. Just you do like I told you and cover for me with Aunt Florence."

She swallowed, and her throat was so dry I heard it as a click. "What are you going to do?"

"I have a plan," I lied. "I can either sit here and explain it to you, and then we can go home, because by the time I tell it to you, Jim Beverly will have gone off to college. Or you can just shut up and trust me."

She stared at me for two more heartbeats and then did as I asked, driving away from the field at the foot of the hill, down the dirt road. Right before she hit paved road, she paused in the shadow of the trees, and I slipped out the door. "Thanks, Clarice."

Her eyes were huge with worry. "This is the stupidest thing I have ever done in my life. Should I wait for you?"

I shook my head. "I'll get home. You need to make curfew." It was only about a four-mile walk. I could hoof it in under an hour. "If anyone asks, later on or tomorrow, not just our parents but anyone, you'll say you took me home. Okay? And don't worry. I have a plan, and he isn't going to hurt me again."

I waited until she nodded, uncertain but trusting, and then I stepped back from the car. I stood in the shadows and watched her drive away.

The truth is, I had no idea what I was planning to do. I knew that the freshman girl was up there. Maybe I just planned to spy on them. Maybe I wanted to go snatch that girl up and drag her stupid little patootie home. I swear I did not have a plan. But I'll admit I didn't want anyone to know I was heading up onto the hilltop after Jim Beverly.

I ghosted through the woods, circling the field. There were still about fifteen cars, although they wouldn't be there long. A lot of people had an eleven or eleven-thirty curfew. I stayed out of the moonlight, slipping behind the trees. Even after I got to the path leading up Lipsmack, I stuck to the woods, taking a parallel course up through the bracken. I was going slowly, to be as quiet as possible, and because I kept getting caught in blackberry thorns, when I heard someone stomping down the path.

I froze. It was the freshman girl. She was marching down and muttering and cussing. "Who does he think he is, Mr. Big-Shot Jerk-Ass Quarterback, well, he can kiss my butt is what he can do." Her ponytail quivered with righteous indignation. She had a pissy little death grip on her purse in one hand, and a key ring in the other. The keys clashed together angrily with every stomping step she took.

After she was safely past and down, I probably should have come to my senses and followed her. I should have gone home. But maybe I wanted to see how he could have let her walk away, something completely out of character for the Jim Beverly I knew. Up the hill I could hear him calling, "Miss Sally? Come on back, Miss Sally. Miss Sally?"

I got onto the path and walked up. I came out of the woods, and there was Jim Beverly, sitting with his back to me, facing the heaps. The other side of the hill was so steep you could have almost called it a cliff. It dropped off for a few feet, and then leveled into a long, steep slope, all of the slope now eaten by the heaps that reached up in humps, each trying to be the first to get a claw hooked onto the cliff.

On the edge of the small cliff, Jim Beverly was sitting in the gravel, swinging his feet over the lip. I could see how the freshman girl had gotten away. He was so drunk I doubt he could have stood and walked after her without help. The soles of his sneakers lightly brushed the top of the highest heap. He was leaning unsteadily back on his hands, swaying. Just behind one of his hands, sitting upright in the grass, was the liquor bottle. It was tequila. I could smell it on him from where I stood. The bottle seemed outsized, and the golden liquid inside came down to a point, but the bottom of the bottle was square, with a thick glass base.

Jim Beverly had heard me coming. He was talking, slurring his words so badly I could barely understand him. He never turned around. He said, "Now, Miss Sally, be a sweetie and give it a little suck, hey? I swear I'm too damn drunk to fuck. C'mon, Sally, least you can do is give it a little suck, hey? You know I'm feeling melancholy."

He'd lost homecoming for us in the last week. His playing had been off ever since the news of his scholarship came through. He was headed to UNA in the fall, solid, so he could afford to slack off.

The tequila bottle was open, the cap lying beside it. The moonlight on the bottle was mesmerizing.

"Mustang Sally," sang Jim Beverly. "Guess you better blow . . . me, suck my dick."

I walked towards that pretty bottle, getting closer to him, and still, and still, he did not turn around. I kept expecting him to turn, and then maybe our eyes would meet and somehow this moon-washed hill would be like a real place to me and I would yell something at him, call him an asshole or a drunk, and then turn and run home as fast as I could go. But he didn't turn, and I felt like I was swimming towards the bottle, moved by currents, not my own power. It was so pretty and solid and whole.

"Mustang Sally, now, baby," wailed Jim, covering the sound of me carefully screwing the cap back on. From where I stood, staring down at his broad shoulders, his head looked out of place, covered in blond fuzz like a baby's. The back of his neck looked pale and downy, innocent and somehow vulnerable.

It was such a sweet-looking bit of flesh, I thought I might lean down and place a kiss there, closed-mouthed and chaste. The kind of kiss Clarice might give an ugly boy she felt sorry for. I waited for a moment, holding the bottle loosely in one hand, feeling the solid weight of the heavy glass. It was thick, grainy. The glass was bubbled and the bottle had no label. He did not turn. I waited and waited, and when he still did not turn, I took the bottle carefully in both hands, and, going into the good batter's stance I had learned in Little League, I swung it as hard as I could at his head.

People who play baseball, they talk about a sweet spot, and in a way I know what they mean. I am not sure exactly what it is— a place on the bat? something to do with where you hit the ball?—but I know the feeling of the sweet spot. I know when the bottle hit the back of his head, just above the neck; I felt the connection run through me like electric current. I felt the bone of his skull give, and that giving reverberated up into my hands and spread through my whole body. It was all but silent, but I felt the crunch of it, felt him splintering and the shards of bone entering the thick meat of his brain. He slumped sideways from the force of the blow and was completely still.

And somehow nothing had changed, except the singing had stopped. There was no blood. His skin was unbroken. The bottle was unbroken. Nothing seemed broken at all. I stood there until I got the giggles. I stood there giggling and giggling, unable to stop. It struck me that this was inappropriate, and then I realized the word "inappropriate" was a hilarious word to think while standing over an utterly dead body. It sounded like something Clarice would say, pursing her lips with disapproval over my laughter coming right after I smashed a boy's head in, and I dissolved into more helpless giggles.

At last I unscrewed the cap and took three long, searing gulps. The pain of them burning down into my throat shut me up, and there was Jim Beverly, and he was dead, and I had killed him. I looked stupidly at the bottle. Although I had been staring at it, fascinated, before I ever picked it up, somehow I had not registered the fact that this was real Mexican tequila. A dead worm floated disconsolately near the bottom.

I was so surprised that I opened my mouth and the tequila I had swallowed came shooting back up. It fell in a wash down the front of my dress, the fumes of it burning my eyes. Then it struck me that I had calmly puked on myself, and that was the funniest thing yet. I laughed so hard I had to either sit down or wet myself.

When I wound down, I sat there for a minute, hitching and

gulping. I must have been laughing so hard it was like crying. I looked over next to me, where Jim Beverly was lying slumped in a pile. He was absolutely and completely still. I didn't know what to do with him. Even though he was a short skinny guy, maybe five-nine, with an overdeveloped chest and stringy, muscular limbs, he was a lot bigger than me. I was barely five feet tall in shoes, weighed maybe ninety-five pounds. And I was shaking like I had the ague. As I stared at the body in front of me, I was surprised to find that my situation didn't seem terrible or even real. It didn't seem like anything had actually happened. But even so, I knew better than to sit around giggling and puking on my boobs, keeping company with a dead boy until a nice policeman came to cart me away.

I scooted up behind him on my butt and began shoving at the weighty mass of him with my feet. I shoved at him and pushed, and slowly he slid forward and toppled over the edge of the cliff. He landed with a meaty, slapping bounce, rustling the kudzu, a noise so clearly theatrical and fake that I had to pinch myself, hard, to stop myself from giggling again. Then he was rolling down the steep slope.

It seemed that as he rolled, the heaps were rolling, too, rolling in waves like the ocean. It was as if they were alive, grabbing at bits of him, reaching up like they had hands, pulling him in and under, down to Roach Country.

I took the tequila with me and drank it as I made the long hike home. Worm and all.

# CHAPTER

## 3

I GOT TO my office on campus at around six A.M. on Thursday. I knew Rose Mae Lolley would be back, and I didn't want to be home when she turned up. I would have to lie to her, and I wasn't ready. I wasn't even sure I remembered how.

I passed the morning grading papers and fretting. My office was a windowless cube I shared with two other Ph.D. candidates, but this early in the day I had it all to myself. I called Burr twice at home, but he didn't pick up. At nine I tried his direct line at work but landed in voice mail.

I had been born and mostly raised in the South, so I ought to have been able to find a way to reach him. Southern girls are trained from birth up that the way to a man's heart is never through the front door. They may leave a basket of cookies there, and while he's busy picking them up, they're squirming in through a back window. My cousin Clarice would have had him on his knees by now, trying to peel her a grape. But somehow I missed those classes in girl school, or I didn't get the gene.

I had to leave for my Joyce seminar, but as soon as I got back to my office, I tried to get Burr on his cell. More voice mail. I gave up on talking to him directly and decided to call his mama.

I met Burr's mother long before I met him. He was living eleven hours away in Ithaca when I moved up north. I didn't know a soul, having picked Chicago because it was the farthest place from Possett that had offered me a full scholarship.

I really don't recommend moving from rural Alabama to a major Yankee city in one great bounding leap. It's like picking up a prairie dog and dropping him into the Pacific. Welcome to your new environment. I had nothing in common with my fellow students. They were interested in getting fake IDs and laid. I was interested in a 4.0 GPA and a job.

And it wasn't only that I didn't make friends. Everything was so radically different. The looming buildings, the cars in orderly lines on both sides of every street, the streets laid out like a grid. Everything marched in straight lines, all sharp corners and hard edges. There were no curves or hills, no restful place to put your eye for even a moment. Even the people seemed linear. Walking the downtown streets, they all moved as if they were carrying a donor heart in their lunch box. No one smiled at me, and no one made eye contact. If I smiled at them, they sped up and raced past as if I were mentally ill. They spoke in hard staccato voices that shot words like bullets.

I told myself Chicago was exciting and fast-paced. I told myself it had a stark urban beauty. I told myself that before I broke my word to God and went back to Alabama with my tail between my legs, I would drink a Clorox cocktail while leaping off the Sears Tower.

I met Burr's mother in the Wal-Mart. Back in Possett, going to the Wal-Mart over in Fruiton was a huge expedition. The whole family went. You stayed for hours. You knew half the people there and stopped every other aisle to have a long chat about Fat Agnes's festering leg wound or Mrs. Mott's squirrel infestation.

In Chicago, I was living for my Sunday and Wednesday phone conversations with my family. But in between the calls, when I became unbearably lonely, I would head to a nearby Wal-Mart. I would wander the aisles, touching things, having imaginary conversations with people from home, relatives or family friends. I talked to everyone, especially Clarice. I even manufactured arguments with people I had never liked much or at all—even my dead asshole grampa seemed like a touchstone.

I was standing in the ladies' department with my imaginary aunt Florence. As I debated between a blue sweater and a green one, Aunt Florence spoke up: "Honey, you want the blue. That green'll make you look bilious."

I stood blinking stupidly. I had said plenty of things to my imaginary aunt Florence, but she had never answered me aloud before. And I had never in my life heard Flo speak in such a sweet, cozy tone.

I looked up and saw Burr's mother smiling kindly at me. She had full cheeks, motherly-looking cheeks, like downy brown pillows. Her eyes were a warm golden brown, about two shades lighter than her skin. Her face was unlined, but her features had that soft, blurred look some women get as they age, and her bun was streaked with white. She had on a floral-print dress. A church-lady dress. Her voice had a mild, almost Southern slur to it.

I burst into tears.

"Oh, honey," she said, but I just shook my head at her. I

dropped the sweaters on the floor and put my hands over my face and sobbed into them. I realized this was not sane behavior, and tried my best to tamp it back down, but braying sobs kept welling up and bursting out of my mouth. She came over and put an arm around me; I pulled away from her immediately, then gulped and tried again to squelch myself.

"Do you know why folks cry?" she said to me conversationally while I scrubbed violently at my streaming eyes. I shrugged. I didn't much care.

"God gave us crying so other folks could see when we needed help, and help us." She put her arm around me again. I let it stay there, and then I threw my arms around her soft middle and wailed and snuffled on her sloping shoulder. I gave myself up to it, letting a huge hurricane of pent-up weeping come storming out into the Wal-Mart ladies' department.

"Oh, honey," she said again. "You're going to be just fine. And you go ahead and get that green if that's what you want."

She was a minister's widow and a good Baptist. That day she dragged me home with her and fed me on real cherry cobbler, the kind with the pastry you make by cutting butter into flour for half an hour. She talked to me about pastry recipes and the Lord and invited me to visit her church on Sunday. I felt like I owed her for the cobbler and the kindness, so I went.

It was an all-black Baptist church in a decent blue-collar neighborhood. Everyone at that church was so familiar. It was like visiting home. Sure, I got odd looks the first time I showed up. I felt like my skin was glowing with an incandescent white otherness. I could feel the congregation peppering me with sideways glances. But I didn't feel any malice in their gazes. Every person I met and spoke with was soon relaxed and chatting with me about the weather or their children or Jesus. I was just as easy with them. It didn't hurt that I was firmly wedged under the sheltering wing of Mrs. Burroughs. Her husband had been the minister at that church up until his death, and she was universally beloved there.

Later, sitting in American History 101, I realized why I felt so at home at the church. After the industrial revolution came the great migration, as black sharecroppers traveled up to Chicago for better-paying factory jobs and a shot at a new life. But they were all southerners. They formed their own communities, and the culture survived. The people at Mrs. Burroughs's church spoke with long liquid vowels and blurred consonants, cooked everything in lard, moved with a languorous grace that implied it was 100 degrees outside. They could have been my relatives. Without them, especially Burr's mother, I never would have survived my first year up north.

I met Burr when he moved back to Chicago. Mrs. Burroughs had two older girls, both married to military men and gone. Burr was her baby, the first in his family to go to college, much less law school, although his father had been to a two-year Baptist seminary.

If anyone could show me a back door to Burr now, it was his mama. I hit nine for an outside line and dialed. She didn't seem at all surprised that it was me when she picked up the phone.

"I guess you talked to Burr," I said.

"He showed up this morning at breakfast, wanting my sugar toast," Mrs. Burroughs said against a background of glass on glass and running water—no doubt the remains of the sugar toast were being scraped away as we spoke. "He was like a bear with the sorest head you ever saw. I poked around, and when the sore spot seemed to be you, I started waiting for the phone to ring. Took you an hour longer than I bet myself."

I told her all about the fight, leaving out the sex parts. She was his mama and a preacher's wife, after all. But I told her he had given me an ultimatum and walked out, and now he wouldn't even talk to me to see if I was going to knuckle under. Not that I would.

Mrs. Burroughs made "mmm-hmm" noises at me and sloshed water around while I spilled my guts. I could picture her standing over the sink in her kitchen with the faded tea-rose wallpaper. Pictures of Burr and his sisters hung on the walls around the table and lined the windowsill in standing frames. On a decorative shelf beside the fridge, a ceramic mug shaped like a frog stood among bronzed baby shoes. Burr had made that frog at camp when he was about twelve.

When I wound down, she said, "Lena, you know I care for you pretty deep, but you also have to know you aren't the girl I would pick out for my son to love. I don't know if any girl would measure up good enough for a son in his mama's eyes. But if it was left to me, and I had to pick someone, it sure wouldn't be a tiny half-crazy white girl from Alabama, no matter how much I like her as a person." The kindness in her warm voice took some of the sting out of her words.

"But it isn't up to me to make that pick," Mrs. Burroughs went on. "My boy loves you. I think he loves you in a real way he can't walk out on unchanged. I don't think losing you is going to change him for the better, or make him happy. So if you want him like he wants you, I'm not getting in the way of that. But you better know this: If I help you find a way back to him and then you end up breaking his heart, I don't see how I could be anything but done with you. I wouldn't forgive that, even if it put me into hell."

I could hear a little laughter in her voice, but underneath the laughter was absolute conviction. All at once it was as if I were talking to Aunt Florence. The softness and the accent were wrong, but I recognized the steel behind her joking tone. I had no doubt that Mrs. Burroughs meant it.

"I'm not going to break his heart," I said.

She released a loud breath into the phone, and then she said, "Then I'll tell you two things. The first is, you have to give him something he wants. Right now I think he's feeling that everything flows in one direction, from him to you. He's thinking you don't care about him the way he cares for you. So you need to yield some. But the second thing I am telling you is, you better make him bend, too. You don't ever let a man say 'My way or nothing' to you. Not even a good man. Not even my son. And you never say 'My way or nothing' to him. You don't take your sweetheart's love and use it on him. You can do that to your mama, but not your sweetheart." I smiled at that.

She went on, "He's wrong by doing that with you. But you're wrong to put him in a place where he feels so poor he thinks he has to say that. You both need to bend, but I think this time it has to start with you. And that's all I can say to you without breaking confidence. Now, don't you make me sorry I helped you."

"I won't," I said, and I was as sincere as I had ever been in my life.

I had to hurry to Stevenson Hall to teach my afternoon world literature class. I jogged across the quad, toting my heavy leather carryall. Stevenson was a squat two-story stone building with long slitted windows. My class met on the first floor, just inside the gunmetal-gray front doors.

It was the last class of the semester, and all I had to do was take roll and accept the final papers. Some of the students had come by early and left them on the desk at the front. I collected the rest and then wasted a few minutes organizing the stack of folders into my bag and erasing notes left on the blackboard by an earlier class. By the time I was finished, the building was quiet around me. Most of the other classes had not met for the entire period, and there was a good half hour before the next classes in Stevenson were scheduled to begin.

I walked out into the hall, and Rose Mae Lolley was there waiting for me. I froze in the doorway.

She was dressed like a student again, in ratty, fringed jean shorts and a red tank top. She had on scuffed yellow-brown boots and was lounging against the wall with one leg crossed over the other. "Hey, Arlene," she said.

My voice sounded high to me, wavering as I answered her. "How did you find me?"

"They gave me your course schedule up in the English department."

"No," I said. "I mean how did you know I worked here, or my address. How did you even know to look in Chicago?"

"Oh, that," she said. "I talked to Bud."

"Bud Freeman?" I said. "My cousin Clarice's husband?"

She nodded. I pulled myself together and turned and walked away from her without saying anything else, heading out the front doors of Stevenson and across the quad, angling towards the faculty lot.

Rose Mae boosted herself off the wall and came after me. I

sped up, lengthening my stride so that she was dogtrotting as she caught up with me, her little pointy boobies jouncing in her tank top.

"Hold up, Arlene, I just need to ask you a couple of questions, and then I swear I won't bother you anymore."

I ignored her and broke into a jog, heading across the green.

"Stop for a second," Rose said, keeping pace half a step behind me. "I called Clarice, but she wasn't home, and I ended up talking to Bud. He told me you talked to Jim Beverly the night Jim wrecked his Jeep."

I stopped so fast, Rose Mae barreled into me. She bounced off me, and we stood facing each other. Her boots had short heels on them, and we were exactly eye to eye. All I had to do was lie. All I had to do was say "Bud is mistaken. I never saw Jim Beverly that night," and look into her eyes with total sincerity and a bit of mild confusion, as if I was wondering why Bud would think such a thing. But I had years and years of not telling a single lie behind me, and I blew it. My gaze faltered and my eyes dropped, and I knew if I said it now, it would sound like the lie it was, and she would not believe me.

"I didn't talk to him," I said, which was the truth. But it came out wrong, with the emphasis on the word "talk," and she picked up on it immediately.

"But you saw him?" she asked. I didn't answer, and she grabbed my arm, trying to make me look at her. She said urgently, "Where was he? What was he doing?"

I ripped my arm out of her grasp and backed up a step. "I don't know," I said, but that wasn't exactly the truth. Out of sheer force of habit, I found myself adding, "There's nothing I can tell you about this."

She took a step towards me, the end points of her hair swinging fiercely, and she said, "I don't believe you. I know you saw him."

All around us, kids were streaming back and forth like ants, oblivious to the drama unfolding in front of them. If they could ignore Rose as she stalked me across the commons, maybe I could, too. I realized this wasn't a mature or even a rational response, but who said I had to be rational? The question calmed me, because asking it showed me the solution. All I had to do was ask myself "What would Mama do?"

I looked around. We were almost at the center of the quad, and four stone benches backed up against a square flower bed. A hot-dog vendor stood with his cart by the farthest of the benches, and a short line of students was grabbing a late lunch. A few strides to my left was a stand of four oak trees.

I released the handle of my satchel and dropped it to the ground by the closest bench. I left it where it had fallen and walked to the trees, Rose Mae following. I went to the second-largest tree. It had a thick trunk, but a few of its branches were low enough for me to reach.

I jumped to give myself momentum as I grabbed a low, thick branch and hoisted myself up. My loafers slipped on the trunk, and I let them drop off my feet, using my bare toes to get purchase on the bark. I got one foot up on the branch and pushed, reaching for higher branches.

"Arlene?" Rose Mae said. "What are you doing?"

The answer seemed too obvious to say out loud, so I ignored her and kept working my way up the tree. Inside, I was remarkably calm and peaceful. I peeked down. A couple of students had joined Rose Mae at the foot of the tree, watching me shinny up through the branches.

"Arlene, this is ridiculous," Rose Mae called. "Get down here."

I kept climbing around and around the trunk, following the thickest branches I could find. About twenty feet up, I realized the branches were getting too slender to safely hold me. I scouted for a comfortable fork and then wedged myself in it. A few more students had stopped, and one was pointing up at me.

Rose was still at the foot of the tree, yapping like an angry poodle. "You can't stay up there in that tree forever. You have to come down and talk to me."

I thought she might very well be wrong.

"If you don't get down here," Rose said desperately, "I am going to take your shoes!"

A tall, weedy-looking blonde from my world lit class was standing at the base of the tree with a friend, looking up at me. "You are not taking her shoes," she said incredulously to Rose, and she picked up my loafers and held them to her chest. She noticed my satchel on the ground a few feet away, and she and her friend hurried to stand over it.

I settled into the fork and looked out over the campus. I had a good view. A couple of the students who had stopped to watch me climb drifted off and were replaced by different ones. I quit looking down or listening, just closed my eyes and concentrated on the breeze hitting my face. The next time I looked down, Rose Mae Lolley had gone.

I backed and shinnied carefully down. My student dragged my satchel over and met me as I dropped to the ground. I took my shoes from her and slipped them back on.

"Thanks, Maria," I said.

"I wasn't going to let her take our papers!" she said, outraged. "Who was that?"

I shrugged and said, "It's not important," in a steady voice, but when I bent to pick up my satchel, my knees wobbled a bit on me, and Maria leaped forward to grab my arm and steady me. She helped me over to the bench, and I sat down heavily, thinking hard. The little crowd of students was leaving, except one group of three who stood in a clot, blatantly staring at me like I was TV.

"Get out of here, you vultures," I said irritably and flapped my hand at them. I put my head down, breathing hard, and when I looked up, they were dispersing.

Maria sat down beside me, her fingers tapping nervously against her freckled stork legs. At last she said, "Want some of my Fruitopia?"

I nodded and she dug a violently green drink out of her backpack. I took it gratefully and gulped down about half of it. It tasted like liquid sugar.

"Thanks," I said. I handed it back and said, "I have to get going now. You have a good summer."

"Are you okay?" Maria said, but I was already up, grabbing my satchel and heading for my car at a good clip. I'd bought myself some time, but if Rose Mae kept after me, I would eventually shift from acting like a complete lunatic to actually being one. I couldn't leap around slamming doors in her face and shinnying up trees forever.

I was angry with myself for failing to lie when a single good one would have solved everything. It still could. I practiced it in my head. "Rose," I would say, "I don't know anything that could help you. I don't know what happened to Jim Beverly."

51

A passing student raised his eyebrows at me questioningly. I realized that my lips were moving and I had composed my face into a mask of sincerity, widening my eyes and nodding at my imaginary Rose as I walked. I gave him an embarrassed grin and ducked my head down, moving faster. This had to stop. It had to, but I couldn't do it on my own, and I was driving myself crazy trying. I needed help. I needed Burr.

I drove over to his condo. I had no idea what to say to him, but I had to make him understand that we absolutely couldn't be broken up right now. I practiced a speech telling him so, over and over, whipping myself up into a frothy panic as the Burr in my head kept interrupting me and not letting me finish my sentences. I miraculously found a parking space on the same block as his building and wedged my Honda into it.

I took the elevator up to his floor. I didn't think Burr would be home yet, so I let myself in to wait for him. I had forgotten he often took short days in the May lull after tax season. He was sitting in his favorite leather easy chair with his headphones on, no doubt blasting the blues loud enough to kill his eardrums. He hadn't heard me coming in, but when the door opened, he jumped to his feet, staring at me. He pulled off the headphones and dropped them on the chair. I could hear Hound Dog Taylor and the Houserockers, tinny and distant. The armchair was right by the entertainment center, and he reached over and flipped the stereo off.

I closed the door behind me and leaned on it, and we stood staring at each other. I had to have him on my side. I couldn't lie to Rose Mae Lolley, so I had to make him be with me, because without him at my back, helping me, I didn't see how I could win. His mother had told me I had to bend and give him something he wanted, but I sure as hell couldn't take him home to Alabama. I opened my mouth to give the speech I had been working on in the car, but what came out of my mouth was "I think you should have sex with me."

Burr raised his eyebrows at me. "That's certainly . . ." He paused, searching for a word. At last he said, "Abrupt."

"I think you should have sex with me right now," I countered. My voice faltered. "Here, on the carpet."

Burr half laughed, incredulous, and stayed where he was. At last he said, "I think you should have sex with me. Here. On this chair." He extended one arm like Vanna White, modeling the recliner.

I stamped my foot. "I am being serious, Burr. Let's go. Let's do this."

He searched my face, and then he said, "Baby, what happened? You're so pale. Are you sick?" He came over to me and took my hands and led me back past his chair to his big leather sofa and sat me down. "Your hands are clammy. Do you need a glass of water?" he asked.

I shook my head. "I had a Fruitopia." He was temporarily setting aside the fight and the breakup because I was so obviously in extremis. I was flooded with such relief and gratitude that I sagged against him and said, "You remember that girl? The one on my doorstep last night?"

"The one with the Mace?" he asked. "Yeah. That's not an easy girl to forget."

"She's Rose Mae Lolley," I said. The name meant nothing to him. I added, "From my hometown. From Alabama. And she's up here and she won't stop following me, and it's like she's dragged with her everything ugly I left behind me, and she's dumping it all over me and I can't make her stop. She knows where I live, and Burr, she's turned into this relentless, awful girl with political hair and no bra, and she isn't going to ever leave me alone. I can't go to my apartment, and then today she tracked me down at school. There's no place I can go. I acted like a lunatic just to get away from her, and if the head of my department saw me, oh crap. You know he's going to hear about it . . . but I don't know how to get rid of her."

I was clutching Burr's arm and pounded his shoulder for emphasis. "I have to get her off me, Burr. She's stalking me."

"Take a deep breath," Burr said. "You need to calm down. Lena, I'd put you in the ring with any bra-less girl from Alabama. I have no doubt you could kick her ass. In fact, I'm getting a pretty good visual."

I smiled in spite of myself, and he grinned at me and continued, "Here's what I think we should do. Let's put our fight on hold. We can fight later, after she's gone. I'll take you home, and I'll make you that tea you like that smells like cat pee. We'll order a pizza. Watch TV. If she shows up again, you can handle her. I'll be there to back you up in case she gets crazy with the Mace can."

I nodded, relieved. "Burr? We aren't broken up, are we?"

"I don't know," he said. He shook his head, and I let go of him and sat back to study his face. "Whatever is going on with us, let's leave it alone for now."

"I can do that," I said. "That seems good."

We caravanned back over to my place, Burr following me in his Blazer. I had a spot in the lot behind my building, but Burr had to drive around and around the block until a parking space opened up. I waited nervously on the front stoop for him. The sun was starting to go down. When I saw him walking up the block, I got up and went to meet him.

"Find a spot?" I asked.

"Yeah," he said. "In Egypt."

We headed up the two flights to my apartment together. The stairwell was clear, but when we got to my door, I saw an envelope taped to it. My name was written on it in fat girlie handwriting, the kind with the overblown vowels and the perky upstroke at the end of each word.

"The stalker?" said Burr.

"Has to be," I said. "No one in Chicago calls me Arlene."

I took it down and we went inside my apartment. "Hey. My book," said Burr. It was still lying on the floor where I had thrown it. Burr picked it up.

I sat down on the sofa and opened the envelope and read the letter.

*Dear Arlene,*

*I'm really sorry for what happened today on campus. Bud told me on the phone you had not been home in ages, but gave me no indication you were so troubled. May I suggest, not in a judging way, but as someone who knows and is speaking from experience, that you should get professional help?*

*I am going to do as you ask and leave you alone. I am heading now to Oklahoma to track down Jim's best friend from back then. Remember Rob Shay? Well, he is a pro ballplayer now, can you believe it? Minor league, but still. And then I will be in Texas where Jim's brother lives now. I do not know where I will be staying. But after that, say by next Wednesday or Thursday, I will be heading to my last stop, which is Fruiton. I am going to try and stay at the Holiday Inn, the one just off the highway by the Waffle House.*

*I will be there for at least a week, and I plan to spend the time mostly in places that were special to Jim and me, meditating and trying to get a feel for where he might have gone. Surely he must have said something to clue me in back then, and I think if I go back to our old haunts, I might remember something that will help find him.*

*I hope you will find it in your heart to call me, especially if you think of anything that could help me as I follow my quest. If not, I sure understand, as I have been where you so clearly are now. Remember, there is help available if you take it!*

*While in Fruiton, I will also be talking to people who knew Jim, like your cousin Clarice, but do not worry! I will not say anything about the enraged black man you were fighting in your apartment or the tree-climbing, as I know no one can make you get help. Only you can help you! I will say hey to Clarice for you.*

*Remember, it isn't your fault! You do not deserve it! There are shelters if you need to hide!*

*—Rose Mae Wheeler ← married name (divorced now, but I will be registered at the hotel under Wheeler if you decide you can talk to me).*

"Shit," I said, and threw the piece of paper onto my coffee table. Burr picked it up and started reading it. I sat silently, letting him finish, and when he looked up from the paper, I said, "I should have just lied. If I had thought up a good enough lie, I could have nipped this whole mess in the bud. Why didn't I lie?"

"I don't know, Lena," said Burr. "Why don't you ever lie to

anyone? Maybe you should give your cousin a heads-up?" He waved the paper at me. "This girl is not right."

I groaned and dropped my head onto the back of the sofa. This was God. It had to be God. Baptists don't believe in coincidence. I had tried to lie today and failed, even though I wanted to lie. I had tried to fornicate and failed, even though I wanted Burr. God wanted the deal broken for some reason, and the only thing left was Possett, Alabama. God was forcing me back there, step by unwilling step.

My aunt Florence was about to march triumphantly all over her kitchen, lofting her biscuit pans like victory banners. Because the truth was, I had to protect Clarice. I couldn't let Rose Mae Lolley go down to Possett and start hounding her and digging up the past. Clarice knew just enough to hurt me. At the same time, she didn't know enough to realize how volatile her information could be in Rose Mae's hands.

Burr was looking at me meditatively, waiting.

I sat up and crossed my arms. "So, Burr. I'm thinking next week I'm going to go ahead and drive down to Possett before summer quarter starts. I don't know if I'll make it to my uncle's party or anything. But if you can get some vacation time and you want to go down with me and meet my family, now's your chance."

Burr's eyes narrowed, and he looked at me for a long time. I could practically hear the whir and click of his brain as he thought it through. At last he said, "What is in that note that I am not reading?"

I shook my head helplessly at him. "I swore a long time ago I would never go back there, Burr. But now you want me to take you so bad, it's a deal breaker. And yes, maybe there's other stuff going on. I don't want this psycho tracking down my cousin like she was tracking me. And yes, my aunt Florence is still waging her constant campaign to drag me home. This may be three birds with one stone, but you are one of the birds. My favorite bird, actually. The truth is, I don't want to go at all. But if I have to, then I really do want you with me. I need you with me."

He regarded me for a long time, weighing it. Then he said, deadpan, "Woo-hoo. Road trip."

# CHAPTER

——∞∞——

## 4

THERE ARE GODS in Alabama. I know because I killed one. But if you want the truth of it, the way-down-under-everything absolute probable truth of it, it's this: I killed him for Clarice.

I'm not saying personal revenge was not a part of it. I'm not saying I didn't hate him on my own account. I'm not even saying that had my cousin never been born, I wouldn't have eventually made my way up to the top of Lipsmack Hill and laid him out. I am only saying that I believe firmly and with a true heart that in the middle of the moment, in that second when time slowed and I saw every pore on the back of his neck, when I heard his last breath hissing out of his throat, I could have stopped.

There was a pause before momentum took me, and in that endless second, I could have walked away and let him inhale again, let him blink and stretch and turn and see me, let him maybe smile at me and say "Hey, Arlene" in his low-down, drawly voice. But in that moment, I thought of Clarice, and I knew things Clarice would never know. I thought about how innocent she was, how golden, how light seemed to spill out of her and warm everything around her, even me. And I put that up against the hot-eyed, evil way I had seen Jim Beverly watching her, watching with such constancy. I knew what he was, so I did not pause and I did not walk away and he never breathed in again.

I may have dressed my motive up in Clarice's clothes and lent it her perfume, but I'm not pretending she was to blame. I admit the choice was mine. I'm only saying that how much I owed Clarice was a factor. I owed her everything. She saved my life.

When I was little, I hardly knew Clarice, much less her parents or her brother, Wayne. My world revolved around my immediate family, Mama and Daddy and me. It was a regulation happy childhood.

My father was a compact man, dark and wiry. He was firm and resolute, but so soft-spoken that I don't have a single memory of him yelling. My mother wore an apron and made cookies and shopped the PX with the other officers' wives. Sometimes she had nervous spells. She'd lock herself into a closet or wedge herself way far back under the bed until Daddy got home to coax her out. On bad days she became terrified of opening canned foods. But most of the time she seemed like everyone else's mother.

We moved a lot, military base to military base, so I did not grow up knowing Clarice or any of my Alabama relatives well. I saw Clarice and Wayne only at the odd Christmas or Thanksgiving. We would stay at Aunt Flo's house because my daddy did not get along with my asshole grampa. Every morning my father would snap the leash on Wayne's dog, Buddy, and take me and my two cousins out for a long ramble.

But that all changed when I was seven years old. We were living on post at Fort Monroe. Our building was painted a warm white and had tall ceilings. All the walls had long windows, and the floors were honey-colored hardwood.

I was sitting on the floor making a cat out of Play-Doh. I was pinching the cat's head to give him ears when the phone rang. I could hear the background buzz of my mother padding to answer it. Then she said, "Oh, Florence, no." A pause and then she said again, "Oh no. No, no, no." She said more things, and then she hung up the phone and she was weeping. I was frightened, so I did not listen to her words, just kept pinching the cat's ears while Mama's voice washed around me, anguished and hysterical. Daddy held her while she screamed and beat her legs on the floor.

I was pinching so hard the tiny strings of Play-Doh came off into my hands. The cat's head got smaller and smaller until he had no head left.

Mama choked and cried on Daddy, wailing out a story about my cousin Wayne. Something about yellow jackets. Something about Wayne's dog, Buddy. I couldn't understand it. My cousin Wayne was dead, Mama said, and we had to go to Alabama right then, right then, because Florence needed her.

We never went. Because later that day, after my mother had been given her nervous pills and put to bed, my graceful daddy tripped while loading Mama's suitcase into the car. When he fell, his thighbone snapped like a brittle bit of ice, and that's how we found out he had cancer. It was in his stomach and his liver and had worked its way deep into his bones.

We stayed in Kansas while it wasted him and made him frightening and thin. Then it got into his brain until my daddy, who never yelled, yelled all the time in a raspy voice in a military hospital room that smelled like pee. Finally they sent him home with us to die, and he did die. It didn't take as long as you might think.

Right before he died, my mother started taking his pain pills. One for me, one for you, sharing them out. I remember a nurse came to give him injections, too. He was at that stage when they refilled his prescriptions without blinking, and no one worried that he was taking too many pills. Mama started squirreling them away. One for me, one for you, one for later. As he got worse, so did she. Two for me, three for you, four for later.

After he died, Mama spent all her time blankly sifting through bills and sympathy cards without ever opening a single envelope. She went to a new doctor who gave her antidepressants. She took them on top of her hoard of pain pills and her nervous pills.

The army still paid us, but not enough, especially since with Daddy gone, we couldn't live on post. We moved to a town apartment, and I could never remember which green door was ours, they were all so alike.

I couldn't go to the school on post anymore. I got skinnier, and Mama rarely remembered to give me a bath. She was afraid to open the lid on the washer, so I sifted through laundry piles and dressed myself in the cleanest things I could find. I had no friends in the new school. The town kids were unused to seeing new faces every month. They weren't like military brats who must master early the art of instant friendship.

At lunch I stared at my tray and chewed my ratty black hair and the ends of my fingers like a wild thing. I didn't smell very good. The other kids seemed to think that if they touched me, they might catch dead-daddy-itis, and they would lose their daddies and smell bad and chew their fingers until they bled, too. I was probably the only second-grader at Samuel Gompers Elementary who obsessively read *Lord of the Flies* because I could really relate to the pigs.

Aunt Florence saved us. She came roaring up to Kansas in my uncle Bruster's second-best pickup truck to claim us after being unable to get my mother on the phone. Our phone had been cut off because Mama couldn't open envelopes. I could finally find our apartment when I walked home from school. It was the one with eviction notices on the front door.

I remember very clearly hanging limp in Aunt Florence's masterful grip as she shook me like a floppy puppy and said, "Do you not see this child is dying on the vine? Look at this child! Your child is dying, do you not see this?" Aunt Florence dug her hands almost painfully into my shoulders, pressing my feet hard against the floor, grounding me.

My mother stared back, glazed and calm, not seeing. "All right, then," said Florence. "We can fit your good dishes and the china cabinet in the back of the truck, and the rest of the furniture smells like it needs to be burned anyway. Filth. This place is all-over filth. Even the paint smells. You can kiss your deposit good-bye."

She single-handedly packed up what she could salvage. She bathed me and bundled me into clothes she had washed. She bathed my mother and dressed her, too. While Florence marched in and out, filling up the back of the pickup with our things, my mother sat limp and uncaring in my daddy's old armchair, and I watched big-eyed and wary from the floor at her feet. At last I fell asleep there on a clean towel my aunt had put down because she said she wouldn't put an animal in my filthy bed.

The next day Florence loaded us into the cab of the truck and drove us down to Alabama. I rode in between them, my feet dangling down on either side of the gearshift. It was late November, and the trees were leafless and frightening. A year ago, at Christmas, Aunt Florence and Mama had been lovely tall blond ladies, soft and rounded, almost identical. They'd had ninety-watt smiles that showed a lot of square teeth, and shiny eyes as big and round as quarters.

Now, on one side of me, my mother's pretty plumpness had run to fat. She was squashy and amorphous. In the fading daylight, her face look blurred, as if it were made of pale wax that was melting and her whole face might slide off her skull and slither into her lap. On my other side, Aunt Florence had withered and hardened. She was a stick figure, and her skin was so dry, her arms and cheeks were chapped and ashy. Her mouth seemed permanently clamped into a lipless line. I could see the intricate bones of her wrists, and the unmovable grasp of her skeletal hands on the wheel. I sat ramrod straight between them, unable to lean one way or the other and rest.

We got to Possett just past dawn. I was bleary but awake, staring at the town as we drove through it on the main drag. We stopped at both of its traffic lights. Town was three blocks long. At the end of town was the drugstore that had a diner in the back.

On the other side of the street, three small tin outbuildings, like gardening sheds, stood in a neat row. Someone had nailed a single long board across the top of all three of them, and in hand-stenciled letters it read POLICE DEPARTMENT, FIRE DEPT, JAIL.

"Police Department" was too long, and the "ent" crossed over into "Fire Dept's" rightful territory. It occurred to me that the word "department" had hogged up so much room that the fire department had been forced to use an abbreviation. I wondered if they were angry with the police. I would have been.

We left town behind and headed down Route 19, a country road that led through soybean and cotton fields and pastures to my aunt's house. My aunt's neighborhood was converted farmland. There were only about twenty houses, all small ranches on huge lots with room for a working garden or a henhouse. Some had pastureland attached, with a barn for a horse or goats.

Aunt Florence had devoted over an acre to a fenced-in vegetable and herb garden. She had a shed back there, with electricity and running water, and a concrete drive from the main road led to a parking pad beside the shed. The house itself was a white ranch they had dressed up in some very ugly and obvious vinyl siding. It had dark green shutters. We turned down a side road and took the gravel drive that led to the carport.

As we pulled in, I could see my cousin Clarice sitting on the steps that led down from the back door into the carport. She wore a white cotton nightdress with short puffed sleeves, and her knees were tucked up inside the gown. She had turtled her arms in as well, and had folded herself up inside so that she looked like a ball of white lawn with a head.

She stood up as Aunt Florence pulled up the emergency brake and turned off the truck's engine. Her long golden legs appeared as if by magic, and her arms flailed around inside and then found the armholes and came shooting out. To my tired eyes, she looked like one of those pellets you drop in water, and when the casing dissolves, a sponge animal blooms, lovely and sudden.

Florence got out, but Mama wasn't moving. She didn't seem to be aware that we had arrived, just sat slack in the passenger seat, so I stayed by her. Aunt Flo went to rouse Uncle Bruster to unload, and he followed her out of the house in flannel pajamas, scrubbing at his eyes. He lifted me out of the truck with his great big bear's arms. As he set me on the ground, he tousled my hair and said, "Hey there, girlie. Your aunt Flo says we get to keep you. I guess me and Clarice can quit little-girl shopping on weekends, huh?" And then he headed to the back of the truck to wrestle out Mama's things. I supposed on one of their trips back and forth with the bags, they would unload Mama, like so much furniture.

Clarice walked over to where I stood by the side of the truck. She looked pretty and whole and just like herself. She threw one arm around me and started gabbling at me, saying, "I've been up forever waiting. Hurry and come on in. I'm about to freeze." She pulled me towards the house, chattering and friendly.

Clarice was the only thing that felt right. The air in the house was too still, and it was too quiet. The noises of Aunt Florence and Uncle Bruster, dragging our bags and boxes into the house, were staccato and abrupt. It was as if the house swallowed sounds before they could fade away. Sleep-deprived and a little frightened, I imagined the house wanted Wayne with all his boy noise and karate violence to stir it to life.

Unable to help myself, I went first to Wayne's old room. Clarice came with me, one arm still draped over my shoulder. Wayne's room had been stripped. I remembered it with cowboy wallpaper and bunk beds, with Erector-set debris and Lego and action figures strewn all over the floor and desk, Buddy flopped like an extra-large yellow throw pillow on the bottom bed.

Since I had last seen the room, someone had gone after the walls with a razor, scraping the cowboys away and then painting them a stark, institutional white. Wayne's scuffed bunk beds and toy chest had been replaced by an ancient brass double bed and a mirrorless dresser. My dead aunt Niner's padded rocker was squatting by the closet where Wayne's desk had been. Bruster had brought in a load of Mama's things, and two Hefty bags filled with her clothes sat side by side on the new oatmeal-colored carpet. The room smelled so strongly of lemon Pledge and Lysol that it made my eyes water.

"Where's Buddy?" I said, and Clarice looked at me with round eyes, alarmed. She put a finger over her lips and shook her head at me. Then she pulled me away, out and down the hall. She led me by the hand to the cheery, noisy colors of her bedroom. Apple green warred with gold and hot pink. Aunt Florence had put the new oatmeal carpet all through the house, but except for that, Clarice's room was just as I remembered it.

Clarice had always had a thing for daisies; her room was coated with them. Her dust ruffle was covered in yellow and white daisies, and she had added a few daisy-shaped throw cushions. She even had daisy decals all over the ceramic base of her apple-green lamp.

Clarice saw me looking and snatched up the lamp. "Sniff it," she said, scratching at one of the decals and then thrusting the lamp at my face. "It's s'posed to smell like real daisies, but it smells like fake ones to me." I sniffed dutifully at the lamp, wondering what fake daisies smelled like. Burned sugar, mostly. I saw my suitcase sitting on top of one of the twin beds and fell gratefully beside it, breathing in deep to catch the candy-sweet aliveness that was in Clarice's air.

Clarice had always been too grown up and glowing to be real to me, so pretty and assured and tall. At Christmases past I had been the tagalong, smaller and younger and sometimes unnoticed, trailing in the boiling wake Clarice and Wayne left behind them as they galloped about the house. But now this same Clarice flopped down beside me and said, "I always wanted a sister," even though it meant she had to give up having her own room. We fell asleep listening to Uncle Bruster cuss out my mama's china cabinet as he wrestled it down the hall.

The next day my aunt drove us into Fruiton to register me at Mosely Elementary. Florence bullied the school principal into skipping me ahead and putting me in Clarice's third-grade class. The principal voiced some concerns about my age and size, but Aunt Florence talked over him, winning by sheer volume, while my mother drooped uncaring in his office and I picked the ends of my fingers off.

"The child is reading books I don't understand, and you're worried about her 'social adjustment'?" said Aunt Florence. "Arlene here might know what that means, with all her fancy reading, but I don't know any social adjustment. All I know is she's smart as a whip, and in the third-grade classroom my girl will be there to look out for her."

The principal was right in theory. I was incapable of social adjustment to a third-grade classroom. But I would have been just as incapable in the second, where I belonged.

In the third-grade room, it didn't matter. Clarice calmly adjusted everyone else to fit me. It soon became apparent that if anyone wanted Clarice to come to their sleepover or birthday party, or to play on their kick-ball team—and they all did—then they had to invite me, too.

I'd been in school about two weeks when Mama had one of her fits in the middle of the night. She was banging the wall so loudly that she woke up everyone in the house. Clarice and I sat up, and Clarice said, "That's in Wayne's room."

I said, "Mama," and leaped up and went running down the hall, with Clarice a beat behind me.

The banging stopped as I reached the doorway. I looked in and saw Aunt Flo sitting on Mama. Mama must have been banging Wayne's wall with her face, because bright blood was jetting out of her nose. Florence had Mama's shoulders pinned with her knees. Mama was flopping like a trout under her. Florence was grimly silent, riding her, and the only noise from Mama were little grunting puffs that made the blood streaming from her nostrils bubble and pop. Uncle Bruster loomed up behind us, and Florence saw us all there. She snapped, "Call an ambulance, Bruster, and you girls better get. Back to bed. Now."

Clarice took my shoulder and pulled me away. We went back to our room and lay in the dark, listening to the EMTs take Mama away for her first stay at the nervous hospital over in Deer Park.

I rolled over on my side and looked at Clarice. She was awake, looking back at me.

"What's wrong with her?" Clarice said. "Is she sick?"

"I don't know," I said. "She's just weird that way sometimes." I felt cold and small and scared in my bed. "I wish y'all's dog was still here," I said. "What happened to Buddy?"

There was a long silence from the other bed, and then Clarice said, "You know how Wayne died?"

"Sort of," I said. I thought of my mama sobbing out the story to Daddy. Something about yellow jackets. Something about Wayne's dog.

After another long pause, Clarice began talking. Her voice was flat and colorless in the darkness. It was like she was reciting something she had memorized a long time ago.

"Buddy was on a clothesline, tied up to that big pine in the backyard, and Wayne was out playing with him. And I guess they stirred up some yellow jackets. They nest down in holes in the ground. Daddy always pours gasoline in, but he missed this one. It was a big nest, and they all came out pretty mad.

"A few stung Buddy, but for some reason they mostly headed for Wayne. When Wayne went to run for the house, Buddy was running, too, but Buddy was scared and he didn't run right. He was going crazy around in circles. And he got Wayne all tangled up in the clothesline, and Buddy ran around the tree and he kept running around it and winding up Wayne. He tethered Wayne to the tree.

"The yellow jackets, they kept on stinging Wayne. They aren't like bees. They can sting and sting."

Clarice took a shuddery gulping breath. I slipped out of bed and got in beside her, held her hand in the dark.

"So then anyway, me and Mama went outside because we were going to work in the garden. She was carrying a shovel she'd bought new at the Wal-Mart, taking it to put down in the shed.

"We walked out and we saw Wayne. I looked at him, and I couldn't even see that it was Wayne, you know? I couldn't make out his face. It looked to me like his eyes were gone, but I think it was because he was so swollen, they had puffed shut. I think he was already dead. But Buddy was fine. The yellow jackets were gone, mostly.

"But Mama, she took in the whole thing in one breath. She looked there at Wayne lying so still, all tangled in that leash and tied up to the tree, and Buddy sitting by him, and one or two of the yellow jackets whipping around mad, and she understood everything.

"Mama made this awful noise. You never heard a noise like that. No one ever did. Mama went towards Wayne. And Buddy was trying to come forward and meet her, wagging his tail. He was still tied to Wayne, and he was pulling, and it made Wayne's foot move a little. As Mama got up to where Buddy was pulling at Wayne, she swung the shovel off her shoulder and down, right onto Buddy's head. It made this noise, like a crunching-thud noise. It didn't even slow her down. It was so smooth, like swinging a shovel down was a normal part of running for her. Buddy flopped down onto the ground as she passed, and his head was mashed in. But she wasn't looking at Buddy. She dropped the shovel by him and got the clothesline, and she untied Wayne and picked him up in her arms."

I squeezed Clarice's hand in the dark, and we were quiet together.

"So that's what happened," Clarice said at last. "It's weird how time goes sometimes. All that seemed to happen so fast, like in four heartbeats, but it took a really long time."

I said, "When Daddy died, time got very slow. Every day took so long, and it was like Mama and me sat waiting around for the day to be over, but then the next day kept happening, and we had to wait through that one, too. It's better now that we're here."

"It's better for me, too. It's better with you here."

I don't remember falling asleep, but I stayed in her bed with her, and from that night on, she and I were like sisters. I wasn't even afraid, left alone with the Lukeys while Mama was under observation over in Deer Park, because Clarice was with me. We were close all the way up until the night things went bad on us, when we were freshmen in high school.

No, that's not right. We didn't fall apart until after, sophomore year, when I got so secretive and crazy and started "running around." Running around was as close as Clarice would ever come to saying "fucking any boy who would hold still for long enough." I couldn't explain it to her, because in a twisted way, I did what I did with those boys for her. Or at least because of her. Even then she never said one word in public that indicated she was anything less than delighted with me.

The truth is, even when she was barely speaking to me, I never stopped loving her. I can say that with no uncertainty, no matter what else is true. I would have killed for her. And of course, eventually I did.

# CHAPTER

## 5

BURR AND I left for Possett early Monday morning. We were planning to drive the whole fifteen hours in one day, so I had told Aunt Florence we would arrive late Monday night. I wanted to be sure I got there ahead of Rose Mae.

Florence had crowed in triumph when I called to tell her I was coming. I had been so irritated with her that I rang off too fast. I told her I was bringing my boyfriend but neglected to mention that he was black. I also didn't exactly make it clear that we might leave town before Uncle Bruster's party on Friday. Once she met Burr, I thought, the invitation might be revoked anyway.

I'd spent my early childhood years living on military bases with friends of all colors, but at Aunt Florence and Uncle Bruster's house, Burr was not going to go over very well. It wasn't like they had a closetful of giant oil-soaked crosses and pointy white hats, and I had never heard any of my relatives use the word "nigger." But they didn't use it for the same reason that they didn't say "Pass those shitty-ass peas." It wasn't nice.

The idea that black folks were not like us was such obvious and fundamental truth to the Lukeys, and Aunt Flo's relatives, the Bents, that they did not have to use ugly words to point it out. Their prejudice was so ingrained, it was as much a part of them as the Lukey blue eyes and the Bent women's propensity to take to secret drink.

My plan was to get in there, introduce Burr, get disowned, and then check in at the Fruiton Holiday Inn before Rose Mae Lolley arrived. I would intercept her before she descended on Clarice, defuse her, and send her packing with a yet to be determined lie, then get the hell out while the getting was good. With any luck, Aunt Flo would get on the phone with the extended family, and all the Lukeys and the Bents (except Clarice, I hoped) would wash their hands of me. I would never have to worry about going down to Possett, Alabama, again as long as I lived. On the downside, they might lay siege to the Holiday Inn and light us on fire.

We took Burr's Blazer, as it was bigger, and I didn't think my Honda could take the trip. Burr drove the first shift, negotiating the city streets while I read. Once we were on the highway, he got bored and made me put my book away and play car games. Burr and I were not car-game traditionalists. We looked down on plebeian fare like Name That Tune and Road Sign Alphabet, preferring to make up our own games.

We tuned the radio to one of Chicago's few country-music stations and played a game I had made up called My Heart Is a Fart. We'd listen to the first line of a country ballad, then take turns thinking of the dirtiest line possible to follow it. It had to rhyme, and we had to sing it loud enough to drown out the actual lyrics.

Eventually we were drowning out each other, laughing like

lunatics until we were hoarse. We played the game all the way to the Indiana state line, where we started to lose the signal.

Burr turned off the radio and pointed to the WELCOME TO INDIANA sign looming up ahead of us. "Here it comes. Are you ready?" he asked.

The Burroughses had a family tradition on road trips. Burr and I had gone to Wisconsin together quite a few times, and once down to Detroit for a mutual friend's wedding, so I was familiar with it. As we approached the sign, Burr lifted one hand off the wheel and glanced at me. I said, "You know this is a little weird, right?" But I lifted my hand, too.

I turned around in my seat, and Burr sneaked glances over his shoulder. "Goodbye, Illinois," we yelled in singsong, waving our lifted hands as we crossed the state line. Then we faced forward, still waving, and yelled, "Hello, Indiana."

"Don't we trade off driving at each state line?" Burr asked.

"Come on, it isn't even an hour to Indiana, you wuss."

"All right. Let's play the Pants on Fire game," said Burr. He shot me a sideways glance, just a bit smug. I smelled a trap. "I'll go first. Your cousin tries on a dress at a store. She comes out of the changing room, looking like a truck, and says, 'Does this dress make me look fat?' What do you say?"

"Is it my cousin Clarice or my cousin Fat Agnes?" I asked.

"Why do you call your cousin Fat Agnes?" Burr asked.

"That's her name. She's my uncle Luke-John's daughter, and her given name is Fat Agnes Lukey. I keep telling you, Burr, these people you are so hot to meet are moderately dangerous loons."

"All right, fine," said Burr. "Play the game. In this hypothetical, it's your cousin Agnes."

"Then I say no," I said and shrugged.

"Aha!" said Burr.

"No, not 'Aha!' I haven't told a lie," I said. "The dress may make her look bad, but it can't be blamed for making her look fat. Fat Agnes is heavy no matter what she wears."

"Okay, then. What if it's Clarice and the dress makes her look heavier?"

"No way, cheater," I said. "You don't get to change it in the middle. It's my turn."

We played back and forth for a while, making up hypothetical situations and watching the other try to avoid revealing unpleasant truths without being caught in a falsehood. Burr had made up Pants on Fire on the trip to Detroit. He invented it partly to try and figure out how my system of not lying worked, but it was also fun. Anyway, as I had pointed out, the game was probably teaching him invaluable skills he would use every day as a tax attorney. We played for over an hour, exiting once to load up at a drive-through before they stopped serving breakfast at eleven. I liked to eat a lot in the car.

Once we were back on the road and had plowed our way through a huge bag of hot food, I got the pillow and blanket out of the backseat. I pulled on one of Burr's baseball caps and settled in for a nap. I said, "Okay, last one. Your girlfriend—"

"My cute girlfriend," interrupted Burr.

"Yes," I said. "Your adorable girlfriend says to you, 'Honey, will you do me a favor?' "

"Uh-oh," said Burr.

"Uh-oh, indeed. So you say, 'Sure, baby.' "

"Why would I do that without asking what the favor is?"

"Because two reasons," I said, wrapping the blanket around my legs. "One, she's adorable. As we have established."

"I said cute," said Burr.

"Ah, the perfect segue into reason two, which is that this is my hypothetical. So she's adorable, and she asks you for a favor, and you say, 'Sure, baby, I'll do you any favor you need.' Then she says, 'I know you have been hiding a deep and terrible secret from me, and I want you to tell me what it is.' "

"I assume I have been hiding one?" said Burr. "Since this is your hypothetical."

"Of course," I said.

"Fine. I say, 'I won't tell you.' "

"Aha!" I said. I closed my eyes and pulled Burr's cap down low to block out the light.

"Telling her I won't tell her is not a lie."

"But you said you would do her the favor, so if you refuse to tell her, then that was the lie."

"Tricky," said Burr. "So I tell her the secret. If she stops loving me over a single dark secret, she was a bad girlfriend. Unless the secret is something Jerry Springer, like I'm really a woman, or I'm having sex with her mother."

"Then I still get a point, because you didn't *not* tell a lie."

"Wait, what? I didn't lie."

"Right," I said. "Exactly. You told the truth, which is not the same thing as *not* lying. You have to *not* lie to win."

"Let me think about it."

Burr turned the radio on softly. I closed my eyes, but my brain was going ninety miles an hour. As tired as I was, I couldn't stop trying to invent a good enough lie to divert Rose Mae Lolley. Best-case scenario, my lie would make her give up her quest and leave Fruiton, but at the very least, it had to make her stay away from Clarice. My only other option was making up a lie that would keep Clarice and Bud from talking to Rose, but I would much rather lie to Rose Mae than to the nicest relative I had.

"I got it," Burr said. "The only way out is to begin an argument about semantics. I can posit that a favor is something you do, and refuse to answer on the grounds that answering a question is not a favor. In fact, I can say I'm still willing to do the promised favor, but I'm not willing to answer a question. I can tell her if she wanted information instead of action, she should have said, 'Will you answer a question for me.'"

"Brilliant, counselor," I said. I snuggled deeper in the blanket.

"Lena?" said Burr softly. "If I asked you for a favor, would you answer a question for me?"

I peeked out at him from under the ball cap. His eyes were steady on the road, but he was serious. I should have known my hypothetical would take us into dangerous territory. I sat up and pulled off the cap. "There goes any chance at sleeping," I said. "This is the moment you choose to ask me if I have any deep, dark secrets I want to discuss? Right now, on the road trip from hell, when I'm under so much stress my heart could burst at any second?"

Burr grinned and held up one hand. "Truce! Withdrawn! The witness may step down. Feel like driving the next leg? If you can't sleep, I can."

Burr caught a nap, and I drove and listened to the radio. I woke him up in time to say goodbye to Indiana and hello to Kentucky. He was superstitious about that, and I knew if I changed states without waking him up to wave, his head would explode. He sat up blearily, and we did the geographical salutations. I pulled off to get gas and more food. Then I drove us all the way to the point where we bade Kentucky adieu and greeted Tennessee.

"This is now the farthest south I have ever been," Burr said. He took the wheel, but I still couldn't sleep. I sat staring blankly out the side window.

When it became obvious I wasn't going to nap, Burr began a game of What Have I Got in My Pocketses that lasted us all the way to Nashville. This was a game we'd invented, and we played it in the car and sometimes on slow winter afternoons in front of the fireplace at his bachelor pad. We would each make up a long, complicated story. Burr usually finished his first. When he had the plot points down, he would tell me half the story and give me some background on the characters so I knew who was who. The catch was, the stories were always told backwards. So Burr would start at the end and trace events back through time until he got to the middle. Then he would stop telling it and say, "What have I got in my pocketses?"

I had to listen carefully, and he had to tell a story with an ending so inevitable that I would then be able to tell him the first half of his story. Not only able to—forced to. The end had to come out of one possible beginning.

I'd never get the story exactly as he had imagined it. He'd have five plot points in mind, and he'd get a point for every one of them I had to use to get to his beginning. If I found a narrative path around one of his plot points, I got a point. If I said anything that contradicted something he had told me, he could stop me and I would have to go back. After I told the first half, he'd tally up the points. Then I'd tell him mine.

By the time we'd played three rounds, we were almost through Nashville. I was so tired that things were starting to look a bit surreal in the fading light. The edges of objects in my peripheral vision were running together. I was supposed to drive the last leg of the trip, as I had much better night vision than Burr, but I didn't see how I could do it.

"I think we should stop for the night," I said. "I haven't been sleeping well with this trip looming over me, and I'm scared I'll run us off the road. Let's get a couple of hotel rooms and drive the last leg in the morning. I can call Aunt Flo from the hotel. She won't care. She'd rather me be a day late than dead in a ditch."

"Sure, baby," said Burr.

I said, "I'm not putting off your meeting them. I really am too tired to drive."

"I didn't accuse you of anything," Burr said. "I know you're not looking forward to this. But if we're serious, then I have to meet your family sometime."

"We're here, aren't we?" I shot back.

"Yes, but let's not pretend this trip is all about me and what I want, Lena. There are other factors at work here." He kept his eyes on the road and added, "Maybe your family will surprise you. If they get to know me, maybe you and I can change their attitude."

"Right," I said brightly. "It would happen just that way if this was a sitcom. Very special episode. Come on, Burr. This is real life. You can't stick a quarter in someone and push their nose and get any candy bar you like. People don't work that way. I mean, sure, there is cause and effect, but it isn't predictable."

"So you don't think a traumatic or even joyful event can make a difference in a person's life? You don't believe in revelation or epiphany?"

"I think people have epiphanies all the time. Usually they're worthless. Maybe two percent of the time, someone may decide to change some aspect of their behavior. It's like Paul on the road to Damascus. Here's this anal-retentive control freak who likes to run around and persecute Christians. So God knocks him down and blinds him and reams him out. So he stops persecuting Christians. But—go read him. He was still an anal-retentive control freak. He changed his behavior, but I don't believe people can change their essential natures. The things that happen to me just make me more me."

Burr didn't answer. After a few minutes, he said, "There's a Courtyard off this next exit, how does that suit you?"

"Fine, if you're paying," I said. "Otherwise let's hit the Red Roof."

"I'm paying," he said.

Burr checked us into adjoining rooms, and then he went to bring up our bags while I called for room service. I was too sleepy to go eat. We quietly ate club sandwiches in his room, and then I went through the adjoining door to mine. The rooms were pretty standard hotel fare: two double beds with a Monet print hanging above each bed. *Water Lilies.*

I felt sticky from being in the car all day, so I took a shower and then brushed my teeth and combed my wet hair. I changed into the soft T-shirt and leggings I'd brought to sleep in. Then I lay down in the double bed closest to the door between our rooms. We had left it cracked. Burr had a light on in there; he was reading. My eyes felt heated and gritty. I closed them, but still I couldn't sleep.

I got back out of bed and opened the adjoining door, leaning in the frame. Burr was sitting up in the bed closest to me, with a couple of pillows propped up behind him. The bed was still made, and he was on top of the comforter, but he was wearing a white undershirt and a pair of pajama bottoms with lobsters all over them that I had given him for Christmas.

"I can hear you rustling around in here," I said.

He put his book down on the bedside table and patted the open space beside him. "If you can't sleep, come talk to me. I could hear you thinking in there."

I lay down beside him on my back, and he slipped an arm around me. I rested my head on his chest. "What did you hear me thinking?"

"Not so much thinking," he said, "as worrying. I can hear your gears grinding. Nervous about me meeting your family?"

"Of course I am," I said. "Burr, we don't talk much about it. This whole thing where I'm white and you're black."

"Because those are facts," said Burr. "Here's another fact: My car is a Blazer. We don't spend a lot of time mulling that one over, either."

"That's because your car being a Blazer doesn't have any con-sequences except a good warranty. Oh, save me from that. But you're coming down to meet my family now, Burr. Just wanting to meet them, that says something. About us, about where we're heading."

Burr grinned. "Why, Ms. Fleet, are you asking me what my in-tentions are?"

I laughed. "I guess I am. I was thinking about that night we had that big fight and you almost broke up with me. I had this idea that you were going to propose to me at dinner. Was I way off base?"

He was silent, looking down at me. He turned on the pillow,

scooting down until he was lying beside me and facing me, eye to eye. "Yeah, I was," he said.

"Why didn't you?" I asked. He smelled like Crest toothpaste, and under that I caught the warm smoky smell that was Burr.

"When I planned to ask you, I thought you'd say yes. Listening to you work over your aunt, I realized I didn't know what you would say. You never do the little things that show a commitment. I wondered what made me think you'd do the biggest one."

I thought about that for a minute. I reached into the small space between us and found his hand, taking it in mine, and said, "If we got married, things would be different. Not so much for me. I mean, my career is going to be academic, and half of them don't care and the other half applaud our couplehood as a political statement."

"That's the white people," said Burr. "Meanwhile, the black academics, half of them don't care, and the other half see you as a white trophy bitch who has usurped the rightful place of a black woman."

I laughed again. "I'd have to be prettier to qualify as a trophy bitch. I need longer legs and fake eyelashes. Maybe some fake boobs, too. Or any boobs, really."

"You're plenty pretty enough to be my trophy bitch," said Burr. "Lena, I love you, but posit for a moment that love isn't enough. Look at the big picture. We have the same religion, the same politics, we're both careful with money, we both want at least two kids, and we're best friends—that right there wipes out eighty percent of the possible divorce-level fights we could have. As soon as you discover what a god I am in bed, the other twenty percent goes out the window. That's all the stuff that's inside our house.

"The stuff that's outside our house? Forget it. We're used to it. We can bar the door and pull down our shades. It'll be tougher if we get married. And tougher still if we have kids. But as long as it stays outside our house, we'll be fine. I think you're worth it, even if you didn't have the sense to be born a Nubian goddess."

I scooted towards him, wrapping my arms around him and burying my head in his chest. "You're so smart, and you always say the exact right thing."

"Good for me," said Burr. "Now get back to your bed before I ravage you and ruin you before I have officially proposed."

That reminded me of this story the youth minister's wife told all the girls who came to the eighth-grade lock-in at Possett First Baptist Church. Clarice and I were there. In the story there was this beautiful young Baptist virgin, and she was engaged to a Baptist boy. The boy pressured her all the time to have sex, even though he knew it was wrong. He couldn't help but ask, because he was a boy and therefore ruled by his genitalia and not responsible for his actions.

So she, like any good Baptist girl, decided to be responsible for both their actions and steadfastly said no and kept his hands below her knees or above her shoulders, as all good Baptist girls are taught to do from birth on.

The night before their wedding, they went out together to lie on a hill and look up at the stars, and he started pressuring her again. "Well," she thought, "the wedding is tomorrow." And she gave in. The next day her father walked her down the aisle, but there was no groom waiting at the end of it. Instead the best man read a note to her, aloud, in front of everyone. It said, "I can't marry a whore who would have sex outside the bonds of mar-

riage. I thought you were a better person than that." The girl
fainted and her life was ruined, the end.

The story made a huge impression on me at the time. I kept
running it over and over in my head, the betrayal, the public hu-
miliation. "Never, never," vowed the girl who would later fuck
her entire sophomore class, "no, never, will I have premarital sex."
Which of course was the youth minister's wife's whole freakin'
point.

The next night, as Clarice and I lay in our twin beds at home,
I couldn't get the story out of my head and go to sleep. I couldn't
stop seeing myself as the bride, standing there alone in my white
dress, hearing that note read aloud to the entire town of Possett.
I saw myself trying to stagger away, back up the aisle of Possett
First Baptist. Then the congregation would rise as one and stone
me to death.

"I can't imagine how horrible it would be," I whispered to
Clarice, but that was a lie. In actuality, I was imagining it over
and over, with me in the starring role.

"That girl was lucky," said Clarice.

"Lucky?" I said.

"Oh my Lordy, yes, so lucky. What if she hadn't done it with
him? What if she'd actually married him and only found out way,
way later when they had kids and she was totally stuck?"

"Found out what?" I said, not getting it.

"Found out that he was the kind of person who could do
something so mean to someone he was supposed to love," Clarice
said.

I told the story to Burr, but by the end he was barely listening.
He was smelling my hair and his hands were roving and I lost the

thread of it. I caught his hands in my own, between us, and we were very close together. "Back, devil," I said.

Burr growled like a bear. Then he took one of his hands out of mine and pointed emphatically at my room. But I did not move. My body, pressed close to his, was tired and limp and easy. I felt as malleable as warm wax. I thought, "Why not now, here, at a moment of my choosing." If I chose it from this place, so quiet and still, it seemed possible that it could be nothing more than love and sin.

Burr was right when he said I had other reasons for going home. He was getting what he wanted, but it was incidental to my own agenda. I was on the way back to Possett, and once there, I planned to lie, so my deal with God was as good as broken. I let go of his hand and wound my arms around him and kissed him, pressing myself bonelessly into him, quiescent and pliable.

He said my name into my mouth, maybe as a warning, but I broke the kiss and said, "Do you really want to question this? Do you really want to have some sort of talk right now?"

He kissed me again and I took that for no. I let my hands run over his body and wound my legs around him. Something broke in him then, and he slid one arm under me, around my waist, pressing me up and into him. He was moving me, and I felt such strength in him, in the flex and retraction of the muscles under his liquid hot skin.

I looked up at him, stayed with him, although I felt sleepy and slow, as if I were half a beat behind as he was surging. There was pleasure in the heat of him against me and then in me, pleasure in his pleasure, and over it all, this blanketed feeling of safety, as if he were storming all around me but I was lying quietly in the eye, moving with him, painlessly alive and present.

After, we lay looking at each other in the light from the bed-side lamp, solemnly, for quite some time. Then he reached over me and clicked it off. I closed my eyes and was almost instantly asleep.

# CHAPTER

## 6

I SPENT THE last week of summer before my sophomore
year at Fruiton High sitting in front of the television. When
school started up again, I knew I would have to see Jim Beverly.
He would be sauntering through the halls, passing out his easy
grins like party favors. I'd smell his spoor in every room of the
building. Even now, miles away from him, I couldn't bear to
think that he was somewhere alive in the world, breathing in and
out, probably having a wonderful time torturing mice or beating
up a baby.

A world with Jim Beverly in it was a constant wash of gray
tones that shifted around me as the morning talk shows faded
into a four-hour block of soap operas. The heated conversations
about love and betrayal were white noise, mercifully blanketing
my thoughts. One morning as I lay mutely on the rug, I happened to shift my dull gaze heavenward and gasped, my TV
trance broken. There, in glorious Technicolor, glossy and thick,

clinging to the ceiling by his six hairy feet, was the grandfather of all Alabama roaches.

In Chicago, when someone says, "Eeek, a roach!" they mean a prim little buglet is mincing its way up the wainscoting. In Alabama those same words mean something completely different.

I had never seen an Alabama roach when my mother and I moved back down to live with Aunt Florence, Uncle Bruster, and Clarice. I was just a kid. My second night in their house, I went into the hall bathroom to brush my teeth. Before, I remembered it had had kid wallpaper with fat baby dinosaurs scrubbing themselves in bubbly bathtubs. I guessed Aunt Florence had put the wallpaper up after she had Wayne. It had been primary colors, very boyish. But like his bedroom, the whole bathroom had been purged of anything remotely Wayne-like. The walls were now a soothing mental-institution pink, and the dinosaur shower curtain had been replaced by a pink plastic liner. On the floor was a loopy throw rug. It was striped in bright pink and blue and yellow and shaped like a tropical fish. The floor was made of tiny white tiles, like rows and rows of square teeth, scrubbed so aggressively that the grout between was almost as white as the tiles.

I opened the drawer by the sink and saw that Clarice had Angel Gel toothpaste. This was a kid toothpaste, new on the market. My mother, back in the days when she bought toothpaste, always bought regular old Crest. Angel Gel was pale pink and opalescent, and I squirted a generous measure onto my brush.

Something caught my eye, a large black spot on the Pepto-Bismol hand towel. Just as I looked towards it, the spot launched itself, spreading, shooting towards me with a buzzing, mechanical hiss. It landed on my toothbrush. Its mouth unfolded, separating into four parts, and it clipped a neat slice out of my pink toothpaste.

I threw the toothbrush away from me, hard, and then the whole world went into slo-mo. I watched the toothbrush spinning through the air, and as it fell, the creature clinging to its tip launched itself off the bristles, spreading its wings again and zooming in agonizing detail towards my head.

I fled shrieking down the hall, and that was my introduction to the Alabama roach, also known as a palmetto bug. Ever since that moment I have hated them with a black passion. The thought that one might touch me while I was sleeping, or run over my foot as I walked upstairs, haunted my summers.

This one, now on the den ceiling, was close to four inches long. He was hanging upside down right over my face.

I rolled quickly away and ran for the kitchen. I had the house to myself. Uncle Bruster was on his mail route. Aunt Florence was out working in her huge vegetable garden, where she spent most of her mornings. This was before she thought to put a lock on the cabinet where Mama's meds were kept, so she had dragged Mama down to the garden to keep an eye on her.

Clarice was sunbathing in the yard. She had wanted me to lie out with her, but I had chosen to mope inside, pale and sweating in three layers of black clothes.

On top of the refrigerator, Aunt Florence kept a noxious green spray bottle full of a solution called Dead Roach. It's always been my theory that Alabama roaches are organized. The poisoned ones run home so their families can eat them while they're dying. The babies take tiny bites, ingesting enough to get a resistance to whatever killed Daddy. But they couldn't resist Dead Roach. It was vicious. Warnings all over the back label advised that its fumes alone could blind you and the actual liquid could melt human flesh. If a pregnant woman came within fifty feet of it, she would probably bear a child with fangs and chitinous wings.

I ran back into the den with it and sprayed up, coating the monster. He shivered and clung and then fell to the floor. I kept spraying him as he ran in ever decreasing circles. I saturated the rug. The cloying burnt-sugar smell of poison clouded the entire room. But still he kept crawling, around and around, his movements disjointed, like the lurching of a cheaply made windup toy. He was dying by inches, and it seemed to go on for a long time.

I took off my shoe, intending to finish the job manually, but I couldn't seem to bring myself to smash him. He was pitiful, and I started to feel sorry for what I had done to him. He was so strong-willed, so determined to live, and he had no chance. He was like me, poisoned inside and out, only he was doing a better job of staggering on. I sank into teen melancholia and lay on the floor beside him, keeping him company until he inevitably lost his battle.

That's where Clarice found me. Lying on the floor next to his corpse, clutching my shoe to my chest, rocking myself and sniveling. Clarice smelled like baby oil and exasperation. She prodded me gently with one pink-tipped toe.

"Arlene," she said. "When's this going to stop?"

She helped me up and dragged me off to our room. She left me to get a cool washrag from the bathroom, then bathed my face. She gently pried my shoe out of my hands and played at Prince Charming, unlacing it and shoving it back on my foot. Clarice, taking care of me once again, remained serene and smooth while I sweated and snuffled, excreting vile fluids from every pore and orifice.

I let her minister to me, but half of me wanted to crawl under the bed, and the other half wanted to bite her. I was like the man who almost burns up in a fire. Months later, he's still jumping at the sight of matches, and everyone else is bored with it. They want to be able to have a smoke in peace, but oh, can't light up here. Mr. Trauma won't like it.

"I don't know how I'm going to go to school on Monday," I said. "Clarice, he's going to be there."

She busied herself tightening and retying my laces. "You're not going to think about that, we decided." Her voice was steady, matter-of-fact. "That didn't happen. And he's a senior. You get through this one year, and then he'll be gone."

"He'll see me. He'll look at us, and he knows everything about me," I said.

She looked up from my shoe, and her eyes narrowed. "He doesn't know . . . he doesn't know"—she dropped her voice to an outraged whisper—"shit! Not about you or me." I was so shocked to hear that word come out of her pretty pink mouth that I stopped puling and actually listened to her.

"This was your decision, Arlene," she said, her voice cool and level. "You are the one who said it never happened, and I said okay because I didn't know what else there was to do. And that's good, it was a good idea, but now you have to make it be true. You can't say it never happened and then creep around everywhere looking like, well, looking like it sure as heck did. Are you saying now it did happen and I have to try and unerase my whole brain or whatever and lie around the house with you and help you be all smelly and traumatized?"

"No," I whispered. "It never happened. We weren't even there when it didn't happen. We agreed."

"Then get off your butt. Now. Get in the shower. You smell like mold. Put on some clean clothes. Ones with, like, a color. And then let's grab a ride to the mall and spend every penny my mama gave us for school clothes."

"On what?" I said.

"School clothes, dummy," she said. "Pretty things, not my daddy's old work shirts dyed black and stacked three deep. If I didn't know better, I might think you were enjoying all this drama. It stops now. We are going to eat pretzels with cheese and see all our friends, and you are going to smile and act like a human. If you can't do it, if you walk around the mall like a ghost, then everything changes. Because I won't go to school to-morrow and pretend everything is fine unless everything really *is* fine." Her voice was rising in volume and pitch. "So you make it fine. Now. Or admit it isn't. But you can't make me keep making it fine for both of us while you wallow around and suffer. You have to help me. You have to help me make it fine. I have to be this perfect shiny girl, happy-happy every minute, and I can't do it by myself, Arlene."

She was shaking. For the first time I saw the crack in her smooth facade, and I realized I'd misjudged her terribly. She was doing this because we had agreed that it had never happened, and the cool and constant sunshine she exuded was nothing more than an act of will.

"I'll get in the shower," I agreed. "I'll make it fine."

And I did. I did exactly what she said. By the time Aunt Flo and Mama came in with a basket of tomatoes, I was dressed in a long peach-colored flowered skirt with a matching crop top and sandals. I had clean hair, brushed and everything. I had on lip gloss and mascara. Clarice was dressed, too, and we were sitting at the kitchen table.

"Hey, y'all," I said. "Can we maybe get a ride to the mall?" Mama didn't look up from setting the tomatoes in a row on the kitchen windowsill, but Aunt Florence stared at me with a faint and wary hope dawning in her eyes.

I curled my lips upward and showed her my teeth. Florence ripped off her sun hat and hurled it onto the kitchen counter, stumbling over Mama in her haste to get to her keys.

At the mall, safely out of her mother's earshot, Clarice said, "You don't know what I've had to do to keep Mama off you all summer. I have told my nice mama so many lies! I said you were mooning over a boy, the boy liked another girl, the other girl was being mean to you about it whenever you left the house . . . I'm surprised my tongue hasn't caught fire and burned itself right out of my head."

"I'm sorry I didn't help you more," I said.

"You're helping me now. That counts for a lot."

We linked arms and went to spend Aunt Florence's money. I found out the more I played at being fine, the easier it was. I could sit up in the driver's seat of my brain and watch myself pretend to be Arlene. Well, not really Arlene, more like Clarice Junior. I sparkled and said, "Well, hey!" to all her friends.

We bought the clothes she picked and tried on trampy things her mother wouldn't let us bring in the house, much less wear, and we giggled like real girls. By the time we were ready to call Uncle Bruster to come get us, I was able to smile like a well-trained monkey and answer questions about my summer on complete autopilot. I was shocked by how easy it was. The surprising thing was that Clarice had figured out how to do it before I had. Historically, I had always been the better liar.

We were walking back to the food court to hit the pay phones when we saw him. Jim Beverly was sitting with some of the other football players, all of them scarfing down tacos and acting rowdy. They were just being boys, I suppose, but the whole scene felt sinister and larger than life. Their gestures seemed slow and exaggerated, their voices strident but indistinct. I had the impression of loud talk, raucous laughter, but no idea what was being said. I slowed, but Clarice clamped an iron hand on my arm and kept me marching.

We had to pass by them to get to the phones. We could have circled out, but I suppose Clarice thought that was too obvious. So we headed past them. Clarice's jaw was set, her chin lifted. To a stranger, it would seem as if she were totally unaware of them, but her eyes were glossy and bright. They looked plastic. They were dead things in her pretty, proud face. I was a skeleton beside her. It was as if I had no skin to soften the stark grin of my skull, no tendons or muscles to keep my bones from clashing and jangling together, chipping and splintering as I walked.

We came abreast of the rowdy group when one of them, it was Bud, lifted his hand and said, "Hey there, Clarice." Several of the other boys lifted their hands, too, Jim Beverly among them. "Clariiiiiiiice," one of them hooted.

We both nodded and smiled, jerky as puppets, and continued the death march. The food court darkened. If there were any other girls present, I couldn't see them. Among the chairs and tables, the eyes of boys shone like hot lamps, all of them fastening on Clarice, who walked by plastic and proud, unknowing. And then they were behind us. I sensed those eyes following my cousin, inching out into the air on stalks to stay close to her. I felt, more than thought, a sudden promise. I knew how to make up for it, this whole summer. I knew how to make up for everything. I would protect Clarice. I would be her secret knight.

We entered the hallway where the bank of pay phones stood. And I was fine. I was back in the driver's seat, watching Arlene and Clarice dig in their purses for change, and the worst was over. I had seen Jim Beverly, and I had neither spontaneously combusted nor used his plastic Taco Bell spork to pop out one of his eyes and dig deep into his brain.

Only a single school year separated me from the moment I would smash his head in with a bottle, so it was more like a reprieve than a cure. But at the time it felt like a small flavor of miracle.

Bud had left the football boys to follow Clarice. He came into the hallway before either of us had dug up phone change. "You calling for a ride?" Bud said.

"Yes, we're done here," Clarice replied, smiling at him. Jim Beverly and most of his crowd were from Fruiton, but Bud was one of us. A Possett kid. We'd known him since grade school. Clarice indicated the host of bags at our feet. "We are flat broke and happy as clams."

"I'd take you, but I only still have my learner's for four more months. My dad is coming by at five or so to get me. We could take you on home and save your folks the drive."

I was smiling my big fake-ass smile, already shaking my head, but Bud was looking at Clarice. And Clarice was nodding. "That'd be sweet, Bud. Just let me call my folks and tell them." She went back to digging in her purse, but Bud whipped out a handful of change and extended it to her on the palm of his hand.

Clarice picked out enough for the phone and simpered, I swear to God, she simpered at him.

"Clarice, it's not even four-fifteen yet," I said, nudging her foot with mine, but she ignored me and made the call.

"Hey, Arlene," said Bud, as if he had only at that moment noticed me.

Clarice hung up the phone and said, "All set," smiling up at Bud. Way up at Bud. He'd been junior varsity as a freshman and looked like he'd shot up another four inches over the summer. He spent his summers in Mississippi with his grandparents and then went to a sports camp, so we hadn't seen him at church.

"Come on and I'll buy you girls a Coke while we wait."

I nudged Clarice's foot harder. It was one thing to walk past Jim Beverly, but if she thought we should sit beside him at a table and drink a Coke so she could flirt with Bud Freeman, she was insane. And anyway, Bud Freeman? What was Clarice doing flirting with Bud Freeman? Bud had always been extremely sweet, the sort of boy you'd trust with your sister, but maybe not the brightest bean in the patch.

Plus, this was a boy who, at the age of six, had eaten a worm. We saw him eat it. He ate that worm whole. And no one had dared him to or made him, he had just taken it in his head to do it. And now Clarice was giving him a kissing look, like she wanted to kiss him on his worm-eating mouth. I nudged at her foot again, practically a kick this time, panicking because she actually seemed to be considering it. Clarice glanced at me.

"I'm not thirsty," she said. Bud nodded, visibly deflating, and she quickly added, "Arlene and I wanted to walk down to Baskin-Robbins and get a cone, but we didn't want to carry these bags all that way. Maybe you could help us?"

Oh, she was smart. Baskin-Robbins wasn't in the food court. It was at the other end of the mall. She'd combined an escape route for us with a request for a man to tote her things, a clear sign of romantic interest. Also, she was going to get him to buy her a sweet food you licked—a love food, Clarice's borderline-slutty friend Janey would call it.

Bud gathered up all the packages, flexing his mighty thews, while Clarice googled at his forearms in a parody of female appreciation. He seemed to eat it up, though. We headed back across the food court, Bud leading the way. Clarice sailed ahead of me to walk with Bud, and I followed, churning in her wake.

Jim Beverly was still there with his crew of football boys and toadies. I kept my eyes on Clarice, and it was easier this time. Maybe, I thought optimistically, it would be easier every time until I didn't even notice him. Until he didn't even exist. But then my eyes, of their own volition, snaked sideways to peek at him. He was watching Clarice walk. His gaze was proprietary and lingered on her ass. I looked away.

At Baskin-Robbins, Bud bought three cones, and we sat down on some benches near a stand of ferns in the middle of the mall hallway to eat them. Bud and Clarice were in full flirting mode now. I passed the time people-watching. I watched boys, mostly. Boys roving in packs, boys alone, boys being dragged along by mothers on a mission. Not one of the boys noticed me watching. Because when they came into our orbit, each and every one of them was much too busy staring or sneaking glances at Clarice. Even the men, I noticed, men with wives and children, paused to drink in the sight of Clarice tossing her shiny hair and laughing at something not funny that Bud had said.

I looked at her, too. I tried to see what they saw. I knew she was pretty. She had always been exceptionally pretty. But I tried to look at her like a man might look at her. I tried to think like Jim Beverly. I saw then how soft she was. She still had a toddler's Cupid's-bow mouth, exquisite, but not her own. It was the mouth of every pretty baby. She looked so pliable. I saw how easily she might be pushed into shapes.

There was no edge to her, no hard place, no angle. Nothing stopped the eye, just soft curves that led you gently down to look at the next curve, which led you on to the next. Her baby cheeks took you to her neck, then to her soft shoulders, to her high breasts, to the dip of her tiny waist, to the flare of her hips, her rounded bottom leading into her endless golden-brown legs. Her skin had a bloom to it. It looked silky and vulnerable, easily bruised.

I looked away. A boy in the endless stream of boys was standing by the Baskin-Robbins, watching Clarice. There was always a boy watching Clarice. It seemed there always had been, I had simply never been so aware of them before. This boy I knew. He was another Possett boy, and in our sophomore class, although only because he'd had to repeat eighth grade. He wasn't stupid or lazy. He'd had cancer. He'd gone into remission and been a miracle. I remember when he entered our class, he was bald as an egg. He was also a skinny little guy with troubled skin and eyes that were sunk too far back in his head. Clarice was out of his league, and he knew it. He was taking her in furtively, in gulping glances.

I got up, dropping the remains of my cone in the trash, and walked over to him.

"Hey, Walter," I said.

He started guiltily, caught. "Hey, Arlene." He shuffled his feet a bit.

"Walter, you're sixteen, aren't you?"

"Yah," he said.

"Cool. You got a car?"

"Yah," he said. "Well, not my own. Not yet. But my dad let me drive his today." Even then, caught, with me breathing up into his face, his greedy eyes kept straying to Clarice. He couldn't seem to stop himself.

So I stopped him. I said something guaranteed to stop him. I said something like "Why don't you show me your car. If it's got a big backseat, maybe we could do it."

He stared at me, shook his head. I could see he was trying to process what "it" I could possibly mean. He flushed a dark, earnest red. Then he said, "Arlene, you shouldn't say stuff like that. You shouldn't kid around like that. I mean, we're Baptists."

I said, "I wasn't kidding around." I pressed the back of my hand casually over the fly of his jeans. Something flexed against my touch. I felt it move like a fisted hand, uncurling. I took my hand away, but I could still feel the ghost of movement prickling across my skin.

Walter forgot we were Baptists. He grabbed my hand and started leading me at a canter past Baskin-Robbins, towards the mall's side exit. As we zoomed past the benches, I yelled, "Clarice, Walter's going to show me his car real quick. We'll be right back."

"Meet us at the front," she called back. "Bud's daddy'll be here in twenty minutes."

We hurried out to the parking lot, and Walter led me to his car. We were practically sprinting. The side lot was full, so Walter started up the car and we drove around to the back of the mall where there was no public parking. We stopped behind a Dumpster. Then we sat there for fifteen long, silent seconds. Walter stared at me. He looked both hopeful and terrified. My own face felt blank. I was in the driver's seat, watching Arlene get ready to fuck Walter Fiercy.

"Walter? Are you a virgin?" I asked.

He shook his head. We both knew he was lying.

"Are you sure?" I asked.

"I'm sure," he said, lying. "Are you?" he added hopefully.

"No," I said, and he flushed again. I could see in his face that he believed me, and that he knew I did not believe him. I could read his mind, but I was a closed book to him.

I said, "Come on, then. Since we both know what we're doing and all." He flinched at that, weaker than me. I stared him down, as if daring him to do something, do anything but sit in his daddy's car with his hands in his lap, looking at me with drowning eyes. He didn't know what to do, and I let him flounder there until my ownership of him, of this moment, was a living thing between us.

Then I climbed over into the backseat, and he followed.

"You got something?" I asked. He looked puzzled, and I said, "You know, something. Like, something."

Understanding dawned, and he fumbled in his wallet for the rubber he had probably carried there since he was twelve. I helped him get it on, and we did it. It didn't take long, and it didn't hurt much. I was bone-dry, tight with disinterest, but the condom was lubricated. What held my attention was his utter seriousness, his total concentration. His eyes were closed, and he seemed to be suffering through some internal drama that was utterly divorced from me, and yet I was causing it, and I resolved it for him.

The next morning I woke up and my bed was full of blood. I

stared at it, uncomprehending, and then panicked. He had broken me, and I would never be able to have babies. Probably I would hemorrhage and die of bad sex, and worse, the doctors would tell my aunt Florence what had killed me. But then I realized it was only my unreliable period showing up a week early. I felt very forgiving towards Walter then, and through Walter I felt forgiving towards all boys. I didn't even like Walter, but I was extremely grateful to find out so immediately that his ancient rubber had done its job.

As soon as Walter finished, I pushed him off me and checked my watch. I had about four minutes to get back to meet Clarice. We hurriedly straightened our clothes, and then he drove me to the front entrance where Bud and Clarice were standing. All our bags were piled at Bud's feet. I hopped out of the car.

"That's your car?" Clarice said to Walter, looking questioningly at Mr. Fiercy's huge boat of a sedan.

"My dad's," Walter said to her. But his gaze had changed. It slid over her and off as if she were made out of Teflon. He'd just screwed the closest thing she had to a sister, and she was a closed door. He would have to dream of different pretty girls now. I realized he was looking at me. I looked back, raised my eyebrows at him. "What?"

He said, "I'll call you later, Arlene."

"Why?" I said.

"I thought, I mean I just . . ." Bud and Clarice were looking at him now, too. "I thought we could be lab partners," he fumbled out. "Chemistry."

"Oh," I said. "I'm taking bio."

"Yah, well," he said. "Okay, then." He drove off abruptly in blushing confusion.

Clarice poked me in the side with her elbow and said, "Walter Fiercy totally likes you!"

I shrugged. "Well, I don't like him." And that was the end of it.

After that, every one of the boys I led astray was another roadway to Clarice that I saw as closed. I admit the logic was flawed. But at the time it gave me a sense of control. It was like I was protecting her in the only way I could. And also, I admit it, the sense of power was addictive.

For a few moments, I owned every boy in my class, one by one, and in an order of my choosing. They lost themselves in me while I remained grounded. From each boy I stole a moment where I was totally myself and they were dissolved, not even people. And each time I stayed myself a little longer. The Arlene Clarice had made me become after she found me mooning over a dead roach, this smart and smart-ass girl, became less of a lie with every boy. I was a battery, charging myself up with them.

Until one day I was strong enough to follow Jim Beverly and some stupid little frosh I didn't even know up Lipsmack Hill. And I killed him.

I said fucking those boys was effective. I never said it was healthy.

# CHAPTER

## 7

I WOKE UP lying in the crook of Burr's arm, feeling shy in only my panties, with the hotel sheets pulled up to my chin. The digital clock beside the bed said it was barely past five, but Burr was awake, too. When he felt me stirring, he took his arm out from under my head and propped himself up on one elbow, looking down at me in the dim light. He wasn't embarrassed or shy at all, and I longed to stay right where we were, in the hotel, as if I had no relatives waiting to dissect me and no past rising to destroy me.

I sat bolt upright, clutching the sheet to my chest. "Shit," I yelled. "Burr, I forgot to call my folks last night and say we were stopping over to sleep!"

He slapped himself in the forehead. "I meant to remind you. We're about eight hours late. Your mama'll be worried."

"Mama nothing," I said. "Aunt Florence will have burst something by now. Hand me the phone."

"Won't they be sleeping?" he said.

I shook my head. "They're all up. Aunt Flo may have already headed out to her garden by now, if she isn't pacing the house and calling upon the Lord to send a rain of fire down upon my head."

He rolled over to his bedside table and flipped on the lamp. Then he rolled back, bringing the phone with him and resting the base of it on his chest.

He picked up the receiver and held it out to me.

I took it but paused before dialing. Burr was sprawled in the bed beside me wearing nothing but a sheet. He was long in the torso and lithe, with broad shoulders and narrow man hips. He was perfectly at ease. Hell, he was perfectly everything.

Burr caught me looking at his body and grinned, again propping himself up on one elbow, setting the phone on the bed in between us. He waggled his eyebrows like a lech. "Why don't you call later?" he said in a low-down, nasty voice.

"Behave," I said sternly. "Listen, Burr, you have to be quiet. I mean dead quiet. And none of that 'I think it's funny to torment my lover when she's on the phone with her parents' crap you always see in the movies. Swear?"

He held up three fingers like a Boy Scout and nodded.

"The problem is that I don't know what to tell her," I said.

Burr shrugged. "Tell her the truth."

"Are you on crack?" I yelped.

"I meant, tell her we stopped over because you were too tired to drive. You don't have to tell your devoutly Southern Baptist aunt the truth, the whole truth, and nothing but the truth."

"Right," I said, and I took the phone.

"Why do I feel like I'm back in high school?" he said, grinning. "Scared Mom'll find out what I'm doing."

That irritated me. "You're a Baptist, too, Burr. You're not supposed to have sex before you're married, either. You want me to call your preacher's-wife mama and tell her what we did last night? You know good and well it's a sin—"

"People sin, Lena," Burr interrupted. He sat up and reached for my hand. "People in love sin a lot. God invented sex. He knows how it works. Don't forget, we also believe in forgiveness."

"Not if you do it on purpose," I said. "You can't just say, 'La la la, this is what I want to do, and I can always get forgiven later!' There's a moment, Burr, a moment where you can choose, and if you choose what you know is wrong, on purpose, how can you ever come back from that?"

"Lena, that's some hard-ass screwed-up theology you've got there. I'm willing to sit here naked in the bed with you and debate redemption, but only if you can look me in the eye and tell me truthfully that the only reason you never threw down with me before last night is because we're Baptists."

I looked away, trying to take my hand back, but Burr wouldn't let me go. He said, "The first time I kissed you, you leaped off the sofa like it was on fire and said, 'Did I tell you that I'm celibate?' But you didn't want to talk about it. You're still not ready to talk about it. That's fine, but let's not pretend it's not there. Something you won't say is between us, in this bed, and it's important for me to say I know it's there."

I wouldn't look directly at him. I shook my head, but I kept my hand in his. "I have never lied to you, Burr. Not once," I said.

"And we both know what that's worth," Burr said, but he was smiling. He tugged at my hand until I met his eyes. "You're no liar, but you're devious enough to be a litigator. Don't worry. You picked a man who can read tax code and date a celibate for two years. That's some serious patience. I have zero doubt in my ability to wait you out. And I have zero doubt that you're meant to be my girl."

I nodded. Then I lifted the phone and dialed. Florence picked it up before the first ring was halfway over. "Arlene?" she said.

"Hey, Aunt Flo."

"Are you all right?"

"Yes, I'm—"

"Are you hurt?"

"No, we're fine, I—"

"Hold, please," Aunt Flo said. I heard the clatter of the receiver being dropped on the counter on her end, and then I heard her calling my mother. She was loud enough to make sure I caught every word. "Gladys? It's your daughter. She must be calling to tell you she is dead and in hell and to ask you to dip your finger in the water and come and cool her tongue, as she is tormented in the flames. Surely she is dead and in hell, because nothing else would explain her not showing up and not even calling you, her own mama, to keep you from pulling out all your hair with worry. I am so sorry she is dead and in hell, but at least they have phones there . . ."

From farther away, I heard my mother yell back, "Tell her hey for me."

Florence picked the phone back up and said in a tight, angry voice, "Your mama says . . . hey."

"Tell her hey back?" I said.

"I can only assume," said Florence, "that this call means you are not coming, and it's so late because you did not have the courage or courtesy to at least tell us earlier and save us the agony."

"No, Aunt Florence, we are coming. We're more than halfway there. Burr doesn't see well driving at night, and I got so tired we had to stop over at a hotel. I was so punchy I forgot to call you, and then I fell asleep."

"I assume Burr is this boyfriend? This boyfriend you say you are bringing?"

"Yes, Burr is my boyfriend."

"Mmm-hmm," said Aunt Florence. "So. You'll be here later today?"

"Yes, ma'am," I said, feeling twelve years old.

"So if and when—and I mostly mean if—the two of you show up, I hope you know he will be sleeping on the sofa, while you will be in your old room."

"Yes, Aunt Flo, or if you'd rather, we could get rooms at the Fruiton Holiday Inn."

Aunt Florence inhaled and said, "You can stay here. For now I suppose there is nothing for me to do but begin my vigil anew."

"We'll be there today, I promise."

"I will believe it when I see the whites of your eyes," said Florence.

"We'll be there," I said.

"What sort of a name is Burr, anyway? It sounds unreliable. Does this 'Burr' have a job, or is he at that school of yours?"

"He's a lawyer, and it's his last name. His last name is Burroughs."

"Arlene," said Aunt Florence, "later today, if and when I see the whites of your eyes?"

"Yes, ma'am?"

"I am likely to start shooting."

"Yes, ma'am," I said.

She hung up.

I released a shaky breath and set the receiver gently in the cradle. Burr took the phone and put it back on the bedside table. He turned the lamp off while he was over there, and then flopped backwards onto the bed.

I stayed sitting up with the sheet still clutched to my chest. "Burr?" I said. "I hope you know last night was a onetime thing. It was probably a bad idea, but we did it, and I'm not sorry, and I don't blame you. But don't start thinking we're going to frisk around fornicating like rabbits all the time."

"All right," said Burr, but he reached up and took me by the shoulders, turning as he pulled me down so that we were lying face-to-face. He kissed me, and it was a serious kiss, filled with intent.

When he came up for air, I said, "I mean it, Burr. Don't get ideas."

"I'm not having ideas," said Burr. "I'm just kissing you. While you're naked." He grinned wickedly, and then he bent his head to me again, rolling me onto my back as he trailed a warm string of kisses down my neck to my collarbone. He dislodged the sheet as he went.

I lay beside him, a little stiff and a little wary, but I did not move away or get up. I should have, but some secret place in me did not want to, and anyway, I had broken my side of the deal with God for real now. I had been on the way to Possett, and planning to lie to Rose Mae, but nothing had really been done until last night. The pact was broken, and I couldn't unfornicate by saying no now.

"Once we leave this hotel room, all this stops," I said.

"Sure, baby," Burr murmured into my throat.

I had meant it as permission, but Burr, the king of the roving hands, was behaving himself mightily. He kept his free hand in the Baptist-sanctified safe zones, on my waist, my shoulder, and my hip, where he paused, probably surprised to find the panties I had slipped on in the night. Then he stretched out his arm across my body and put his hand in mine, squeezing briefly before turning his hand over so the back of it was cradled in my palm.

"Put it where you want it," he said.

He was kissing me again, and I realized he was inviting me to play the game we always played when we made out. It was the game where his hands roved and my hands moved them, controlling them, placing them where it was safe for them to be. But this time it was backwards. He moved his hand and placed it palm down on my waist again, with my hand over it. I pulled it up to my breast. He lingered there briefly before sliding on past, up to the innocent flesh of my shoulder.

I kept moving him, placing his hands on all the off-limits places I had spent so much time and energy defending from these same hands. As always, the power of it got to me. The ability to make his big hands do what I wanted, to go where I pushed them, was an aphrodisiac. I closed my eyes.

He stayed quietly beside me, not moving anything except the hand I controlled as it moved on my body. As he touched me, my grasp on his hand loosened, until my fingers rested on his as lightly as they might rest on a planchette. I couldn't tell if I was moving him or he was moving me. Then I was sure it was him, and I was clinging to his wrist, digging my nails in a little. His big body was still and quiet, innocent, but his hand was moving, and it did not stop moving, and I dug my nails into his wrist, and then I came, my eyes opening, surprised.

As I was coming against his hand, he was already moving over me and into me. That was surprising, too, that he could feel so good to me, pushing slow inside of me in the aftershocks of my orgasm.

I wrapped myself around him as he moved, and he smiled at me and said, "Don't look so shocked." Then later he said, "I think you should marry me." Before I could answer him, he took my hips and pulled me up tight against him and buried his face in my long hair, shaking. We lay together, very still.

He rolled off of me and pulled me with him so I was lying half stretched across his chest. His eyes were sleepy and sweet, drifting closed.

I dug the point of my chin into his chest, hard, and his eyes opened. "We have to get on the road pretty soon," I said.

"It's not even six," he said. And then his eyes closed again and he was gone. I lay beside him, wide awake, feeling his body become warm and heavy as he drifted deeper.

"Burr?" I whispered. He did not answer. "I will marry you," I said. I waited another full minute, but he did not respond, so I knew he was really out.

I would tell him yes when he woke up. I would tell him I would marry him because I loved him, and that was true. But more than one thing can be true at the same time. We were almost to Alabama. And there wasn't a statute of limitations on murder. I knew this from Burr's books. I also knew from these same books that it was sheer insanity to return to the scene of your crime. And being in Alabama, vulnerable and distressed, I might accidentally tell him.

The truth was, I wanted very badly to accidentally tell him. If we got married, I could relax in the knowledge that a husband cannot be forced to testify against his wife. Boyfriends can be forced to testify against you all day long.

Until Burr, I never wanted to tell. I didn't even want to tell Clarice, who had been present for my motive and alibied me during the crime. I never had any need to tell Aunt Florence or Bruster, much less Mama. I had no desire to confess to my preacher, cry on my youth minister, or whisper salaciously to his virginity-obsessed wife. I didn't want to discuss it with God, although of course, God had seen everything.

In a seminar I took on Greek mythology, I read about a cursed king who whispered his secret to the river. Ever after, the rushes murmured "King Midas has donkey ears" whenever the wind blew. He deserved it. He was an idiot.

But the day I realized I was in love with Burr, I also realized I wanted to tell him. Underneath it all, I was an idiot, too. I wanted to cup his ear in the dark and whisper it to him. I knew how to begin.

"There are gods in Alabama," I would say. "I know. I killed one."

I imagined it as a game. Burr and me playing What Have I Got in My Pocketses, this time for keeps. Begin at the end, with the murder itself. Tell him about the walk up the hill and the bottle. Then I would move to motive, tell him everything Clarice had meant to me, and how I had to protect her from the things I understood. Then I would tell him about the dark summer I spent sweating it out in black clothes, weeping over roaches. I would tell him about all the boys, starting with screwing Walter Fiercy in his daddy's sedan while Clarice had some ice cream and fell in love with her future husband. I had practiced those parts of my story for over a year now, waiting for the time when I could finally tell Burr. I had the back half of my tale down letter-perfect, knew it word for word.

I would stop in the middle, and Burr would tell me the beginning. It ought to be easy for a tax attorney with a romantic yen for criminal law. "What have I got in my pocketses?" I would ask, signaling that it was time for him to take over. Burr was good at the game, and in this case, hadn't I made it easy for him? My motive, my catalyst, though unspoken, was laced all through the endgame of my story. I had crafted my portion carefully, so there was only one place he could begin.

Burr would tell it to me the way he always did. He never said, "Once upon a time." He liked to lay out the facts in orderly rows, as if delivering a closing argument. I saw him in his dove-gray suit, performing to an empty courtroom. No one there but me, both judge and witness.

"—Fact one: Jim Beverly did something very bad to you at the end of your freshman year at Fruiton High.

"—Fact two: Aunt Florence did not allow you and Clarice to date as freshmen, unless both of you went—it had to be a double date.

"—Fact three: Jim Beverly was a god at that school, and Clarice was a goddess. If he had asked out anyone, it would have been Clarice. You were just along for the sake of the rules, probably with some boy who owed Jim Beverly a hefty favor as your date.

113

"—Hypothesis one: Your date would have ditched out early, trying to peel you away with him as per Jim Beverly's plan. You, extremely protective and enamored, almost worshipful, of Clarice, would not have abandoned her.

"—Fact four: Jim Beverly, as we saw on Lipsmack Hill, drank to excess, and when he drank to excess, he became crude and sexually aggressive.

"—Hypothesis two: He became sexually aggressive with Clarice in some remote area. Only you were there, your date having ditched you back in hypothesis one. You tried to protect her, both of you fighting him. There was violence, and there was blood. Perhaps Jim Beverly hit Clarice in the fray, and she fell back. Perhaps she banged her head on something. It may have knocked her out. At any rate, she went down, leaving you to fight Jim Beverly alone. And then the fight changed, didn't it, Arlene?

"Which leads us to a conclusion. Doesn't it, Arlene?"

And there my fantasy stopped, because the real Burr never called me Arlene, and even in my fantasy, I couldn't make him speak his conclusion aloud. Sometimes I could get his mouth to move, lips forming the words "Jim Beverly raped you." But I could never hear his voice. In my head, he wanted me to say it instead of him.

My phantom Burr, looking at me with raised eyebrows, expectant and hopeful. "Just say it." Because even in my dreams, Burr was Burr. Burr the patient could wait all year for me to say it. And Burr the idealist would believe that saying it would make everything all better. Won't it, Arlene?

First say it only to him. That's one step out of twelve or so. Then go to some meetings full of damaged women. Say it more.

It feels so good to say, because what's a little murder between archenemies if he raped you? If I said it enough, it would buy me forgiveness, and I knew better than anyone that forgiveness is instantly addictive.

Once I got started, how would I ever, ever stop? Now I couldn't just talk. I would have to cry. Roll on the floor and sob and wail. Say it over and over, every week, until I was using it as a purge, a flagellation, using it like the Greeks used theater. Cry more. Call Mama and scream, "Lookit, see what happened while you gobbled down your nervous pills and hid from the canned peas." Now it's a weapon. Tell the man on the crowded bus, see if he won't give you his seat in abject apology for his revolting sex. Now it's a device. Just say, "Jim Beverly raped me."

Say it until I am redefined! Lena the murderer? No! Arlene the victim! Say it again and again in an enveloping mantra because that makes me feel so much better, and I move past it and through it and then go on national television to talk about how past it and through it I indeed have moved. I am Arlene, little skinny ugly lovable victim, not Lena, attractive, educated, self-assured, and oops, a murderer. Not if I say it. If I say it, I am simultaneously forgiven and raped and damaged and holy. And what does Lena matter as long as Arlene feels so much better, and if I will only say "Jim Beverly raped me," I will be forever justified in my right raped rightness.

Fuck that. I have no right to purchase such a cheap and easy absolution. I wanted Burr to be my righteous advocate, to say it for me. Make my excuses to yourself, Burr, forgive me and love me, but don't ask me to take that ride with you.

I would never say it because I never never lie, and saying "Yes, I killed him, oh but Burr, he raped me, he raped me" is to say that I am the victim here. That's just not true. I'm not. You want to find the victim? Ask yourself "Who's dead?" Arlene the victim is a lie, and I will leave the lies to lawyers.

Yeah. Okay. I admit that I had a bad time. But you know what really made me feel better, Burr? I'll tell you what made me feel better. What made me feel better was walking up to the top of Lipsmack Hill and smashing his head in as he sang, and making him quiet forever.

I never said it. I never said he raped me. But at last, in the gray hours of dawn in the quiet, safe space after Burr became my lover, after he gave me my first orgasm, I made him say it for me. He was dead asleep beside me, his angular face made softer by sleep, and I whispered to him, "What have I got in my pocketses?" I told him everything, moving my lips in the rising light, slowly and silently, forming every word but letting no sound escape.

"There are gods in Alabama," I began. A practice run, because I knew the day was coming when we would play this game for keeps. I stared down at his sleeping face and took us both through it, all the way through to "Okay, I said fucking those boys was effective. I never said it was healthy."

My open-eyed, imaginary Burr laughed at that line. I knew he would, he always did, and I played it for his laugh. And then, pristine in his dove-gray suit, my manufactured Burr at last agreed to speak for me.

"Of course, of course I know," he said. "You hated Jim Beverly. He hurt you, he was dangerous. He went after Clarice, and when you tried to protect her, Jim Beverly raped you. He was a bad, bad man. Of course you had to kill him. He was evil incarnate, and he raped you." Then he grinned at me, sure he'd gotten full points in our game. He was sure he'd seen what I had in my pocketses, sure he had won.

I smiled for him, throwing up my hands as if defeated, not speaking, because I still was not ready to lie. The truth was, my imaginary Burr had lost on points. There were things that he had missed. My little last secrets.

Not least among them, Burr and Jim Beverly were brothers in a way. The only men I'd ever loved.

# CHAPTER

# 8

I WAS PROBABLY the only girl in the freshman class at Fruiton High who didn't have a crush on Jim Beverly.

At first Clarice also seemed unaffected, but the sillier girls all but swooned when he walked by, as if he were every member of Duran Duran rolled into one pair of Levi's. I didn't get it. He wasn't that smart and he wasn't that good-looking. In my opinion, he was actively ugly—short and bandy-legged, monkey-faced, barrel-chested, the whole package topped with a close-cut crop of baby-fine blond hair. I shrugged off the mass crush to football insanity.

Me, I don't think I had enough hormones running to have a crush on anyone. A boyfriend was something I wanted in a vague "other girls would envy me" way. I couldn't yet see any other use for one.

I was a year younger than the rest of my class, and a late bloomer to boot. The only curve I possessed was a little round tum left over from childhood. Aunt Florence called me Miss Betwixt and Between as if it were my name.

Barbie's Dream House bored me, but I hadn't started my period. Boys were mystical, distant creatures, but I longed for ruby-red lipstick. My mother absently handed me hers when I asked, but Aunt Florence told me my mouth looked like a baboon's butt and took it away. Then Florence and Clarice took me to the mall and bought me rosebud blusher and gloss, and a triple-A training bra. Meanwhile, my mother stirred her coffee until it was dead cold, staring dreamily over my head while her left eye leaked clear juice.

Clarice was blooming like a tulip. I suppose I must have been jealous of her. But not much. How could I be jealous when she was so kind to me, and so different? I couldn't aspire to ever be a Clarice. After all, she was tall where I was tiny, blond and ripe where I was dark and scrawny, outgoing and open where I was secretive and silent. She was popular and I was her dreaded barnacle, the obstacle course on every double date, the dead fly you got with every perfect bowl of cream-of-Clarice soup.

And she had things I couldn't imagine having. Breasts. Confidence. A real mother. Since I couldn't imagine possessing Clarice's life, I couldn't have hated her. I couldn't have.

Instead I decided to hate Rose Mae Lolley.

I could imagine being Rose Mae Lolley. I followed her up and down the halls of Fruiton High. I knew the routes she took to her classes long before I could go to my next class without checking my schedule. I ghosted down the halls in her wake, trying to learn her walk. At home, in secret, I practiced her pet facial expressions, like her "I am hanging on your every word, handsome boy" face, where she tilted her head left, widened her violet eyes, and pursed her mouth into a thoughtful pucker.

After about three weeks of this, me thinking I was very James Bond and undetected, I lost sight of her in a long hallway filled with banks of lockers. I continued on cautiously, knowing we were two turns away from her next class. But I could not see her anywhere. Then she popped out from in between two rows of lockers, and there we were. Eye to eye.

She hissed at me, letting her breath out between her teeth like a cat, and looked me up and down. She said in a fierce whisper, "Quit following me, you little freak." Then she pinched me as hard as she could with her dry baby fingers, turned her back on me, and stalked off. I had a purple and yellow bruise on my arm for days, shaped and colored like a pansy. In the dark, after Clarice was asleep, I licked it and licked it.

Before Clarice entered as a freshman, Rose Mae Lolley was easily five times prettier than any other girl in the school. In spite of that, I resembled her. A little. She was tiny, with long dark hair, like me. And we were alike in other ways, too. One of her parents was dead. Rumor had it her dad liked his beer and wasn't in the running for the Most Stable Parent Award. But there my imagined twinhood with her ended.

I was made of bones and, when naked, resembled nothing so much as a fetal chicken. Rose Mae Lolley had genuine girl hips in spite of her tiny frame, and they swayed slowly and hypnotically as she walked. Her shoulders were so frail that her high-set, pointed breasts seemed bigger than they were. She had long slender limbs that moved as if she were underwater. Her hair was as dark and lustrous as mink, falling in a thick, dead-straight sheaf past her shoulder blades. She had a full, naughty-looking mouth and huge eyes that explained the origins of the word "limpid." Her body seemed almost boneless in its graceful movements.

She was slow to smile, slow to speak, slow in everything she did. This may have been due, in part, to her severe anemia—Rose Mae Lolley was so iron-deficient that her doctor had sent in a note saying she was permanently excused from ever dressing out for gym—but her languid movements looked like pure grace.

Jim Beverly called her Rose-Pop.

She'd been his girlfriend since they were freshmen, and they were juniors now. There was some hope, though. Four times, the sophomore girls trumpeted gleefully to the freshman girls in the bathrooms, four times last year they had broken up. And each time Jim Beverly had dated another girl for a few weeks. Rose Mae had not dated at all. They weren't a stable couple, the sophomores said over and over. They would crash and burn again, and someone else would get a shot at him.

I would leave these bathroom sessions not caring a fig about Jim Beverly, and go station myself in a place I knew Rose Mae had to pass on the way to her next class. I'd quit following her, just as she'd asked. Not my fault if she chose to walk past the places I happened to be.

It wasn't love, exactly, this obsession I had with Rose Mae Lolley, but it was passion. It felt like an animal running and tickling and scrabbling inside me, almost enjoyable. Envying Rose Mae Lolley was the warmest thing in my life.

I had a recurring fantasy. A car crash. My mother and Rose Mae's drunken daddy on an ill-fated journey down an oil-slicked road.

They come from opposite directions. I am clinging to the passenger seat. I beg my mother not to drive, implore her. She is weaving dreamily and does not realize how dangerously fast she is going. Rose Mae Lolley is in her drunken daddy's car. Rose and I see each other, know what will happen as the cars careen towards each other. For a split second before impact, our eyes meet. "Oh no," mouths Rose, "oh no, no, no!" Then we crash.

My body shatters the windshield, slides across the crumpled hoods, getting torn and wasted as it goes, smashes through the other windshield and falls, broken and dying, onto Rose Mae Lolley, whose drunken father at least cared enough to make sure she was buckled in. Rose and I are face-to-face, my ruined length pressed against her. I am taking my last breath from her mouth.

I am bleeding uncontrollably. I have the clarity and vision of a dying saint. I see the soul of my mother, a wisp of white vapor, slip free from her body. It struggles in the air like a fish trying to swim upstream, but then is sucked inexorably down into hell. I see the soul of Rose Mae Lolley's father lose the same struggle. And still I have not looked away from Rose Mae's face. My saintly vision is panoramic. I see all. I feel my own soul slip its moorings. Rose's eyes widen.

She is fine and whole, unscathed. A tear spills from my eye at the unfairness of it all. She is a bitch and a pincher who has everything. I have nothing, and now I die, alone except for her, and she sees me only as a disgusting pile of bleeding flesh that is soiling her. My soul rebels. It does not float up; it swims as hard as it can, trying to force itself back into my crumpled form.

But that body is dead, useless, and my soul turns instinctively to the closest source of warmth. It burrows deep into Rose Mae Lolley's body. So surprised, so unprepared is she, that her soul is shoved out almost immediately. It is a dirty gray thing, so insubstantial it neither sinks nor rises, just puffs out of existence like smoke.

Then I am looking through beautiful limpid eyes at the dead thing pressed on me, and I shove it away.

There was more. Handsome firemen getting me out of the slag heap of twisted metal with the jaws of life. The drunken father's surprise million-dollar life insurance policy. Clarice, taking my hand and saying, "At last, a friend who is my equal." The homecoming crown. And yes, in this fantasy, I inherited Jim Beverly. He mainly stood by me at school events where I was being feted and whispered things in my ear like "Rose-Pop, you are so different now, so sweet and fine! Before I was only with you for your looks and because you were easy, but now! I must have the whole package!"

But the crash was the main thing, the part I played over and over, lying in my bed after Clarice was asleep, licking the place where my pansy bruise used to be.

In October, Jim Beverly and Rose Mae broke up again. He buzzed around Clarice, but she was dating a boy on the baseball team pretty consistently at that point, so he settled on a chirpy redhead named Dawna from the sophomore class. She had him for three dates, and then he was back with Rose again.

After he ditched her, Dawna wasn't so chirpy anymore. I don't remember seeing her around much after that. She all but dropped out of the popular kids' social rounds. Or maybe it just seemed that way to me, watching from the fringes of the social scene. I was there only because Clarice invited me to go along with her. And because of Aunt Florence's insistence that Clarice double with me until she was sixteen. So I went to the movies and the games and all the good parties with Clarice and her friends, and I had a string of dates who owed huge favors to Clarice's baseball boyfriend.

The weather was turning cold, and watching Clarice organize our winter wardrobes, I was suddenly struck by the fact that I had never seen Rose-Pop naked. No one had, except presumably Jim Beverly. All fall she had dressed in long flowing skirts and silk blouses with poet sleeves. The fabrics were so sheer and fluttery, you didn't question but that these were warm-weather clothes. Still, they covered her from neck to knees.

Now, as winter came, she changed her look, sporting black leggings that fit her lithe body like a second skin, topped with clingy sweaters. Except for her face and hands and sometimes her neck, I never saw her skin. When she wore a skirt, she'd put on opaque tights, avoiding even the appearance of flesh. And thanks to her doctor and her so-called anemia, she never had to change for gym. I began to wonder if I wasn't buying a pig in a poke, fantasy-wise. What if she was covered with horrible chemical burns? Or warts? Or bright red patchy birthmarks so that, naked, she looked like a pinto pony?

I couldn't get to sleep at night without the fantasy, I was that addicted to it. I would drift off as I imagined living inside Rose Mae, but as I slid into sleep, it would all turn terrible. I would unbutton Rose Mae's blouse with Rose Mae's fingers, only to find my new bouncy little titties were Ziploc bags of cherry Jell-O stuffed into her bra. Rose Mae's chest was as blank and flat as a boy's. I would rip the bra off and see two shallow pockets of scars, as if something with long-clawed hands had scooped my breasts away, and then I would wake up again, lathery and panicked.

I had to investigate. But how? The girl never took her clothes off. At one point I considered staking out her house, but I was foiled by the logistics: I would need a ride to Fruiton and a ride home. A hiding place. Binoculars. A camera. To not get shot by her drunk daddy. I prayed she would try out for the school play so I could catch her in the dressing room. I cursed her for not being a cheerleader like all the other super-popular girls, so I could hide and watch her as she put her uniform on.

Finally it happened almost by accident. Rose had 11:10 lunch, and every day she and a gaggle of cronies would stop by a certain girls' room to fluff their hair and put on fresh lipstick before sitting down to eat with their boyfriends. They would look under the stalls for feet and, if no one was there, indulge in a bit of quick and nasty gossip while they preened.

I took to getting there first. I would slip into one of the stalls and crouch on top of the toilet seat, peering at Rose through the cracks.

One day she lingered after the bell had rung and the other girls had gone. After the door had closed behind them, she waited a moment, then bent down carefully with her habitual slow grace to do another scan for feet. I made myself stone, scared to make the slightest sound in the bathroom.

She turned back to the mirror, and then she lifted her shirt. I stopped breathing. Reflected in the mirror, Rose Mae Lolley's pale belly was patterned in black, like a marble cake. I stared at her midriff trying to make sense of what I was seeing. Then my eyes refocused and the picture resolved itself.

I was looking at bruises. There were fresh black bruises on top of old purply-blue bruises on top of almost faded mustard-yellow ones. She had a huge one, brand-new, on her back, low and to the left of the vulnerable knobs of her spine. She slowly lifted her shirt higher, until I could see her breasts nestled in a white cotton bra. It was laceless and virginal. She gently peeled down one of the cups. Her breast was a black rosebud rimmed in purple.

I had a yell in my throat, and it might have gotten out of me, but at that moment Rose and I heard girls' voices outside the door. She tucked her breast back in its cup and jerked her shirt down, wincing. It was the fastest I had ever seen her move, and immediately I understood the constancy of the slow grace I had envied.

That night I whispered to Clarice across the aisle that separated our narrow beds, "Jim Beverly hits his girlfriend."

"Oh, hush, Arlene. He does not," she said.

"Rose Mae Lolley pulled up her shirt today in the girls' room. She's a walking bruise."

"Why do you have to be so dramatic and jump to conclusions?" Clarice said irritably.

"I don't. I saw her. He beat the stuffing out of her."

"He did not!" Clarice sat up and glared at me.

"How do you know?" I said.

"How do you not know? Everybody knows. Jim Beverly doesn't hit her! Rose Mae Lolley's daddy is a mean drunk, and he hits on her when he's been drinking." She flopped back down onto her pillows. I sat up and peered at her. Her eyes were wide open, glaring at the ceiling.

"I didn't mean to make you mad. I thought—"

"No, you did not. You didn't think. You gossiped." But her tone had softened. She turned onto her side and curled up, cupping her cheek in the palm of her hand, looking at me. "I'm sorry I got tempery, but I hope you haven't been spreading that around."

"No," I said. "I only told you."

"I'm sorry I snapped at you. I didn't want you to say that, because I have my own way of thinking about him. I mean, in my head, a little bit, I think of him as someone really good. Maybe even like some sort of hero."

I stared at her. "Oh my God," I said. "You like him!"

"Hush," she said, but she sat up, too, and tucked her knees into her nightgown and wrapped her arms around herself. "I'm going to tell you something. It's gossip, but oh well, I'm telling you anyway, but don't you spread it, okay?" She stared me down with fierce eyes until I nodded. "Okay, last year Jim Beverly and Rose's daddy got in a fistfight."

"Like a real fight?"

"Yes, a real one. Jim dropped her off from a date, and her daddy was drunk in the yard and tried to beat on her. Jim wouldn't let him hit her. Rose's daddy sprained Jim's arm so bad, Jim had to sit out two games! Of course, last year Jim was only junior varsity, but still."

"You completely have a crush on him!" I said. "And you kept it a secret from me."

"I do not," she said, and then we sat there very quietly, both of us, because I don't think until that moment, Clarice had ever lied to me. "Well, if I do, I didn't tell you because it crept up so gradual I didn't see it. And then it was embarrassing. Everyone has a crush on him for all these dumb football reasons. But that's not why I like him. I like him because he isn't like those other football boys. He sticks with one girl, and he tries to protect her, even from her daddy. And he doesn't drink like the rest of them do. Or he hardly ever drinks, anyway, because she doesn't like it. Maybe it isn't so much I like him in particular as I think I could really love a boy like that, who treated me that way."

"He does too drink," I said. "Don't you remember that Halloween party at Missy Carver's? He got so blind drunk he put his fist through her mama's picture window and ripped out a hunk of the rhododendrons."

"I know what he did. I was there," she said, irritated again.

"So that isn't gossip. We both saw it."

She shrugged. "You know how boys are. So, okay, sometimes he does drink, but like only twice a year. And it's poison to him. He gets crazy. After we left Missy's, I heard he got in a fight with Rob Shay and Chuck and roared off and smashed up his dad's Corolla so bad you couldn't hardly see it was a car. Rose broke up with him over it, remember? He started dating that Dawna just after. Whenever he drinks, if Rose even hears about it, that's when they break up. Then he's so sad he stays drunk until she takes him back. And she always does, and then he stops. Don't you see, that's something else he does for her, even though all the other football boys drink all the time and cut up like mad."

"I can't believe you are this in love with him and you didn't tell me."

Silence from the other bed. Finally she said, "I admire him a little, is all. And anyway, we shouldn't gossip. Now go to sleep."

So I did. Slept like a baby, too, now that I had my fantasy back to settle myself down. Now I knew how to play it. My new body was bruised, but the evil man who had given me those bruises died in the crash.

But after my conversation with Clarice, the fantasy started to change. I got less interested in the car crash and more interested in being Jim Beverly's Rose-Pop. Or not even Rose-Pop, exactly, but a girl like that. A pretty girl a boy like him would love enough to fight for.

At school I didn't follow or watch Rose Mae Lolley so much as I watched how Rose Mae and Jim Beverly were together. I watched Clarice watch them, too. She drank them in, in barely noticeable glances. She was subtle. A person not watching for it would easily miss how constantly she kept an eye on them. A person who knew Clarice less would never pick up on how aware she was whenever Jim Beverly was in the room.

I noticed he was never cruel to the school goats like some of the other football boys were. In fact, if he was around, they didn't seem to act that way. It was as if his presence was enough to hold them back. I noticed how careful he was with Rose Mae, his arm always draped cautiously along her frail shoulders, never roughhousing with her.

I noticed these things because Clarice noticed them. Clarice changed him for me, and I couldn't see him as the fictional character the other freshman girls made up to love. That cocky football boy they had invented was repugnant to me. The one Clarice was making up, though, him I could love.

In my dreams I saw him as the boy he would be without the astounding talent for landing a pass in the loving arms of his receivers. He wasn't good-looking enough or smart enough or funny enough to be popular if it wasn't for that arm. He'd just be sweet, a sweet boy with a slow Alabama smile that could melt a girl. A plain talker who told my mother to get over herself and quit banging her head on the floor if she had a bad day. A fighter when words did him no good. I started to look less like Rose-Pop in the fantasy, and more like regular me. Especially since I was slowly losing the puppy tummy; I could see the beginnings of what might someday be a waist. My nipples stopped being flat pink spots and started pushing themselves outward, dragging breasts out of my unwilling body.

That spring, in May, Jim Beverly got roaring drunk at a gulch party, blacked his friend Barry's eye, and used a tire iron to smash out the back window of Barry's truck when Barry wouldn't fight him. Rose-Pop ditched him again. This time, she vowed, it was really over and done. I heard her tell her friends as I crouched silently on top of the toilet in the girls' bathroom. Her eyes were red from weeping, but her shoulders were set and her mouth was screwed up into a determined wad.

Jim Beverly was free.

He was up for grabs for any girl who could get him, and Lordy but they were all trying.

The day after Rose-Pop dumped Jim Beverly, I woke up feeling grumpy and oddly out of sorts. I'd dreamed my old fantasy. I had been in Rose's body, looking at my face in a mirror. Rose's spirit had looked back at me, laughing at me for taking over the day after she had ditched him for good, knowing I would never have him.

I stared bleakly into my half of the closet. I never had problems picking out clothes. I just reached in and pulled out something that fit. But that day I gazed with distaste at everything I owned, shifting my weight from one foot to the other. Clarice finally moved me gently out of the way and pulled out my khaki pants with a braided belt and my loafers. She fished a chocolate-brown and gold pullover out of the drawer and handed me that. Then she stood staring moodily into her own half of the closet for so long that I was groomed, dressed, and eating breakfast before she made it into the bathroom.

All morning I knew exactly where Jim Beverly was in the school, although I never saw him. I didn't even pass him in the halls. It was as if the radar map in my head that had been used to track Rose-Pop for so long had switched to another channel. Now he was the red blip of heat cruising down the south hallway while I was staring into my locker, irradiating the bio lab while I mooned through math, dressing out in the gym while I moped around the library.

At lunch, wending my way through our garish turquoise cafeteria, I saw Clarice sitting with her borderline-slutty friend Janey. Clarice usually got to sit up on the stage with the seniors because she was dating that baseball boy, but today she and Janey were down below at one of the long tables. With Clarice gracing it, the table would fill up fast, so I took my tray of congealed lasagna and Jell-O and hurried over to her.

"I broke up with Justin," she said as I sat down next to her, and then she gave a slight shrug. Her cheeks were very pink, and I noticed she was wearing a clingy lightweight sweater set she usually saved for church.

Janey said, "Oh yeah, Clarice is on the loose!" Then her eyes narrowed and she said, "Guess who else is on the loose, and oh my God, guess who else is coming over here." She was looking over Clarice's shoulder, and I knew he was coming, could feel him approaching our table on my imaginary radar map. The heat of him was toasting the skin right off my back. Clarice shrugged again, calm and casual, but her eyes were very bright.

I could not stand it and turned to look. I saw him weaving his way through herds of girls who set themselves like snares in his path. He avoided them all, a guided missile locked on Clarice.

Janey was sitting on Clarice's far side, so Jim Beverly sat down by me, straddling the table's bench as if it were a horse, facing me.

"Ladies," he said. "Got room for a refugee?"

"Of course we do, Jim," burbled Janey, preening. But Jim Beverly wasn't looking at her. He was looking through me and speaking directly to Clarice.

Clarice smiled at him and started poodling around with her hair, twirling one finger in it. "Refugee?" she said.

"Yup," said Jim Beverly. "I'm a refugee in the dating wars. Maybe even a casualty."

"Have you been wounded?" said Clarice. "Should I get you a Purple Heart?"

Janey leaned desperately around Clarice and said, in a voice that left the borderline and teleported her miles into slutty territory, "Poor baby, show me where it hurts. Maybe I can kiss it for you."

Jim Beverly barely spared her a glance and a half-smile. "Yeah. Me and Rose-Pop went boom." He grinned ruefully. I sat between them, feeling like the wall that separated Pyramus and Thisbe.

"I heard," said Clarice. "Me and Justin broke up, too, so I know how you feel."

"I heard," said Jim Beverly. "I was thinking maybe we could get together. Tend each other's wounds. Cry in each other's beer. That kind of thing."

Clarice was going to wear her shoulders out what with all the shrugs she was throwing, I thought bitterly.

"I'm not one for crying over spilled milk," she said, and I stood up abruptly, cutting off their view of each other.

"Let me get out of your way," I snapped.

Clarice looked up at me, stricken. "Excuse me, Arlene, I wasn't trying to be rude!"

But I was already struggling out of the small space, trying to swing my legs out from between the attached bench and the table without touching Jim Beverly. I got free of the bench and was reaching for my lunch tray when Jim Beverly snaked one arm around my waist and pulled me down again. I was suddenly perched on his knee. I went immediately still, shocked into silence.

"Hold up there, speedy," said Jim Beverly. "Didn't mean to be an asshole."

"Yes, really, it was rude of us to talk around you," said Clarice.

"I'm not mad," I managed to say. My throat was caked with glue. His hot hand was on my waist, steadying me, and the heat of his leg was soaking up through my pants. I felt something in my belly, down low. It was a muted cracking feeling, as if something glass that was muffled in a towel had been stamped upon and broken, followed by an odd gush of warmth between my legs.

"Maybe you can give me a hand, Arlene," said Jim Beverly. The warm hand at my waist moved. He slid it up my back, under my hair, and I felt his callused palm cupping the prickling flesh at the base of my neck. "Your sister here says she won't come cry over milk with me, so what do you think I should do?"

"Cousin," I squeaked, but he wasn't listening.

He reached up with his other hand and put one finger on my chin, pulling down and then pushing up, making my slack mouth open and close like a puppet's. He spoke for me in a high-pitched voice. "Gosh golly, Clarice, Jim Beverly is totally flirting with you, and you are shooting him down! Poor, poor Jim!"

Clarice laughed, and I pushed his hand away, blushing and confused. The spot of warmth at my core was on the move, running like a trickle of wet heat from belly to crotch.

Clarice said, "I didn't say I didn't want to go somewhere with you. I said I didn't want to go somewhere with you and cry." Janey could have made that sound filthy, but coming from Clarice, it sounded at worst mildly naughty and flirty as all hell.

I stood up abruptly, meaning to make some sort of excuse and flee, but as I leaned over to pick up my lunch tray, I happened to glance down. There, on Jim Beverly's knee, stark against the almost-white of his super-faded Levi's, was a spot of dark blood as big as a half-dollar. I froze, appalled, staring. In that moment I felt myself catch fire and spontaneously combust, burning up in half a heartbeat to nothing but a crisp cinder. When the burning passed, I was still standing there.

Jim Beverly saw the blood on his leg, and then Clarice saw it. The three of us froze in a tableau of horror.

I did not know what to do. There was nothing to be done. The period I had begged God to send me had finally arrived, and there I was bending over to get a lunch tray with my bloody ass in khaki pants facing the rest of the cafeteria.

My eyes met Jim Beverly's, and I don't know what he saw there, but before I could sprint to the nearest ocean and drown myself in it, he jumped to his feet, whipped off his letterman's jacket, and draped it over my shoulders. It covered me to mid-thigh. He put his arm around me, anchoring the jacket and holding me in place.

"Maybe I can call you about this later, eh, Clarice? Me and Arlene here need to go down to the office."

Janey looked up at us, blank and uncomprehending. She couldn't take in the fact that Jim Beverly was leaving the table with me, so I knew she hadn't seen. I did a quick scan of the cafeteria. No one was screaming with laughter or pointing at me.

Clarice said, "Do you want me to . . ." and then trailed off, uncertain how to finish.

Jim Beverly, perfectly at ease again, acting like this was the most natural thing in the world, gave Clarice one of his slow grins and said, "Nah. We got it, don't we, Arlene?"

I nodded dumbly, and he pivoted, pulling me with him. He walked me out of the cafeteria, his arm still over my shoulder. People were staring now, but I was pretty sure it was only because they couldn't figure why a scrub like Arlene Fleet would be draped in Jim Beverly's holy jacket and cuddled up under the shelter of Jim Beverly's immaculate passing arm.

We headed down the hall towards the office. The horror and mortification were slowly morphing into almost weepy gratitude.

"I'm so sorry," I whispered. "I'm so sorry. I didn't know that would happen."

"Pfft," he said. "Forget it. Let's go call your mom to come get you."

"You don't have to walk me down to the office," I said.

"Yeah, I do," he said. "I gotta call my mom and have her bring me some new pants."

I felt dark red heat flush my face and started apologizing

again. "I am so sorry, I really did not know. I never, I mean, I didn't know that would happen today."

He gave my shoulder a squeeze and said, "Hey, kiddo, don't sweat it, really. Chalk it up to what Coach calls a PPD—poor planning day."

"But I couldn't plan, I mean, I never had to plan before." I realized what I was telling him and flushed even harder.

"Well, hey, cool for you, then, huh? No need to be embarrassed." He grinned like a devil and added, soft and dirty, "I'll tell you a secret. You ain't the first female to change from a girl to a woman while sitting in my lap."

I laughed, startled, and then looked down, suddenly feeling okay. In that moment I loved Jim Beverly so fiercely I would have dropped on top of a mud puddle and let him walk over me to save his shoes.

When I killed the rapist, the foul-mouthed drunk, I killed this boy, too. And this boy had a mama who thought he hung the earth, and a proud dad. He had two older brothers, and he had Rose-Pop. He had friends. Before Burr could defend me, he had to know this part. Arlene the monster killer was a lie, because this other boy existed, too. Burr had to know I understood what I had done. I knew you couldn't kill only the pieces that needed killing, and leave the pretty parts whole.

# CHAPTER

## 9

WHEN I SAW the WELCOME TO ALABAMA THE BEAUTIFUL sign looming up ahead of us on the highway, I clutched Burr's arm. "It isn't too late to turn around and go home."

Burr goggled at me and then started chuckling. "Yes, it is," he said. He lifted his hand, still laughing. "Goodbye, Tennessee," he called.

I echoed him: "Goodbye, Tennessee."

He faced forward, and the Blazer crossed the line. "Hello, Alabama."

"Yes, hello, Alabama, you big green whore," I said sourly, not waving.

That hit Burr just right, and he lost it. "You big green whore? Green whore?" He was laughing so hard, tears were starting in his eyes. He thumbed the button, and his window scrolled down. He yelled out the window: "Hail to thee, Alabama, thou Verdant Trollop!" He laughed and laughed, sticking one hand out the window and waving. His laughter was contagious, and I found myself giggling, too. "Greetings, Emerald State of Tarts! Lo! I am here to fuck your white women!"

"With my big black dick," I said, sotto voce.

"With my big black dick," he bellowed. He was laughing so hard between yelling at the state that he was practically choking. I lost it, too, and both of us were hooting with tears streaming down our faces.

"Blind," Burr choked out, and he slowed and pulled off the highway onto the shoulder. A few cars whizzed past us as I leaned against the dash and laughed and laughed until my stomach ached with it. Burr was clutching dizzily at the steering wheel, trying to breathe. I closed my eyes, pulling in oxygen, until Burr and I had ourselves mostly under control.

It was quiet for a moment, and then Burr said, "What the hell is that?" I opened my eyes. He was staring past me out my window. I followed his line of sight.

"Oh," I said, sobering. "That's a heap."

"A heap?" said Burr.

"It's kudzu. It's a plant, like a vine. It's all over Alabama. It eats anything it touches, just climbs right up it and covers it and kills it."

The heap outside my window had coated a row of dizzyingly tall pines. I could still see the basic outline of the trees underneath. The heap undulated in a sinister stretch, slowly reaching back towards itself from tree to tree, lacing itself higher, sending grounders out, looking for something else to climb.

"Let's go," I said.

Burr wiped his eyes and then put the Blazer back in drive.

There was very little traffic, and he pulled back onto the highway and gunned it.

The speedometer said he was going about seventy, but it felt to me like we were moving at the speed of light, whipping around curves and over hills. Florence and Bruster were ahead of us, and with them my addled, grinning puppet of a mother. The rest of my lunatic family surrounded us, scattered in a fifty-mile radius. Rose Mae Lolley was aimed at our location, heading at us from Texas on a collision course. And somewhere in the wilds of Alabama, whatever was left of Jim Beverly was waiting for her to find him.

I had promised God I would stop systematically fucking my way through Fruiton High School. In fact, I had promised to stop fornicating completely. But truthfully, up until I fell in love with Burr, cutting sex out of my life had been more of a relief than a sacrifice. I had promised God that I would go into exile and never return to Alabama. But if God had my relatives, He would happily promise to stay out of Alabama, too.

I had always known the heart of the deal was my promise to give up lying. It was as if I had broken the smaller, more self-serving vows as practice, using the plan to go to Alabama as a flimsy excuse to be with Burr, and using the fact that I had been with Burr to push myself across the state line. But in the darkest corner of my mind, in the savage place that shuddered if a black cat crossed my path, I believed that as long as I did not lie, the deal was still intact.

I'd had a chance to lie to Rose Mae in Chicago and had blown it righteously. The pressure of the promise I had made caused me to falter at the most important moment. I could not afford to be caught unprepared again.

It occurred to me that if I broke the vow now, bloodlessly, told some smaller lie, when I met Rose it would all be that much easier. There would be nothing left to break.

Perhaps it was fortunate that I was headed into the clutches of Aunt Florence, the dogmatic grand inquisitor. Florence, who never inferred anything, would be waiting to get me alone. She had ten years' worth of interrogation on every possible fragment of my life ready in the hopper. If she got her teeth in me, she would worry at me until I broke and gave her the truth, the whole truth, and nothing but the truth. But perhaps I could use my practice lie, my vow-breaker, to distract her or even defuse her. And if I could get a lie past Flo, Rose Mae would be a piece of cake.

"Baby, where's that bag of popcorn?" Burr asked. I got it out of the backseat and opened it for him.

"I think I want to tell a lie," I said, passing him the bag.

"Just a sec, let this moron pass me," said Burr. A guy in a red Celica hurtled past us on the right. "That's new. What lie?"

"I think we should tell my aunt Florence and everyone that we got married," I said.

Burr had the popcorn propped between his thighs, eating it as he drove. His mouth was full, and he coughed a little. Once he got the bite swallowed, he said, "Why would we do that?"

"Because a boyfriend is tenuous. They could launch a pretty good full-scale racist-alert war against a boyfriend. But on the Southern Baptist Church scale of sins, a divorce is probably worse than a black husband," I said. "If we're married, then they have to take us both or leave us. I don't want to give them the option of me and not you."

140

Burr shook his head, fishing out another bite of popcorn. "Should I prepare for pillowcase hats and flying bullets?"

"No, it's not that they're Ku Kluxy, Burr. They're just garden-variety backwoods Alabama racists. But Aunt Florence? She's ruthless. She has no ruth at all. And assuming she doesn't flat disown me—big assumption—if she sees any seam between us, she is going to pick at it and do her damnedest to get us apart."

I racked my brain, trying to sufficiently explain the power of Florence. Finally I said, "Let me tell you a story. Growing up, our closest neighbor was Mrs. Weedy. She was an older lady. A widow with no kids. But she had this pet chicken named Phoebe. And she loved Phoebe insanely. I mean that literally. She was not mentally well on the subject of Phoebe. And whenever my cousins Wayne and Clarice did something great and Aunt Flo would try to brag on them, Mrs. Weedy would interrupt with a long tale of Phoebe's latest accomplishments.

"According to Mrs. Weedy, Phoebe understood English, liked country music, had political opinions and a passionate personal relationship with Jesus. But all Phoebe ever did really was drop chicken poop and scratch around.

"After Wayne died, Mrs. Weedy came over with a ham-and-green-bean casserole and told my aunt Flo, 'Honey, I know exactly how you feel. I can't imagine if I lost Phoebe! Phoebe and I will pray for you.'

"Clarice told me this story. She was only eight when Wayne died, but she remembered Mrs. Weedy coming by with the casserole. She watched Aunt Flo's fingers get whiter and whiter as she clutched the dish. After Mrs. Weedy left, Clarice watched Florence deliberately open her hands and let the casserole dish fall and smash on the floor.

"About two weeks later, Mrs. Weedy did lose Phoebe. Clarice told me she was playing out on the porch, and she heard Mrs. Weedy calling until she had no voice left, and Phoebe never came. And the next day my aunt Flo took Mrs. Weedy a chicken chili cheese pie and said how sorry she was."

Burr was silent for a long time. "Am I to infer that the chicken part of the chicken chili cheese pie was—"

"Infer what you like."

"And did Mrs. Weedy eat the pie?"

"Licked the platter clean, according to Clarice."

Burr handed me the half-full popcorn bag. "I think I'm through with eating now," he said. "Your aunt Florence is hard-core."

"It's not that big a lie, is it, Burr?" I said. He was watching the road. "You did ask me to marry you this morning." I looked down into the depths of the popcorn bag. "Did you mean it?"

In my peripheral vision, I could see Burr's hands flexing on the wheel. "Yeah, I meant it," he said slowly. "Are you saying yes?"

"I did say yes," I said to the popcorn bag. "But you were sleeping."

There was a pause then, a pleased silence, and Burr said, "So, we're engaged. How about that?" He took one hand off the wheel and tucked it around my thigh, just above the knee. "I planned to do a better job. I have a ring. I was going to do the restaurant thing. Take you to hear a good blues band, get champagne."

"The way you asked was pretty good, I thought," I offered, still shy. I shook it off and added, "Anyway, if we're engaged, it's barely even a lie. It's more like telling a pre-truth."

Burr laughed out loud at that. "What happens at the wedding if they already think we're married?"

"Oh God, no, I don't want a wedding, Burr. I don't want anyone but us. If I had a wedding, Aunt Flo would mobilize the entire family like the Fifth Infantry. She'd flog them into rented vans and point them at Chicago. And I don't mean just Uncle Bruster and Mama and Clarice. She'd dredge up my vicious aunt Sukie and her hell spawn. She'd snatch my great-great-aunt Mag out of the nursing home and load the trunk with the ashes of my asshole grampa and Saint Granny. And that's just the Bents. She'd get Bruster's whole tribe, Dill Lukey and Uncle Peaches and Luke-John and Fat Agnes and all nine million of my wild boy cousins, and they'd head to Chicago to try and stop the wedding. It would be like the traveling-freak-show version of *Guess Who's Coming to Dinner.* I'd much rather we did it just us, on the quiet. Your mama could give us a reception in the fellowship hall at church one Sunday after services."

Burr widened his eyes. "You've just described every man's dream wedding."

The story was pushing at me again. There are gods in Alabama. The urge to tell, to spill everything out onto his lap, to set it down and rest, washed over me in a wave. "Can it be soon? Really soon?" I said.

"Baby, I'm good to go the day we get home," said Burr. "You're worried about being pregnant?"

I boggled at him because, stupidly, that hadn't occurred to me. I started counting days, working backwards in my head. "It's not likely," I said. "But when I was a girl, my aunt Florence always said to me and Clarice, 'If you are on the battlefield, you can get shot.'"

Burr smiled at that. "Soon, then," he said.

"Really soon," I said, and he nodded. "And let's lie."

Burr said, "That seems a little—"

I interrupted him. "You know, nothing like sex can happen at my aunt's house. Thin walls. I would die. But if we tell them we're already married, we can sleep in the same room."

"Sold," said Burr. "I'm pro-lie."

"All right, then," I said, and ate a little popcorn. "Is your cell phone charged? I think I'll do better on the phone. It's been a long time since I told a lie. And maybe you better pull off the highway. I feel like I might need room to walk if I'm going to do this."

Burr took the next exit. There wasn't anything there but a Shell station with an attached diner, surrounded by rolling Alabama pastureland on one side and woods on the other. Burr was heading for the Shell, but I said, "Don't pull in. I don't want the people or the truck noise." He cruised a few hundred feet before pulling onto the shoulder.

I said, "You get out, too. I might need the moral support." We were next to a rail fence surrounding a long, thin pasture. Two fat ponies and a creaky old horse were ambling about in it. When we got out, the ponies glanced up and then went on grazing, but the horse started meandering slowly over to investigate. He was a swaybacked, ancient yellowed thing with a Roman nose. The hair around his mouth had gone entirely gray.

Burr, a city boy to the core, watched the horse suspiciously while I dialed. He said, "Do you think he's upset I parked here?"

"No, I think he just sees the popcorn bag," I explained. "It's ringing."

"Arlene?" said my aunt Flo. "This better not be you."

"It's me," I said.

"I said it better not be," said Aunt Flo. "What's the excuse this time? Aliens abducted you back to Chicago? You suddenly had to take a side trip to Guam? Lay it on me, Arlene, I have been waiting for this call all day."

The horse reached the fence and put his nose over. Burr took an ultra-casual step back and leaned nonchalantly on the car.

"I'm not calling to cancel, Aunt Flo. We're about two hours away. Maybe less."

I tilted my head and pushed my shoulder up to secure the phone, then dug out a small handful of popcorn for the horse. I offered it on the flat of my hand, and he started nuzzling it up with his prehensile lips. A few kernels of popcorn fell to the ground. I couldn't tell if my hands were shaking or if the old horse had knocked them off.

"Lena," Burr whispered urgently, "should you be doing that?"

I flapped the popcorn bag at him because I couldn't hear Aunt Florence.

"—not calling to say hey, so you might as well spit it," Florence was saying.

The fatter pony's ears pricked up when he noticed the horse was getting something, and he started over at a trot. The second pony followed him. They were pretty, brown roly-poly things. The fatter one's sides jiggled as he trotted over.

"Now look what you did," whispered Burr.

"Aunt Florence, I just wanted to call before we got there and explain why we stopped over last night." I took a deep breath and did it. I lied, flat and plain. "Yesterday we stopped in Tennessee and got married."

There was a long silence on the other end of the phone. The ponies arrived at the fence and flanked the horse, questing forward with their noses and trying to press him out. I held out popcorn for the fatter one first, as he seemed the most desperate about it. I was happy for the distraction. If I thought about feeding ponies, it was easier to let lies slip out of my mouth, almost as if I wasn't noticing them.

"He could take your finger right off," whispered Burr. "Look at those teeth."

I shook my head at him and almost dropped the phone.

"Married," said Florence in a dire, deep voice. "You got married."

"Yeah, we pretty much did," I said.

"Well. Thank you so, so much for calling to tell me this." Sarcasm flooded the phone and spilled out, soaking me. "I appreciate the news bulletin. Is there anything else you want to tell me while you are passing on this tidbit? Is your new husband that your family has never met an ex-convict, for example? Or are you just knocked up?"

As she spoke, I wiped my horse-feeding hand on my jeans and grabbed the phone, holding it a little away so Burr could hear. The cell phone's tiny speaker distorted Aunt Florence's powerful voice, and from this distance it sounded like nothing more than the quacking of an enraged duck. I put the phone back to my ear.

"I'm not pregnant, and he's not a convict. I told you, he's a lawyer. But while I've got you, I guess I should tell you he's black."

I clipped the phone between my chin and shoulder again. There was a long silence. I shared out another handful of popcorn among the horse and the ponies. Burr was watching me, rubbing his hand across his lips.

Finally she said, "What do you mean, he's black? You mean he himself is black? A black man?"

"Yes. By black, I mean he is black."

Florence took a deep breath and then spoke, her voice dead cold. "I am hanging up now, Arlene. I will take this up with you and your secret black husband when you arrive."

"Yes, you'd better go quick," I said. "You have less than two hours to get on the horn and tell everyone that Arlene married a black man just to piss you off. I wouldn't want Aunt Sukie to have live kittens if you don't get to prep her before Uncle Bruster's party. We have a large extended family—may I suggest a phone tree?"

"What is that supposed to mean?"

"A phone tree," I said. "It's where you tell everyone you call to call two more people, and they tell their people to call two more—"

"Don't sass me. I head the Baptist Women's League, I think I know what a phone tree is, Arlene. We will discuss this further if you actually show up, with or without your secret and possibly made-up black husband. I am not stupid, Arlene. I guess now I am supposed to say, 'Oh no, if you have invented a secret black husband, then you can't come home and ruin your uncle's special day, so scamper on back to Chicago with my blessing.' Is that your plan?"

"Don't be ridiculous. I am not making Burr up. You know I never lie." I stopped speaking abruptly, because saying that I never lied was a lie now.

"Oh yes, that's right," said Aunt Florence. "You don't lie unless your mouth is open and words are coming out of it." And then she hung up.

"I don't usually lie," I said to the dial tone. I hit the red button and handed Burr his phone back. The horse stamped a front foot, and the ponies gazed at me in popcorn-induced adoration. "That's all," I said. "Go graze, you spoiled things." But they didn't speak English, so they stayed at the fence, craning their hopeful noses at me.

"I'm terrible at this," I said to Burr. "I don't lie ever." My hands were shaking. Fornicating had been much easier.

"I know, baby," he said. We got back in the car and buckled in.

"I shouldn't have lied. I shouldn't have even called. This gives her time to line up snipers around the driveway."

Burr merged back onto the highway. I turned the stereo on and slipped in one of Burr's Skip James CDs. I was in a blues kind of mood. I jacked it up pretty good, and James's eerie falsetto filled the car. I didn't feel like talking. Burr seemed to catch my mood and drove us silently, one hand tapping out odd rhythms on my thigh.

We listened to the CD twice through, and just as it was starting over, we hit the turnoff onto Route 19. I turned down the volume and told Burr to hang a left.

"If we kept going, we'd come to Fruiton," I said. "This way, in about ten minutes we're going to shoot through scenic downtown Possett. I believe it is obligatory to make the standard small-town joke, so allow me to say 'Try not to blink.'"

"Check," said Burr.

We wound our way down 19, passing through all three blocks of downtown Possett and then through clutches of ranch houses. After that, there were lengthy stretches with nothing but fields on either side of us. In another four miles, we started to see a few houses again.

"Coming up ahead on the left," I said, "that's Mrs. Weedy's house we're passing. She died five or six years ago, and I don't know the folks who took it. That big fence is around my aunt Florence's vegetable garden, and that white frame up ahead, that's us. Turn in the gravel drive, that concrete one will take you back around to the garden and the shed."

The house looked just the way I remembered, neat and tidy, with its green shutters and door gleaming. The hydrangea bushes out front were trimmed and orderly. Florence had put some sort of blooming creeper in the front bed, and its big white flowers were bobbling lazily as if they were nodding at us. Florence and Bruster had come out on the front porch and were sitting in their respective rockers, watching for us. Burr slowly crept us up the gravel drive. He stopped short of the carport, and we got out and walked around to the front of the house.

They rose together as we approached, Florence in one of her nice housedresses, sinewy and tall. Uncle Bruster stood behind her, a great big bear of a man with sloping shoulders and tufts and wisps of gray-blond hair sticking up on his bald head. He looked like he had put on some weight.

I was surprised by how much ten years had aged him, while Aunt Florence looked just the same. With a shock, I realized that she had looked dried and gaunt and twenty years older than she should have when she first came up to rescue me and drag my mother back to Alabama. She had done all her aging when my cousin Wayne died, and Bruster, who was her senior by several years, was only now catching up.

Aunt Florence's mouth was firm and her gaze was hard, unwavering, but her big hands betrayed her. They were clamped together in front of her, and her dry fingers were worrying at her wedding ring. She had long spider-thin fingers with big knuckles like knees, and her band hung loose and spun as she twisted at it. Uncle Bruster was sizing Burr up with cool blue eyes, but Florence barely spared him a glance. Her eyes were fast on me.

"There you are, then, Arlene," she said as I approached. "You're still no bigger than a minute."

Burr was coming up behind me, and I felt better knowing he had my back. "Yep, I'm still me." They came down the steps, and we met on the strip of sidewalk in front of the flower bed. The bigheaded blooms on the creeper were nodding so cheerfully that I wanted to stamp them down and smash them into stillness.

"This, I take it, is your husband?" said Florence. She nodded towards Burr without looking at him, her eyes steadfast on me.

"Yes, this is Burr. Wilson Burroughs, I mean. Burr, this is my aunt and uncle, Bruster and Florence Lukey."

"Ma'am," said Burr, politely nodding. He held out his hand to Bruster and said, "Nice to meet you."

After a brief pause, Bruster took his hand and pumped it briskly up and back down. "Hey howdy," he said, in an inappropriately grave tone. I felt a bubble of absurd laughter building in the back of my throat and quashed it. Uncle Bruster let go of Burr's hand, and Burr put it on my shoulder, anchoring me.

"Your mama's up in the house watching one of her shows," said Florence, her eyes flicking to Burr's hand on my shoulder and then back to my face.

"I guess we better go on in and say hey," I said.

"Yes, I guess you better," said Florence. But as I stepped forward, her big hands shot out at me, as if her arms were on springs. I flinched, but she didn't hesitate, grabbing me and yanking me forward against her. My face was squashed on her unyielding breastbone, and she was pressing her nose into the top of my head, burrowing into my hair, breathing me in. She smelled of waxy, sharp lemons and ammonia, as if she had scrubbed her dry body down with Pledge and Mr. Clean right before we arrived. Her smell was so shockingly familiar and homey that I found myself clutching at her back and squeezing her as hard as she was squeezing me.

She let me go just as abruptly, and Burr's hand came back to my shoulder, steadying me. I blinked hard, twice. "Ten years is too long," she said. "You little turd."

"Yes, ma'am," I said, quavery.

Then Bruster grabbed me and gave me a great big leathery bear hug, whispering, "Hey, girlie," in my ear. I had forgotten that, how he always called Clarice and me his girlies.

"Arleney?" I heard my mother say, and I looked over Uncle Bruster's sloping shoulder. Mama had come to the screen door. Bruster let me go, and I walked up onto the porch, Burr following close behind.

Mama had aged, too, hard and badly. Her little pretty face was mired in a lined sea of fat, and her blond hair was stringy and faded to the point of being colorless. She was wearing some sort of awful red-print muumuu with big green fronds and yellow blooms splashed all over it. The muumuu had short sleeves, and her doughy arms quivered as she clapped her hands. "There's my girl," she said. She held open the door for us, and we went on in, Mama patting ineffectually at my shoulder as I passed her. "There she is," she said again.

"Burr, this is my mama," I said.

"Ma'am," Burr said again, shaking her hand.

"You're a lawyer, Flo says?" Mama said, patting vaguely at his shoulder and keeping the hand he'd extended clutched in her paw.

"Yes, ma'am, I am," said Burr.

Mama turned to me and said, "He doesn't talk very much like he's black, does he? I mean, if we were on the phone, I would probably guess he was black. He has a black voice, but he doesn't talk black."

"He's standing right there, Mama," I said. "You're holding his hand."

"Oh, that's right," Mama said. And then to Burr, she added, "I'm just surprised how well you speak."

Burr was staring at her openmouthed, not quite sure how to respond. "I'm a credit to my race," he said at last, very mildly, and cut me a fast, sly look that told me he hadn't lost his sense of humor or his temper. Yet.

"Let's go sit down," said Florence. "Who wants iced tea?"

The living room was just as I remembered it, stuffed with furniture from the seventies and dominated by Florence's squatty sofa. It was burnt orange with a blue and gold paisley print, and when Mama sat down on it in her muumuu, the color clash was enough to make my eyes bleed. Burr and I sat down next to her on the sofa, and then Florence and Bruster perched across from us in the high-backed velvet chairs on the other side of the coffee table. Florence immediately jumped up and went to get everyone tea, and once the glasses were passed around, she reperched, and we all sat there looking at one another in a congealing fog of silence.

"You aren't wearing rings," Florence said.

"I know," I said. "Like I said, we only got married yesterday. Kind of spur-of-the-moment."

I felt a blush rising and buried my face in my glass. The tea was so sugary that the first sip made my teeth ache, and a sad mint leaf floated hopelessly on top of the ice.

"One would hope you are at least a Baptist," said Florence to Burr.

"Yes, ma'am," said Burr. "In fact, my father, before he died, was the minister at the Baptist church Lena and I attend."

Florence's eyebrows shot up at the "Lena," but she shrugged it off and pressed doggedly on. "Southern Baptist?"

"The Southern Baptist Church is not a strong presence in Chicago. We're American Baptists," said Burr.

"I imagine you could find one if you were looking," said Florence tartly. "The Southern Baptist Church is everywhere."

"Strong presence," said my mother dreamily, mimicking Burr's inflection.

I took Burr's hand.

"Are you planning on having children?" said Bruster, leaning forward.

"I don't know. I thought I would talk about that with Lena privately before discussing it with you." I pressed Burr's hand, hard.

"It's not very fair to them if you do, now, is it?" said Bruster.

Burr was pressing my hand back just as hard, but I did not think he was aware of it. "I'm going to choose to misunderstand that," said Burr. "That's the most polite response, under the circumstances."

"What?" said Uncle Bruster.

"Misunderstand," said Mama, still trying to re-create Burr's accent. "Circumstances."

Aunt Florence interjected, "Sissy Mack from over to Fruiton has a daughter up in Wisconsin going to school, and she found a Southern Baptist church, you know, Arlene."

"He really is very well spoken," said my mother to the air.

"Well, I done gone to lawyerin' school," said Burr in his driest voice, quirking up one eyebrow. "I be making good yipyap wif my mouf."

Florence, Bruster, and my mother stared at Burr in varying states of offense and quizzical disbelief. The room felt so hot that I would not have been surprised had I looked up and seen the ugly orange drapes ablaze. The heated silence stretched up, unbearable, and just as it crested, the front door crashed open and everyone jumped.

"Arlene? Arlene?" I heard Clarice calling, and her beautiful voice came in like a breeze, cooling the room. I heard the clatter of many feet, and then Clarice was in the doorway, flanked by two grinning blond boys and topped off by a pretty, fat girl baby perched on one hip. Clarice's blond hair tumbled around her face, and she seemed lit from within, as she always had. Her simple presence seemed to bathe the room in balm.

I stood up and she charged at me, practically leaping over the coffee table to get to me, the baby giggling as she ran and the boys surging after her. She clutched at me, laughing. "Oh, Arlene, you came! You really came!"

Up close I could see the beginnings of crow's-feet around her eyes, could see she was a bit heavier in the hips after three babies, but it didn't matter. She was still exactly Clarice. "Arlene, lookit, it's Bud!" She gestured to where Bud was waving and saying

"Hey, y'all" from the doorway. "And you've never even seen the kids except in pictures. This is Pete. Petey, give your auntie Arlene a big hug. He's our oldest, and this mess here is Davey Bud, and this is our Francie. Here, hold Francie, isn't she a peach?"

The baby came to me without protest, clipping her fat little legs onto my waist and breathing sweet milk breath up into my face. "Ba," she said and touched my nose.

"And you have to be Arlene's husband, yes?" Clarice turned to Burr.

"Yes, this is Burr," I interjected.

Burr stood up, too, and she grabbed his hand in both of hers, looking up into his eyes and grinning. "I couldn't wait to meet the man who could catch our Arlene. You must be a fast runner!"

"Yes," said Burr. I could see he was still smarting. "My people are notoriously good athletes."

"Really?" said Clarice. "Well, you and Bud will sure get along, then. His people are, too. One of his brothers went to college on a football scholarship."

Burr searched her face, trying to tell if she was being disingenuous, and I recognized his faint surprise when he realized she wasn't.

Within two minutes of entering, Clarice had total control of the room. She started micromanaging, sending her boys with Uncle Bruster to feed the goats across the street. She jump-started Florence into catching me up on all the family gossip, the only topic that could reliably peel Florence off the perfection and wonders of the Southern Baptist Church. Clarice worked hard to include my mother, perching beside her on the arm of the sofa and pulling her into the conversation, giving who's-who asides to Burr so he could follow Great-aunt Ida's botched hip-replacement saga and the latest exploit of slutty cousin Cinda. Bud sat in the chair Bruster had vacated, watching his wife work the room with quiet adoration, the same look he'd had when she was just a girl and he'd bought us ice cream down at Baskin-Robbins.

The baby seemed determined to jam her little finger all the way up my nostril, so Clarice took her back and put her down on the floor with some toys. Francie pulled herself up on the coffee table and tiptoed around and around it, holding on to the edge for balance. She babbled softly to herself while Aunt Florence talked. After a bit, we heard Bruster and the boys come back in the front door. They settled down in the den, watching some sort of cartoon, by the sounds of it.

Aunt Florence wound down and went to start supper, and Mama wandered off the other way, towards the den. Clarice and I gave Burr the grand tour. The front of the house was built in a circle, with the front hall leading into the living room, and the living room leading into the dining room where Clarice's older boy, Petey, was setting the big table for all of us. An open archway led into the kitchen, and the back door there led out to the carport. Aunt Florence, cool and unreadable, watched us as we passed through.

The kitchen had a breakfast nook with a swinging door to the den. Uncle Bruster had talked Davey Bud into changing the channel, and baseball was on. My mama sat in the back corner, overflowing her armchair with her mouth slack and her eyes half closed. Bud had joined his sons and was watching the game. Clarice shooed at him and said, "Honey, go get their things in from the car. You know they have to be exhausted."

"Just a sec, it's two and two," he said. Clarice shook her head at him in mock exasperation and said, "Well, take the baby for a minute," and handed off Francie.

We left the den and went down the hallway, stopping to look at the wall Aunt Florence had coated with family pictures.

"Is that you?" Burr said to me, pointing.

"Yes, and that's my dad, and that was Mama. Mama says I was born pure Fleet. She could never see even a speck of Bent." My father and I were both small and dark and wiry. We stared solemnly at the camera with identical reserved expressions, almost lost in the sea of tall blond Bents and Lukeys surrounding us. Mama was on Daddy's other side, pretty and plump, clutching his arm and grinning at him, ignoring the camera.

The door to the room I had shared with Clarice was shut. We wandered past it, following the line of pictures down the wall while Clarice pointed out all the people who would be at Uncle Bruster's retirement party.

"I'm not sure if we're going, Clarice," I said, but she ignored me and walked Burr down the wall. We ended up right in front of Aunt Florence's door at the end of the hall, looking at a recent picture of my great-great-aunt Mag. The lines around her mouth were brown with snuff.

"That's Mama and Daddy's room, and here right next door is where Arlene's mama sleeps. I guess Bud should put your things in here, as she's got a double bed. Arlene, your mama can sleep in our old room."

We left Florence and Bruster's door closed and opened the door to Mama's room. It had not changed. No pictures broke up the industrial flat expanse of the white walls, and a mirrorless dresser squatted lonely near the closet. The double bed was made. Hospital corners—Aunt Florence's handiwork. The closet door was shut. A basket of magazines sat on the floor beside my dead aunt Niner's old padded rocker. If the small bedside table had not been littered with crumpled tissues and half a glass of water, you would never guess a person lived in the room.

"Where's your old room?" Burr asked me.

"Back up the hall," I said. "Past the bathroom."

"The door closest to the den?" asked Burr. When I nodded, he said, "Let's stay in there."

"But this has the double bed," Clarice said.

"We don't mind cramming in," Burr said, and I said, at the same time, "We don't want to displace Mama."

"Allrighty," said Clarice, shrugging. "If I can ever peel Bud off that game, I'll have him put the bags in there."

"I'll get them," said Burr. He headed back up the hall. Clarice started to follow him, but I put a hand on her arm, stopping her. When Burr had disappeared around the corner into the den, I said, "I need to ask you, have you heard from Rose Mae Lolley? From back in high school, remember?"

"Not me, no. Bud talked to her, though. He said she called the house."

"What did Bud tell her?" I asked, a bit more urgently than I had intended. "Do you know?"

"Not really. You know men, they can't recount a conversation word for word. They just give you a two-word summary and then go mow the lawn." I was gripping her arm too hard, and Clarice's brow furrowed in concern.

"I thought it was probably about the reunion. We're coming up on ten years. I know she asked about you, and Bud gave her your address." Clarice put her hand over mine. "Arlene, it was about the reunion, wasn't it? Rose Mae Lolley wasn't . . ." She trailed off and then said, "It was about the reunion, right?"

I didn't want to lie to her, so I said, "Clarice, her class graduated two years ahead of us."

Clarice pulled away from me. She wrapped her arms around her middle and looked down at the floor. "I should have thought to call you. Warn you. I didn't think of it that way when Bud said she'd called."

I hadn't meant to get into this with her, but looking at her pale face, I knew I had blown any chance at keeping it casual. I said, "You never told Bud? Oh no, of course not, because if you had, he never would have told Rose Mae how to contact me."

Clarice swallowed hard. "I never told anyone, Arlene. You said it never happened. We agreed." She glanced up at me and then added, "Don't look at me that way. I would bet money you never told Burr."

"He's your husband, Clarice," I said.

"Well, Burr is your husband," Clarice said.

"Not exactly," I said. It just popped out.

"Oh my Lord!" said Clarice. "Arlene, what the heck is going on? What are you doing? Why are you this way? Why can't anything ever go in a straight line with you, one step after another, one, two, three, four?"

"Keep your voice down," I hissed. "I am going to tell Burr. And we are getting married. Really soon. Immediately. It's barely even not true."

Clarice's breathing had quickened, and she was spinning her wedding band unconsciously, exactly the way Florence did when she was upset. I opened my mouth to say more, but Clarice gave a barely perceptible shake of her head and cut her eyes up the hall, behind me.

I looked over my shoulder. Aunt Florence was standing at the head of the hall, holding my suitcases. "Every man in this house is stuck on that game," she called down to us.

"I'm not done with this," Clarice whispered as I turned and went up the hall to help Flo.

Aunt Florence opened the door to our old room and went on in. I went inside after her, and Clarice stopped in the doorway behind me.

"Oh my God," I said.

Clarice's side of the room was just the same as it ever was. Her childhood lovey, Mr. Bun, was on the daybed, which still sported the old apple-green checked comforter and green shams. Her cheerleading trophies were still up on shelves, and her school desk still had the horse-head bookends with some of her old Trixie Belden books in between. The daisy decals on the apple-green lamp were faded but still attached.

My side of the room was gone. Obliterated. An old washstand stood where my desk used to be, and my bed had been replaced with Aunt Florence's Singer on a sewing table. The rest of the room was dead empty of everything, stripped down and hollowed. It was exactly what Aunt Florence had done to Wayne's room, only Wayne had died, and I was still breathing in and out.

But there was nothing left of me in there, nothing to indicate I had ever slept there. My books were gone. Flo could have sent me my books. And the stupid stuffed panda I slept with as a child, she could have sent him, too. My old dollhouse where the Minkus family had lived was gone. My high school diploma in its Wal-Mart frame was gone. My clarinet. My stuffed animals.

My yearbook, filled only with the hasty scrawls of embarrassed boys because every girl in the class except Clarice had refused to sign it. Gone. Florence's scorched-earth policies had left my half of the room gutted and scraped so clean that not even the dust had been allowed to settle. I stared at Flo in shock, Clarice silent behind me.

Florence set the bags down and looked at me with her unfathomable eyes. "What?" she said. "It's not like you were using it."

# CHAPTER

## 10

THE MORNING AFTER I killed Jim Beverly, I woke up in the gray hour just before dawn. I had passed out in my front yard. I was crammed between the hydrangea bushes and the front wall of the house. Clarice was kneeling beside me, prodding at me and hissing, "Arlene, Arlene." It was warm out, but she was shivering in her baby-doll pajamas. I saw our bedroom window was open.

"I was up waiting for you forever," she said. "I must have fallen asleep. I came out here to look up the road and saw your feet sticking out of the bushes. Oh Lordy Lord, Arlene, we have to get you inside before a neighbor sees you or, God forbid, that stupid paperboy comes. Oh Lordy, but you smell like drinking."

My mouth felt sticky, as if spiders had sealed it with webbing as I slept in the dew. I felt something hard in my hand and realized I was still clutching the neck of the tequila bottle. I sat up, and the world spun, and my stomach flopped and heaved.

"Arlene, now," said Clarice urgently. She stopped prodding me to scrub the sleep from her eyes, and then brushed at my cheek. I had been sleeping facedown in the loamy earth of the flower bed, and a shower of dirt fell into my lap as she brushed.

"If Mama gets one whiff of you, you are utterly doomed." She dragged at my arm and I half walked, half crawled to the open window. We paused there while Clarice beat at me with her hands to get as much of the soil off my clothes as she could. Then, with Clarice boosting me from behind, I heaved half my body over the sill and tumbled inside, slithering sideways to land beside Clarice's desk. I struggled upright and fought hard to keep from puking. Clarice stayed outside to shut the window and put the screen back on.

I sat on the floor, longing for death. I heard Clarice creeping through the house, and then she slipped into our room and shut the door tight.

"Don't tell me that's a liquor bottle," she said. "Hard liquor? You couldn't even go beer?" Clarice pried the murder weapon out of my fingers. I tried to cling to it, but my hands had no grip. I watched her hands holding it, but my brain was too fogged to understand why it bothered me so. It wasn't until she stuffed it under my bed that I thought the word "fingerprints" and realized she shouldn't be touching it.

"Go get in the shower as cold as you can stand it," she whispered. "Go, go. And if you have to throw up, for the love of God, do it quietly."

I did what she said. I stood in the icy spray, and then I had to go to my hands and knees and heave. When I could breathe again, I squatted on my haunches in the spray and let cool water beat down on my aching head. My tequila-soaked brain began to perk up and gibber at me. When you've just committed a murder, you shouldn't immediately drink a third of a bottle of Mexican tequila. Especially if you aren't used to drinking. Right after a murder, you need to be able to think clearly.

"You killed someone," said my brain. I shook my head, hard, and it made the world spin just enough to drive that thought sideways and out. I couldn't think about that now. I couldn't think about it at all. "Okay, then," said my brain, "what about this: Someone is going to find out."

I had to think about that. Jim Beverly's car was at the foot of Lipsmack Hill, and Jim Beverly himself was somewhere on the other side of the same hill. When they found the car, they would find the body.

I clung to the absurd notion that whoever found the body might think he fell down the hill drunk and smashed his head on some tequila-bottle–shaped natural root formation. I tilted my face up into the spray, hoping the cold water could clear my head.

The thought came back again, persistent. "You killed someone. Someone is very dead now."

"Shush," I said out loud.

I had to move him. No, not "him." It was better not to think of it as him. The pronoun made me want to weep, immobilized me on the floor of the tub. I had to move the body. I had to get back out to Lipsmack in the dead of night and drag it out of there and take it somewhere. I had to bury it, or no, I could drop it in a quarry. There were quarries in Alabama somewhere. I had to find a quarry and steal a car and tie rocks to it and drop it down a quarry.

The thought came back again. "Hello. Dead person. Killed by you."

"Good," I said aloud. "And I am glad, so there, so shut up." I sat still again, shocked to hear my voice say these things so strongly, with such truth. On some level I was glad, and that was almost worse than having done it. But at the same time, it was distant enough from me that I could think about which shampoo to use to wash my hair.

Ugly joy and horror were at war far away from me, on the other side of a huge wall of tequila and fear. "I'm sorry?" I said, testing, and was relieved to find that somewhere in the sick numbness that ruled me, I was sorry. I did not know if sorry or glad would win, but I also knew, listening to myself, I wasn't sorry enough to spend my life in jail if I could help it. The problem was, I did not think I could help it.

Rationally, I knew I couldn't move it. I simply didn't have the strength to drag 160 or so pounds of dead, dead weight out of Roach Country. The vines would cling to it and hold it. It was uphill. I couldn't have moved it last night without sitting down and shoving at it with my feet. And that was on open ground. I certainly couldn't go down into the heart of the heaps and drag it uphill. Someone would have to help me.

Bud could get it out of there easily, but I didn't think his boyfriend-in-law loyalty would extend to dragging around dead bodies. Maybe even Clarice could do it, if the two of us worked together. She was tall and strong from gymnastics and cheerleading. But Clarice, my aching brain countered smugly, was firmly against any sort of crime.

The truth was, I thought, standing up and adjusting the water to warm, there was nothing I could do but hope that if they found him, they wouldn't find anything that led them to me. I tried to think it through. Barry had watched me go all the way to Bud's car. Bud had left me with Clarice. Clarice had covered for me with our parents. As long as Clarice kept her mouth shut, and no one had seen me creeping up Lipsmack Hill, or after, staggering home in a dead drunk, or after that, passed out in the hydrangea bushes for God only knew how many hours . . . no sense following that train of thought. I had to sit tight and hope they didn't find him. When they found him, everything would unravel, and it would be only a matter of time until they found me.

I began to pray, desperate and in earnest. "Please Lord, I know You probably don't approve of all this, and it's a bad, bad sin, well, actually, probably, okay, the worst sin there is, but please, Lord, please, don't let them find him."

I stood up and began to wash, getting the cloying smell of tequila off me and praying hard. I scrubbed viciously at my skin with Clarice's loofah until I felt peeled and raw. I washed my hair with Clarice's sacred Raspberry Essence shampoo instead of my almost scent-free Johnson & Johnson. All the while I made extravagant promises to God, silently, but so fervently my lips were moving. "Oh God, dear God, I will stop all that nastiness with the boys. I won't ever fornicate again, and if you help me, Lord, I will never tell another lie. I will get straight A's and get out of this town and never come back, won't even look back, just please, Lord, don't let them find him."

I got out of the shower and dried off. Clarice had crept in at some point while I was bathing. My dirt-covered, stinking clothes had been taken away, and there were a clean pair of panties and fresh PJs sitting on the toilet lid.

I was beginning to understand what Paul meant when he told the Thessalonians to "pray without ceasing." As I dressed, as my head pounded, as my stomach twirled and my intestines looped and writhed, underneath it all was a constant stream of imploring promises going up to God.

I paused at the bathroom door, listening. Mama, I wasn't worried about. She didn't care what I did. Uncle Bruster slept so heavy, I could run a truck through the wall, and if he was sleeping especially light, he might turn over. But Aunt Florence was unpredictable. I didn't hear any movement coming from their room. I walked as quickly and quietly as I could back down to our room.

Clarice was in her bed, sitting up with the covers bunched around her waist. Our light was off, but I could see her clearly in the dawn light coming through our windows. I closed the blinds.

Clarice had unmade my bed. She had taken the trouble to try and put a hump in it with our shams, so if Florence had glanced in during the night, there was a tiny chance I might not get busted. I pulled the shams out and piled them on the floor and crept gratefully in and lay down. In the back of my mind, I was still churning out a long repetitive stream of terrified prayer, but my body was too ruined to allow me to feel as frightened as I should have.

I could hear Clarice breathing, fast and shaky. She was almost panting.

"I'm sorry," I said, knowing it wasn't enough.

"Where have you been?" Clarice whispered fiercely. "I have been going crazy, and you are off getting drunk on hard liquor? What happened? Did you see him? Did your plan work? What happened?"

My throat filled up with fifty good lies, and I opened my mouth to release them, and then closed it again fast before any could escape. I had promised God not ten minutes ago in the shower that I would never lie again if He would help me.

"Arlene," Clarice hissed. "I know you are sick and tired, but you are not going to sleep until you tell me what happened."

I spoke slowly, checking every word for truth before releasing it. "I got about halfway up Lipsmack, and that girl, that freshman, was coming down already." True.

"Was she okay?" whispered Clarice.

"She seemed fine. She was mad, though. He'd been rude to her. So anyway, I went on up."

"Why on earth!" said Clarice.

"I don't know." True. "Anyway, he was sitting with his back to me, up by the cliff, and he was so drunk I didn't think he could stand up. And his tequila bottle was behind him." I paused to edit bits out of the next part of the story, and to offer an explanatory prayer to God. I told Him that not saying something was not the same as telling a lie. Lightning did not come through the window and strike me, so I assumed God agreed. I went on, "I snuck up behind him, and he didn't hear me. I put the cap on his tequila bottle, and I picked it up. When I went back down, I took the bottle with me, and I drank tequila all the way home." All true.

"He never knew you were there?"

"No," I said. "He was very drunk, Clarice, and he was singing really loud."

In the dim light, I saw the white flash of her teeth. Clarice was smiling at me the way she used to before I started up with all the boys and she got so angry with me. "Good for you," she said. "I bet he reached around looking for that tequila and could not figure out what was going on. I bet he crawled around looking for half an hour with no clue. You really got him, Arlene. You really played a good one on him." Somewhere in the middle of speaking, her grin had faded and her voice had gotten louder. It cracked, and she said, "That stupid bastard. That stupid, stupid bastard." She was crying. "I was so scared for you."

I slipped out of my bed and took five wobbly, world-spinning steps to hers, saying, "Shove over," and slipping in beside her.

"Don't cry, Clarice," I said. I had to go slow and careful, to make sure I wasn't lying. "I know taking his tequila doesn't pay him back. He is—he was a bastard. I remember. We say it didn't happen, but we both remember. He almost killed me. Forget the bottle. The only thing that matters is that freshman girl. She came down safe."

She nodded, snuffling.

"Also you have to keep it down or Aunt Florence will come in here like the wrath of God, wanting to know what's going on," I said.

"I think Mama must already be out in her garden. It's Saturday. She must have been going out the back door as you were going in the window and I came up the front. Otherwise she'd already have busted us."

I was starting to lose consciousness, so I slipped back into my own bed. My eyes were closing, but I had enough presence of mind to say, "Clarice? One thing? Please don't tell. I don't mean just your mama, I mean anyone. I don't want anyone to know I went up there and took his bottle and got drunk and all, okay? Let's pretend like I came home with you." I was sick and sleepy, and my heartbeat was thundering in my head.

"I wouldn't tell anyone," said Clarice. "Oh, except I already told Bud."

I sat up so abruptly that the room tilted around me and I almost threw up in my lap. "What, why?" I said, when I had enough breath back to speak.

"You didn't come home. I wanted Bud to go look for you, so I called him on his phone. You know his mama lets him have a private line in his room, so I didn't wake his folks up. He reminded me I still have his car so he couldn't go out looking. We were going to go look for you this morning if you hadn't turned up."

I flopped back down in the bed, my stomach churning. "Did you tell him where I was? Or what I was doing?"

"Not really," she said. "He doesn't know. I mean, he doesn't know about Jim Beverly or last year. But I told him you were going up Lipsmack, and I may have said who was up there or . . . I don't remember, exactly. I was so afraid. But I will tell him not to tell anyone. If it ever comes up, we'll say that I borrowed Bud's car and took you home from your date with Barry because you got sick. And I'll tell Bud you got drunk and are embarrassed about it, and that he has to keep his mouth shut or you'll be grounded forever."

"Don't forget," I said. "Don't forget to tell Bud to stick with that story." Then it seemed I closed my eyes for less than a minute before a horrible banging clatter was invading my ruined head.

"Up, up, up, girlie," Uncle Bruster was bellowing outside the door. "Your aunt Flo has breakfast almost ready, and everyone is waiting on you."

I groaned. Clarice's bed was already made. The clock said it was eight-thirty, and that meant Aunt Florence would have paused in her gardening to make our traditional Saturday-morning family breakfast. After we ate, there would be family chores, and I would probably die, hopefully before the police arrived to arrest me.

Unless we had company, we always ate in the kitchen. Uncle Bruster was ensconced behind the paper, and next to him, my mama was peeling the white parts away from her fried egg and hiding them in her napkin. She had ringed the unbroken yolk with petals made of torn pieces of biscuit. Clarice, across from Mama, shot me a quick look as I entered, and from her expression I could tell I looked as green as I felt. I sat by Clarice, my back to Aunt Flo, who was frying up more eggs in the bacon grease.

A platter of glistening pink bacon was emitting vile fumes, and I watched in horror as Uncle Bruster reached out blindly and picked up a piece, taking it behind his paper to devour it. I heard his thunderous crunching and longed to crawl under the table and heave and hopefully choke to death on my own vomit. Aunt Florence came to the table and slid two eggs onto my plate, cooked over hard till they were almost crunchy. They glared up at me balefully, moist and glistening with droplets of fat. I glared back.

I looked up, and Aunt Florence was still standing over me, regarding me with a jaundiced and suspicious eye. I hastily picked up a fork and began choking down the eggs. Aunt Florence remained, looming over me, watching me eat. She'd seen hangovers before, but not in me or her daughter. She was probably trying to talk herself out of identifying my malady.

"Mama?" said Clarice. "Are me and Arlene supposed to weed the strawberry patch today? Or what else needs to get done? Because I want to go on and get started. I'm supposed to meet Bud at his football practice."

Florence was not deterred. "Arlene, are you sick?" she said.

I did not answer. I had just promised God for the seven hundredth time that I would not lie ever again.

"Yes," said Clarice quickly. "She is totally sick. Bud went to shoot pool with Clint, and I brought her home in his car last night. There is definitely a very bad stomach flu going on at school, and I definitely think she has it."

Bruster looked out from behind his paper. "You're looking a little peaked, girlie."

I kept my head down, forking up another bit of egg and praying.

Aunt Florence stepped away, and it was like a weight being hefted off my stomach. I gratefully set my fork down, and then started as Aunt Florence reappeared beside me. She set an icy-cold can of Coke down beside my juice and said, "Drink that, it will settle your stomach. Let me make you some dry toast. And then you go back to bed. Bruster has to run some errands for me, and I have a lot to do in the garden. Are you going to be all right by yourself, or do you need someone sitting with you?"

"I'll be fine," I said.

"All right, then," Florence said. "Clarice, you can go on over and meet Bud after breakfast. You girls can weed the strawberries one afternoon this week, when Arlene feels better."

"Poor baby," said my mother, taking a piece of bacon to give her egg daisy a stem. "Did you get it from a boy?"

I stared blankly at her, and then Clarice launched mercifully into a stream of mindless prattle. I took sips of the wonderful, bracing Coke and had to fight the urge to hold the icy can up to my aching head.

Aunt Florence brought me toast. "You eat that," she said. "That will help you."

After breakfast I went back to bed, but for the longest time, I could not sleep. I stared at Clarice's shams and prayed and prayed and prayed. I had been raised to believe that prayer could move mountains, if only you had faith the size of a mustard seed.

"Mountains be damned," I whispered to God. "I need a body moved."

# CHAPTER

## 11

CLARICE FORCE-MARCHED everyone into cheerful small talk all through supper, but eventually she had to leave to get her babies home to bed. That's when the real cat-and-mouse began. Florence wanted to get me alone so she could peel me like a grape, but Burr and I would not be separated. Burr wouldn't even take the garbage out unless I came with him to show him where the big can was. And he stayed in the kitchen drying the dishes as I washed. Florence told him to leave the dishes to womenfolk and tried to shoo him out to watch TV with Bruster.

"Real men aren't afraid of housework," said Burr, and Florence was halfway to shooting me an approving look before she remembered he was both black and hampering the inquisition and squelched it. Then she told him the dishes didn't need drying at all, they could air-dry in the drainer.

"All right," said Burr, "I'll rinse, then. Shove over, baby." He bent deep at the knee to bump my hip with his. As I finished scrubbing each dish, I handed it to him, and he rinsed with elaborate care, so close our elbows kept banging together as we tried to work. The message couldn't have been clearer if he'd whipped up some epoxy and glued me to his leg.

Florence gave up for the moment and sat down at the kitchen table, biding her time. I glanced back over my shoulder and saw Florence the inexorable sizing me up, effortlessly containing five thousand pounds of tension in perfect, coiled stillness.

Burr and I claimed trip exhaustion and fled to Clarice's old bedroom after Bruster trundled off to bed. Uncle Bruster kept farmer's hours out of lifelong habit. My mother stayed dozing in the armchair at the back of the den. Florence had already fed Mama her evening meds and relocked the pill cabinet. I pecked at her cheek and murmured, "'Nighty, Mama." Her eyes were half open, but only the whites were showing, and she did not respond. Florence watched us go down the hall in silence.

I took the bathroom first and brushed my teeth and washed my face. Then I changed in Clarice's room while Burr was in the bathroom. I had just pulled my sleeping shirt over my head when I heard Florence rapping at my chamber door.

"I'm not decent," I called, which was true on many levels, even though I was completely dressed.

"Just saying good night," she said through the door. "I am tucking in your mama."

"Good night, Mama. Good night, Aunt Flo," I called cheerfully. Mama said something back, and I heard Florence say, "Here we go, Gladys." I crept to the door and pressed my ear against it, listening to Florence's footsteps, like percussion, giving a beat to my mother's shuffling gait. I got into Clarice's bed and pulled the covers up to my chin. My mother and Florence were in Mama's room. The walls were so thin that even with the bathroom be-tween us, I could hear Mama coughing in sharp barks like a trained seal.

A few minutes later, Burr came in. He was wearing the same undershirt and lobster pajama bottoms he'd had on briefly at the hotel.

"The water here tastes funny," he said. He peeled off the undershirt and climbed in the bed, crawling up from the bottom to take the space by the wall. It was strange to see him lying be-side me, bare-chested, in a bed. I had dated him for two years, but barring a few summer pool parties and last night, he had been, for the most part, fully clothed. Now here was this body, tucked into bed with me, smelling of Ivory soap and man. His bare chest was unfamiliar, and yet it had my best friend Burr's head on top of it.

I was fine with it until he said, "Tight fit," and put his big hands on me. He turned me away from him, then pulled me back so we were nestled together like spoons in the small bed, his back pressed to the wall. As he moved me, my spine tightened, and my limbs stiffened in an almost automated resistance.

"Lena, relax," he said. "I feel like I'm holding a mattress spring."

"I can feel you," I said. "You're thinking about it."

He pulled me backwards, tighter against him, his hand low on my belly. "I'm a guy. I'm always thinking about it. At this point, I have at most four red blood cells bringing oxygen to my brain."

That made me laugh, and the momentary tension dissipated. Burr's body radiated heat, and I could feel his breath stirring my hair.

I put my hand over his and settled against him. Eventually

Burr's breath evened and slowed, and his whole body grew heavy and relaxed. I stayed close to him, getting used to the feel of him beside me, counting his heartbeats. Moonlight was coming in the slats between the blinds. It was a full moon, and my pupils were so dilated from staring into the darkness that the room seemed bright as day. Burr stirred a little, and his hand shifted to my hip. He was dreaming. His body was pressed against mine, and I could feel him wanting me even in the depths of his sleep.

I heard a bed creaking, loud in the silence of the house. At first I thought it was Mama getting up to roam, but the firm tread coming down the hall disabused me of that notion. The bedroom door swung open slowly, quietly. I narrowed my eyes to tiny slits and pretended to be sleeping while Florence stood in the doorway of the room, watching us. She stood there for a long time, three or four minutes. In the moonlight her face seemed expressionless. I had no idea what she was thinking.

"Arlene?" she said softly, just a breath above a whisper.

I did not answer.

"I know you're awake."

I was absolutely still.

"Arlene, you need to come talk to me."

I remained silent, playing possum.

"Girl, you best get your little butt out here and talk to me!" she said, louder, and Burr shifted, making a small noise in his throat. Florence froze in the doorway until he settled.

She whispered, "People who are really asleep don't hold their breath, Arlene." Then she closed the door, and I heard her heading back to her room. I lay in the darkness for a long time, staring at Florence's sewing machine in the place where my bed used to be. At some point I fell asleep.

In the morning Florence was filling the house with the smell of eggs frying in bacon grease by the time Burr and I were up. Clarice's old alarm clock said it was after seven, so I knew Bruster would have already left for work. I wrapped myself in my robe and turned my back while Burr pulled on his running shorts and a T-shirt. When I looked back over my shoulder, he was laughing at me. I grinned back at him and then hid my face in my hands.

We went out through the den and into the kitchen. Florence was standing at the stove, cooking, and she did not turn around or look at us when we came in. Her shoulders were set, and her spine was ramrod straight. She was like the poster child for angry good posture.

"Where's Mama?" I asked.

Florence shrugged. "In her room getting dressed. She already ate."

"I came to say good morning, Aunt Florence," I said. "I'm going to hop in the shower."

"You can sit down and eat a breakfast," she said. "Yours is almost done, Arlene." I obediently sat, and Florence spoke to the window over the stove. "How do you take your eggs, Burr?"

Burr said, "Like Lena's, over soft."

Florence said, "Arlene likes them over hard." She picked up her spatula and lifted two eggs out of the cast-iron skillet. They had been cooked until the edges looked like brown lace. She dumped them on a plate and snatched up some bacon from the drainer and threw that beside them. She slopped grits onto the plate and then grabbed a biscuit so hard she smashed its top in. She marched over and banged the plate down in front of me, but immediately picked it back up, saying, "Or she used to ten years ago. I guess you would know better than me how she likes her eggs now." Her mouth was back in its hard, tight line.

"They look fine, Aunt Flo," I said. "I like them both ways." But she was already taking away the plate. She dumped the whole breakfast in the trash and got four more eggs out of the fridge. She cracked them violently into the iron skillet, and they sizzled and popped in the bacon grease.

"I haven't cooked the girl an egg in ten years," said Aunt Florence, picking out bits of shell. "It's not like she would call me up and say, 'By the way, I like my eggs a new way now.' It's not like she was thinking I would ever cook her an egg again."

Burr raised his eyebrows and mouthed "Wow" at me. I shrugged.

We sat quietly while Florence abused the food and threw it onto plates. Then she slammed the plates in front of us. "I was going to say to you, Arlene, that you can run to bed all tired and hold your breath, but sometime you are going to have to sit down and talk to me. But then, see, I realized, thinking about it, that I am wrong. You seem to have lived just fine ignoring me for ten years long-distance, so what's a few days ignoring me in my face." And with that, she headed out the back door towards her garden.

I popped out of my chair and was after her before she left the carport. "That's not fair, Aunt Florence. I call home every Sunday, and most weeks more than that."

Burr had gotten up after me and followed us outside. Aunt Florence whirled around to face me, and I took an involuntary step back. I ran into Burr, who stood his ground, a solid wall of warmth at my back.

"You think you are such a smart little missy, but you are not that smart," said Florence. She was so angry that her grammar cracked and shattered. "You don't talk to me about nothing, Arlene, not nothing, and you know it. You sit up there all high and mighty in your Yankee town, thinking I am some ignorant old countrywoman, but I know you, smarty britches. I know why you won't talk to me or come home. And maybe I am dumb like you think, because I keep believing one day you are going to stop punishing me and forgive me. But I guess I am wrong about that, too, you resentful little turd."

"Forgive you?" I said, dumbfounded. "Aunt Florence, I don't have a clue what you're talking about, and I am certainly not punishing you."

"Really?" said Florence, her voice flooded with disbelief, and she looked at Burr for a long, ugly moment. "Go hold your breath in the house, Arlene. Nobody wants you out here." She turned her back on me and stalked off towards her garden, and this time I did not follow her.

Aunt Florence had been filling in blanks. I, more than anyone, ought to have known she would. I managed to go through life never lying by pausing in the right place, and people almost always filled in what they wanted. Clarice had taught me that. So Florence thought I had stayed away from Possett for ten years because I was mad at her because of some ancient fight or something she had made up in her head. And how was I supposed to fix that? I had no way to absolve her except the truth. I saw Jim Beverly for a moment in my mind's eye, lying in the earth, waiting for his Rose-Pop to come and find him. I shook my head, shook it away. How could I tell her? So far I couldn't even confess to Burr.

Burr whistled, long and low. "That is one fierce woman," he said. "I see where you get it."

"Get what?" I said. "And what am I supposed to do now?"

Burr took my hand. "Now you come eat breakfast, and then you have a shower."

We went back in and sat down at the table. No one made biscuits like my aunt Flo, and when I made myself eggs, I cooked them in Pam. This breakfast was like eating the sweet parts of my childhood, and it made me choky and regretful.

"By the way," I said to Burr, "just because I'm sitting here like a dork, weeping over my eggs, don't think I haven't noticed what a good man you are. You could make the situation a thousand times worse if you felt like getting shirty."

Burr shrugged. "This isn't anything new. I've been black all my life, and there are racists in Chicago. All I ask is that you remember you owe me when we get married and my sister Geneva calls you a she-pirate who has hijacked a black woman's rightful mate."

I nodded. "Deal."

After we finished eating, Burr told me he was going to try to run off his three-thousand-calorie breakfast while Aunt Florence was busy in the garden. He headed out the front door, and I caught a quick shower and got dressed. I was brushing out my hair in the bedroom when the phone rang. After six rings, when it was obvious Mama wasn't going to answer it, I grabbed the Princess phone on top of the desk. It was Clarice.

"I was hoping it would be you. What's going on, Arlene? You need to talk to me," she said.

"I just had a screaming fight with your mama, and I need some Excedrin and an early death. Maybe you could come out here later?" I opened up the desk's top drawer. Clarice's old pencils and scrap paper were gone, replaced by a local phone book. I pulled it out and flipped through to look up the Fruiton Holiday Inn.

afternoon. It's Field Day at the boys' school, and
somewhere away from my mama," she said.

agreed to meet up in Fruiton the next day at the mall. I had
shop for Uncle Bruster, anyway. In the worry over Burr and
Rose Mae Lolley, I had forgotten to get him a present for his
retirement.

As soon as Clarice hung up, I tapped the button to get a dial
tone and called the Holiday Inn. No one named Rose Mae Lolley or Rose Mae Wheeler had checked in yet. But it was only
Wednesday. Rose had said in the note that she might not make it
down to Fruiton before Thursday night. I would have to keep
checking and make sure I caught her before she got to Clarice
and Bud. I was relieved she hadn't shown up yet. I still did not
have my miracle lie ready, the one that would make her leave
Fruiton and stop searching for Jim Beverly.

I needed Burr's good brain. If Burr was helping me, the two of
us together could figure it out and come up with a plan. If only
we were actually married. Once we got married, it would be safe
and I could tell him everything.

Burr's laptop case was sitting at the foot of the bed. Aunt Florence must have thought it was one of our suitcases and brought
it in. I got out the laptop and set it up on Clarice's desk. I knew
his log-on, so I signed in and went online. I went to Alta Vista
and in twelve minutes had found a site that told me everything
I needed to know. Alabama did not require a blood test or a
waiting period before issuing a marriage license to people over
eighteen years old.

Fruiton was too close. Someone who knew my family might
see us. But Mobile was only about an hour away. I went back and
found the Web site for the Mobile County clerk's office. I followed

a few links and got to a page that told me that any notary could perform a marriage ceremony in Alabama. For thirty-four dollars, we could get a license and be married that same day in the same building. We could get ten dollars off the license if we signed an affidavit certifying that we had read and understood something called *The Alabama Marriage/Family Law Handbook*. The handbook was available as a PDF file, which meant they hadn't transcribed it, they had scanned the actual document into the computer and uploaded it.

I opened the file. The pamphlet had a green cover with a picture of a happy bride and groom, both lily-white and as wholesome as Ward and June Cleaver. I heard Burr returning from his jog and called, "I'm back here."

He came in the room, sweating and breathing hard. "The hills almost killed me," he said. "I'm used to running on the flat. Meanwhile, your mother is in the front yard. Doing something. What, exactly, is a mystery to me."

I scrolled past the cover to the first page of the pamphlet and started reading. "Is she in the street?" I asked.

"No."

"Is she fully dressed?"

"Yes."

"She's probably fine, then." I half stood so I could see out the window into the front yard. Mama was out there, wearing an aquamarine and yellow muumuu and red galoshes. Over the muumuu she had donned a voluminous clear plastic rain poncho and a matching plastic hat. There wasn't a cloud in the sky. She was dragging a large Hefty bag behind her, and in her other hand she had Uncle Bruster's trash pole, which she was using to viciously stab a pinecone. She had to stab three or four times before the pinecone stuck, and then she put it in the bag and walked a few steps, searching. She found another pinecone and began stabbing at it.

"She gets like that," I said. "I wonder if Aunt Florence remembered to lock her pills back up this morning. Sometimes Mama gets in her pills."

Burr was behind me, reading over my shoulder. "Should you go check?"

"Florence has the only key, and anyway, if she got in them, it's too late. She'll have eaten some and squirreled more away for later. We'll keep an eye on her." I sat back down.

"What's this?" Burr said, still reading.

"Alabama marital something-something pamphlet."

Basically the pamphlet said that Alabama was concerned about the rising divorce rate, and if we got married here, the state did not want us to get divorced. In order to avoid divorce, advised the pamphlet, we should communicate with each other. This took about two pages.

Then the pamphlet started to explain in excruciating detail exactly what we would need to do when the communication thing didn't pan out and we decided to get a divorce. I scrolled down the screen, skimming.

"Twenty bucks says lawyers wrote this," said Burr.

"Sucker bet, no takers," I scoffed. I flipped down to the bottom of the document and read, "Published by the Alabama Bar Association at a cost of .085 cents per pamphlet."

"Lena, why are you reading this?" Burr asked.

"Because Alabama says we have to." I closed the PDF file and turned around in the chair to face him. He straightened up and looked down at me. "Burr, listen, I was thinking. What if we ran over to Mobile and got married right now?" Burr's eyebrows went up and I talked faster, making my case. "You said you wanted to marry me, and you said soon. This is soon. And what if I am pregnant? And then it would be done and we could stop worrying about it."

Burr's eyes narrowed, and he looked at me silently. At last he said, "No."

I waited, but he didn't say anything else. "That's it?" I said. "Just no?"

"What else is there to say? Yes, I want to marry you. No, I'm not going to Mobile and get it over with as if it were a root canal. I want to get married in my dad's church, by our pastor, with my family there—"

"Geneva won't come, I bet you," I interjected, but he kept talking.

"My mother will. I would think you'd want her there. I'm sorry you're having a post-lie panic attack, if that's what this is, but this is not the solution. We'll be home in a few days. If you're pregnant, you won't be showing next week. We can do it quietly, the way you want. I'm good with quiet. But I'm not good with hasty and ashamed."

I stared at him helplessly, then turned back to the computer. I closed it down and packed it carefully back into its case.

"I really need this, Burr," I said in a low voice.

"Why?" he said.

I didn't have an answer.

He took a deep breath behind me. "I don't know what your agenda is, Lena. I know you have one. You always do. I don't mind that when you let me be on your team. But don't work me.

Don't tell me half the story and expect me to fall in line. At some point you have to decide to trust me."

"Maybe that's what I'm trying to do. But how can I, if you won't marry me?"

"I will marry you. But I don't want a civil ceremony. I don't want to break my mother's heart. And I don't want to spend my wedding night in that bed, listening to your mother cough. I think that's reasonable. Now I'm going to get in the shower, because this is a bad time and place to have a fight. And believe me, we're heading that way."

He walked out of the room. I heard the bathroom door shut emphatically, and then the water began to run. He stayed in the shower a long time. I got up and went to coax Mama in out of the yard.

Burr and I spent the rest of the day being polite and careful with each other. Burr read one of the legal thrillers he'd brought with him. When I went in the kitchen to make lunch, I gave the medicine-cabinet door a tug. It was locked, but then I noticed Aunt Florence had left her keys behind on the kitchen counter. I sighed. No doubt Mama had been in the meds. I took Flo's keys and went back to her room and tucked her key ring in her pocketbook.

I made tuna salad for lunch and then played cards with Mama. Mama was flushed, and whatever she had swallowed had made her chirpy and twitchy. Whenever I could get a break from her chatter, I went back to Clarice's room to call the Holiday Inn, but Rose still had not checked in.

At about three, Aunt Florence came in from the garden. Burr was still reading. Florence took one look at Mama's red cheeks and said, "Gladys, why don't you go get your scrapbooking things." Mama joggled off to her room, and Florence said, "I got in it with you and forgot and left my keys out, didn't I?"

I nodded and told her where I had put them.

When Mama came back, Florence spent the rest of the afternoon helping her do scrapbooking, trying to keep her calm and seated. Uncle Bruster got home at four-thirty, and Florence went to start dinner. Mama was still flying when we all gathered at the dining room table. The clink of cutlery on the plates and Mama jiggling and twisting around in her chair almost made me run screaming into the street.

Burr and I went to bed when Bruster turned in. I called the hotel once more, but Rose was still a no-show. I spent another long night dozing and listening to Burr breathe while my mother and Aunt Florence walked the house. Florence marched Mama up and down the hall until she could get her to go to bed.

The next morning all was quiet. Mama had crashed and was dead asleep in her room, so Florence was systematically searching the house, looking for Mama's pill stash. My money was on Mama. I offered to help with the search, but Florence shook her head. She remained so cool and distant that her earlier relentless stalking began to look appealing. Right after lunch, Burr and I escaped the house, heading for the mall in Fruiton. I tried the hotel a few times before leaving, but still no Rose.

Clarice was already waiting for us by the mall's front entrance, just her and the baby. Bud was at work, and the boys were at school. Her mouth was pulled down slightly at the corners, but even so, she looked pretty enough to be a TV mommy. Francie perched solemnly on her hip, staring me down with smaller versions of Clarice's pale blue eyes. Clarice walked up to meet us and gave me a one-armed hug. Francie used the opportunity to re-move a chunk of my hair.

"What are we looking for?" Clarice said, disentangling my long hair from the baby's fat starfish hand.

"We have to find a present for Uncle Bruster," I said. "How's that for procrastination? I figured you could help us find some-thing he would really like."

Clarice switched the baby to her other hip, and we headed down the mall together. There was one of those knickknack and trophy shops two stores down from the entrance, and we went in. Burr wandered the aisles, picking up business-card holders and pens and desk sets and setting them back down.

Clarice pulled me in the opposite direction. Once we were a couple of aisles over, she said, "What do you mean you're not married? What happened with Rose Mae Lolley? Why did she want to find you? Why are you really home after all this time, not that I'm not happy to see you, but Arlene, what's going on?"

"That's a lot of questions," I said. "The marriage thing, don't worry about it. We are getting married. I think. I hope. Next week, at home. But I couldn't have Aunt Florence thinking he was temporary and picking at us."

"That almost makes sense," said Clarice. "It makes Arlene sense, anyway. Still, if Mama ever finds out, I don't want to be in the state."

"As for Rose Mae, who knows," I said. "She's a nutburger. She tracked me down at my job—"

"She showed up in Chicago?" Clarice interrupted me.

"Yes, at school and at my apartment."

"What did she want?" Clarice said. Her pretty brow was fur-rowed, and Francie gave a peeping squawk. Clarice was holding her too tightly. Clarice loosened her grip and dropped a kiss on the baby's head.

"I refused to talk to her, Clarice. I pretty much closed the door in her face. I had no idea she'd turn around and come down here hunting you." I was doing it again, telling the truth but not the whole truth. I couldn't bring myself to tell a flat lie to Clarice. "Don't worry about it, okay? She's just your garden-variety loon. She said she was coming to Fruiton mostly on some tour-of-memories thing, so bothering you isn't even her first priority. And if she does turn up, you can send her my way. Don't tell her anything, don't talk to her, just get ahold of me, and I'll handle her."

"I can do that," said Clarice. She wrapped her other arm around Francie, holding her close and rubbing her cheek along the baby's head. "If she's crazy, I don't want her near us."

"Good. It isn't much to do with you anyway. I'll handle her," I said, and Clarice looked at me, solemn and trusting.

We went to find Burr. He was at the back of the store, holding a brass cigar cutter in the shape of a bare-breasted mermaid. She was leering and holding up a clamshell that held the blades.

"Perfect, right?" said Burr, and Clarice giggled. The three of us wandered the aisles together, chatting, and I found unexpected pleasure in having one family member who seemed interested in getting to know and like my probable future husband.

Francie got fussy, and we left the shop and walked to the center of the mall. We sat down on the benches by the center-court fountain, and Clarice dug around in her diaper bag. She spooned a jar of peas into Francie's mouth and dragged out some baby toys while we talked a bit more, catching up. Then Clarice started packing up the baby's things.

"I have to go get the boys at three-thirty. Lordy, but the time has flown. Arlene, you should run down to Wolf Camera and get Daddy a new point-and-shoot."

"That's a good idea," I said.

"I take it the present means you won the fight with Mama yesterday morning?" Clarice asked.

"What?" I said, not seeing the connection.

"I'm glad you guys are going," Clarice went on. "I was hoping you would, and I know deep down, Daddy would be sad if you didn't come. Mama is being ornery."

I said, "Burr and I don't know if we're going to the retirement party, Clarice. But that's not what I fought with your mother about. Why would you think that?"

Clarice paused in her packing and said, "Oh, wait. Never mind. I thought Mama was going to— Oh boy. I guess I put my foot in it. Really, never mind."

But I was doing the math in my head. "That's what Aunt Florence was trying to get me alone to talk about? She doesn't want me to come to this retirement party and shame her in Quincy's Steak House? That's it?"

Burr put his hand on my arm, but I shook him off. "No, Burr, hold on. She tortures me for weeks and uses my mother on me, trying to make me come down here for this party, and when I do, she doesn't want me to come to the thing because, what? Burr? Because of me and Burr?"

"Oh, Lordy, I am so dumb," said Clarice and sat down again. Francie stood up on Clarice's legs, tugging at her hair, and Clarice let her. "I am so sorry. I shouldn't have said anything."

"Yes, you should have."

"Lena, why are you so angry?" said Burr. "This is what you

warned me about from the moment I said I wanted to meet your family."

I shook my head. In a way, I was relieved to know that Bruster's party was the reason Florence had been trying to finagle a moment alone with me, away from Burr. But at the same time, I was angry. For ten years I had abandoned her. And in that ten years she'd decided I was still pissed with her over some stupid teen drama or another, and now all she wanted was to ask me to please not bring a black man to Uncle Bruster's party. Where was the inquisition? Where was the peeling like a grape? Some part of me wanted to be peeled, to tell it all, to irrevocably lay it down at the feet of someone, anyone, who loved me, be it Florence or Burr or both.

But if Burr coming to the party was her biggest issue with me after ten years, then . . . then what? Then she didn't love me. If there was to be no inquisition, then she did not truly love me at all, and I was shocked by how much that hurt me. But I should not have been. She was the closest thing I'd had to a mother after my father died and my own mother quit the job. And as much as I wanted to avoid Aunt Florence's questions and recriminations and anger, it was worse, infinitely worse, in fact devastating, for her not to have questions and recriminations and anger.

But probably she didn't. She had stripped my things, cleaned her house of my presence, and if she had fought to bring me down to Alabama at all, it was probably because her precious Clarice wanted to see me. And for form's sake, to keep up the appearance of my mother having some sort of vested interest in life. And all that "punishing me" crap that had been on my mind like a weight was drama to make me ashamed. Ashamed of Burr, of all things.

Clarice and Burr had continued talking over my head, but I had missed a portion of the conversation.

"—maybe thirteen or so," Clarice was saying. She stood back up so she could joggle the baby on one hip. "High school was very different. The middle school and elementary school we went to was almost all white kids, but the high school was bigger. So he takes me aside—"

"Who did?" I interrupted.

"Grampa Bent," said Clarice.

"The dead one I call my asshole grampa," I told Burr.

"Anyway," said Clarice. "He takes me aside and, out loud, not at all embarrassed, he tells me that if I ever date a black guy—and that they are all sure to be after me—no one in the family will ever speak to me again. And this is the man who raised my mama. When she was growing up—"

"That's just like him," I said to Burr. "There's a reason I call him my asshole grampa. But Clarice, he never said that to me."

"Well, that's because you're not . . . well, you know," Clarice said, blushing.

"I'm not what?" I snapped. "What am I not?"

Clarice looked at me, surprised by my vehemence, but mostly embarrassed. "Blond," she said. She shrugged and turned apologetically to Burr. "Grampa Bent thought black men would be more likely to go after . . ."

"Blondes," said Burr.

Clarice said, "Right, because we're . . ."

"Whiter," said Burr.

"Right," said Clarice. She shook her head. "So how could Mama be any other way? That's who raised her, a man who thought that way, in a time when thinking that way was normal.

Oh, crud, I have more to say on this, but I really do have to go. I'm going to be late to get the boys if I don't run. I do hope I see you at Daddy's party. I think Daddy feels so special that you would come home for this, especially since you don't come home for, well, anything else— Lordy, but I can't say a thing without opening a worm can. Burr, I am sorry my parents are this way, I really am. It's embarrassing to have them be this way." She stood up and got Francie installed in her permanent place on her hip and grabbed the diaper bag.

"I don't think we'll come," said Burr.

"Fuck that," I said.

"Arlene, really!" said Clarice. "Watch your mouth in front of the baby. She is starting to talk, you know."

"We're coming," I said. "Can we pick up the cake or anything? Burr and I want to be really, like, involved."

"Oh, Lordy," said Clarice. "You and my mama are just alike, you know that?"

"We aren't a thing alike," I said.

"If you say so, Arlene," said Clarice. "You see it though, don't you?" she added to Burr.

"I see it," he said, nodding.

I glared at them both. "We are going." My hands came together in front of me, almost of their own volition, but I didn't have a wedding ring to twist.

# CHAPTER

⊗⊗⊗

# 12

I WAS STILL praying to God to hide Jim Beverly's body when I eventually fell asleep. I woke up in a panic. I sat straight up and froze there with my heart thumping an erratic tattoo against my rib cage, not sure why I was so afraid, until I traced back what had awakened me. A noise. The doorbell. Less than twenty-four hours since I had killed him, and already my prayers had failed. They had found him. They had come to get me.

I jumped out of bed and slipped into jeans and a T-shirt. I could tell by the light coming in through the window that it was late afternoon, maybe heading into evening. I crept quickly down the hall to the den to hear what was going on.

Clarice was sitting in the den watching TV, and I put my finger to my lips to shush her before she could give away my presence. She looked at me questioningly. She had a pad of paper in her lap and was holding a pencil. I could hear that Aunt Florence had answered the door and was talking to someone—another woman. A lady cop?

Clarice had some stupid Chinese cooking show on, and I couldn't make out the conversation over the prattle about how to fold a ball of meat into wonton paper, whatever that was. I crept over and turned the volume down.

I caught Aunt Florence saying, "Not coming in here—" before Clarice said, "Hey!" and used the remote to pop the volume up even higher. I hissed at her like a cat and flipped the TV off, then stood in front of it to block the signal from the remote with my body.

"Move it, Arlene," said Clarice, outraged, and I flapped my hand at her to shush her.

"—poop on my carpet," Aunt Florence said.

"Arlene!" Clarice growled.

"I need to hear this," I whispered desperately. "I may have to go."

"I wish you would go," said Clarice. "You're blocking the TV. Anyway, why do you need to eavesdrop on Mama and Mrs. Weedy?"

"Mrs. Weedy?" I said. "It's Mrs. Weedy?"

Clarice looked at me like I was brain-damaged. "Arlene, are you still . . ." She dropped her voice and mouthed "drunk" at me, raising her eyebrows high to add the silent question mark.

I shook my head at her.

"Well, it's just Mrs. Weedy and Pippa."

Pippa was Mrs. Weedy's third chicken. Phoebe's replacement, Greta, had died of old age. Pippa was new.

Clarice said, "Can we please turn my show back on? I want to make those dumplings in home ec for my final project. I was writing it all down."

By this time I had recognized Mrs. Weedy's voice, and I could hear her saying, "Because the news I have—well, it's going to hit your girls pretty hard. Pretty hard. I was trying to be helpful, but I can see where that gets a person in this neighborhood. Anyway, you know Miss Pippa is perfectly house-trained. She uses a litter box just like a cat."

"House-trained my— What do you mean, hit my girls?" said Florence.

Mrs. Weedy said, "A student at their school. He's gone missing."

My eyes met Clarice's, and she set down the remote and stood up. We walked together around the corner into the hall so we could hear.

"A boy at their school—hello, Clarice, you pretty thing, and looky, there's Miss Arlene—a boy at your school has turned up missing. I am so sorry to be the one telling you," Mrs. Weedy said.

"Girls, you better get along," said Florence, but Clarice ignored her and said, "Who?"

"I know you know him," said Mrs. Weedy. She was craning around Aunt Florence, her eyes bright and eager, while Flo stood implacable in the doorway. Pippa scratched around chuckling to herself at Mrs. Weedy's feet. "Everyone knows him. He's the quarterback for the football team."

"Jim Beverly?" said Clarice. Automatically her hand reached for mine, and I was reaching, too. We clung hard to each other's hands, so hard we were hurting each other, but Clarice's voice sounded right. Normal, interested, disbelieving. "Jim Beverly is the one gone missing?"

Mrs. Weedy was nodding vigorously. "He sure is! Why, the whole town is in an uproar! And you'll never guess what I found out."

Clarice moved towards the doorway, pulling me by the hand. Florence did not move or even notice us, standing in the doorway as a bastion against all chicken-kind.

Clarice slipped past her and dragged me into the waning sunlight on the porch. She gestured to the rockers and said, "You sit down and tell us all about it, Mrs. Weedy. You want some tea?"

"No, thanks, sweetie," said Mrs. Weedy, sitting down, "I don't have the bladder I used to, you know. Now it seems like the minute I have a drink of any little thing, I'm heading for the potty. Let me tell you, I have quite a tale." Pippa went bobbing down the stairs and started scratching about in the lawn. Florence remained standing stock-still in the doorway, murderously watching Pippa eat up our grass seed.

Clarice and I sat down on the hanging porch swing, our linked hands hidden between us. I did not dare look at her. I couldn't look anywhere for long. I kept bouncing glances at Mrs. Weedy, the chicken, Aunt Florence turned to stone in the doorway, my own feet. Nothing seemed to move when I looked at it. It was like the world was a static slide show that changed only when I blinked. And every time I blinked, I saw another slide from a different show in my mind's eye. The freshman girl, her ponytail jingling in rage as she stomped down Lipsmack Hill. Jim Beverly with his back to me, singing with his feet dangling over the small cliff. That sweet-spot moment, the bottle in my hands connecting perfectly. Jim Beverly, waxy and utterly unmoving.

"Please, God," I whispered, so soft it wasn't any more than a shaped breath. "Did they find his Jeep?" I said out loud.

"Oh, did someone already tell you this?" said Mrs. Weedy, disappointed. Aunt Florence and Clarice both turned their attention to me. I could feel their eyes like hot spots on my skin.

"No, no," I said, panicking. "No, I just was wondering if he disappeared alone or maybe with his Jeep." Clarice squeezed my hand harder, and I managed to shut up before I could ask if they had found his body where I left it or if I still had time to flee town.

"How funny you should ask that, because you know, they did find his Jeep!" Mrs. Weedy said. "But I better start at the beginning." I died several hundred tiny internal deaths as Mrs. Weedy ever so slowly, and with many asides about what Pippa thought, told us about how Jim Beverly's father called the sheriff's office when Jim Beverly never came home last night. And how even though he was only a week or two away from eighteen, the sheriff agreed to start looking for him without waiting the usual forty-eight hours because, after all, this was Jim Beverly and there was a game on Saturday.

She wound her way endlessly through a protracted search, while my internal slide show ran over and over. Enraged freshman, jingling down the hill. Jim singing. Bottle swinging. Jim dead. And then the freshman started jingling down the hill again. Finally Mrs. Weedy said, "And there was not hide nor hair of him at all, anywhere, until around noon today, you know they found his Jeep."

My heart stuttered, and I waited for her to say that search par-

ties were even now beating the kudzu looking for his mortal remains, but she said, "It would have been found earlier, but you
see, the state police found it first. They found it before anyone
knew he was missing, and it was abandoned and smashed. So
they towed it to the impound lot, and they checked on who
owned it, but that never got coordinated with the sheriff, who
was searching for Jim Beverly unofficially because of the football
game, without waiting that forty-eight hours they have to wait."

"Impound lot?" said Clarice.

"Smashed?" I said.

"That chicken is eating the grass seed," Aunt Florence said
blackly. But at least she wasn't looking at me anymore.

"Let me back up," said Mrs. Weedy. "What happened was Jim
Beverly apparently was driving out of town, or towards the highway, anyway, because the Jeep was very near the highway on
Route 19. It was very close to Fruiton, and it was full of beer
cans. I mean, it was rattling with them! Coors. Coors beer cans.
And you know I am not a mother in the traditional sense, but I
do have Pippa, so I joined MADD. Pippa and I both think it's a
crying shame a young man like that was driving all drunken. He
is the football quarterback, and all the young men are looking to
him to see how to behave. So I think he has a responsibility,
don't you?

"But anyhow, he drove right off the road and into a telephone
pole and smashed his front end all up, but luckily they said he
was wearing his seat belt. And that's good! I mean, he was drunk,
and that is terrible, but some of these young men, they don't
wear a seat belt. I have a special car seat I can strap Pippa's carry
case to, that's how serious I am about seat belts, and in this case,
they think it saved his life."

"Saved his life?" I said. In my head I saw him lying dead, un-saved by seat belts, and then the slide flipped and got stuck on the freshman. Her enraged ponytail.

"Yes, saved his life! Because a few hours later, the state police found his Jeep and towed it away to the impound. And he wasn't in it. So he must have gotten out of it and walked away just fine. There was no blood in it, and the door was hanging open like a drunken person got out and walked away and didn't bother to close the door."

Clarice's nails were digging into my palm, but I felt oddly at peace as understanding washed through me. Ponytails don't jin-gle. I had heard keys jingling as the freshman marched resolutely down the hill. I could now see the keys in her hand perfectly in the slide show. She had been angry enough to take his truck, cer-tainly. Better to take his truck than shamefacedly ask a friend for a ride home after Jim Beverly had humiliated her. Better by far than saying to her friend, "He told me to suck him, like I was some sort of prostitute."

The beer cans were his. She hadn't been drunk, I bet, but she was a freshman, so how much driving had she done? She lived in Fruiton, so the place the Jeep was found made sense. She must have run off the road and smashed his Jeep. She had no li-cense, and she'd taken his Jeep without permission, so maybe she panicked. Maybe she went to a gas station and had a friend come and get her. Or her mom. Or maybe she hoofed it all the way home, like me.

"Hitchhiking?" said Clarice. I had been thinking so hard I had missed part of Mrs. Weedy's endless story.

"I know, it doesn't make any sense," Mrs. Weedy went on. "I mean, he's the last boy in the world to run away! Especially with a game today. He's already missing it because it started at four, and they'll use that second-string Bob Duffy, and we can't win with him. Everdale is tough.

"But the sheriff is thinking he must have run away because of the hitchhiking report. The man who saw the hitchhiker didn't say it was Jim, but it was a young man who could have been Jim. The man did not stop, just noticed him. The odd thing is, the young man was not hitching towards Fruiton. You would think if Jim Beverly was trying to hitch a ride after he wrecked his Jeep, he would have been heading home. But he was hitching the other way! At any rate, no one believes Jim Beverly would run away over having some beers, as young men do, and yes, he crashed, but he only wrecked his own Jeep. He didn't hurt anyone, not even himself, so why would he run away? He's not going to lose his scholarship over that sort of thing, a few beers and a wrecked Jeep. Especially with him still only seventeen. And with a game today! But still, the sheriff is thinking now he is a runaway instead of missing."

I sat in the rocker, and my prayers began to change from please to thank you. This could only be the direct hand of God.

And God continued to do what I had asked of Him. At Sunday school, people gave me reassuring updates. Jim Beverly had not been found. Everyone, the police included, continued to assume that the person who had taken the Jeep to Route 19 and run it into a telephone pole was actually Jim Beverly. He, of course, hadn't been able to do that, being dead. But no one else possessed this contradictory evidence. No one could find him or figure out where he had gone, but then they were looking in places where one might reasonably expect to find an alive boy with a bad hangover.

By evening services, the gossip mills had ground out fresh information. Jim Beverly, it turned out, was failing two classes. He wouldn't be going to UNA. He'd lost his scholarship. His case was reclassified. He was no longer missing. He was officially a runaway.

The prevailing theory was that Jim Beverly, humiliated, in a haze of drunken despair, had run off the road drunk, then staggered down the highway hitching a ride to anywhere but here. The freshman, without ever mentioning her grand theft auto, had confirmed his extreme drunken state and vile mood.

So he'd effectively vanished. Well, a lot of kids do. And the priority on runaways, especially male ones who are seconds away from their eighteenth birthday, and especially when they suddenly aren't going to be big college football stars on TV, is very, very, very low.

Within a few weeks of his fall from godhood, he was old news, and there were many other things to talk about. But Clarice watched me more than she used to, and her eyes were cool and serious. Neither of us seemed to be sleeping well.

For my part, I was waiting for someone to find his body. I knew someone would have to find it. All I could do was pray. I prayed for two things, first for time and rain and animals and bugs to erase all traces of my presence. And secondly I prayed for some sort of forgiveness, because I was beginning to understand what I had done.

I couldn't help but be glad the rapist was dead. I had a secret, fierce joy that I'd erased him from the earth, and I felt the earth was better with one less rapist on it. But I had also killed someone's son. His father's picture in the paper, worried and earnest, haunted me. I had killed the boy who'd fought for Rose Mae

Lolley, and at school she wafted through the halls, tiny and lost
with black circles under her luminous eyes. The rapist and the
boy who gave me his jacket to cover the blood on my pants and
made me laugh my way out of shame were the same boy.

No one but me knew he was dead, so no one could mourn
him, and in my imagination, the rain dripped through the thick
leaves of the kudzu onto his face. He would stay there until
someone found him or until God gave me up.

One night a week into my vigil, Clarice slipped out of bed.
"Shove over," she whispered. I turned onto my side and pressed
my back to the wall to face her as she climbed in beside me.
When we were children, she had slipped into my bed all the
time, and we had whispered endlessly to each other until we
fell asleep. But she had not come over to my side since I had
morphed into a slut. The last time I could remember her join-
ing me like this had also been about Jim Beverly, and she had
held me as we'd whispered back and forth, "It never happened.
It never, never did."

"Don't you talk," she said. "Just listen. You don't have to talk.
I figured it out."

I felt her arm reach for me under the covers, and I took her
hand. "That night, out at Lipsmack Hill, the night you got in
Bud's car and asked me to cover for you and then came home so
late, drunk. I know what happened.

"I put it together. Because I remembered you were with that
boy before you came over and got in Bud's car."

"Yes, I was with Barry," I said. "But Clarice, I am done with
running around with those boys."

"I remembered that Barry works in the front office at school.
He sometimes does the morning announcements. He told you,

didn't he? He told you about Jim Beverly's failing grades. That's why you felt like you could go up on Lipsmack after that freshman. That's why you sent Bud away and asked me to cover for you. That was the plan you said you had. You knew Jim Beverly was not going to college and that he had ruined everything and that he wasn't going to be so special anymore. And you thought, if he wasn't so special anymore, if he wasn't Mr. Big Quarterback, then maybe, if you told, maybe someone would believe you. If both of us told, someone would believe us.

"But I know you would never really tell, Arlene. We never even talk about it between us. But Jim Beverly didn't know that.

"You didn't just take his bottle, did you? Barry told you he was flunking out, so you went to talk to Jim Beverly, and you bluffed him. You told him you knew about his grades, and that no one would cover for him anymore, and you told him you were going to tell. And that's the real reason he left town. You drove him out.

"Everyone thinks he ran away because he was ashamed of failing out and losing his scholarship. But you and I know better. He hasn't got any shame in him. You threatened him, and you made him go. Oh, Arlene, how could you be so brave and stupid? He could have done anything."

I pressed her hand in the dark. I said, "I was serious, Clarice, when I said I was not going to run around anymore. And I am going to be an honest person and a better person. I promised God. And I hope you can forgive me."

She hugged me tight then, and she said, "It's all done, and we will never talk about it anymore. It's finished."

We lay in the dark together for a while longer, and the peace that settled between us was the only peace I had. I clung to it, knowing it was only for a little while. By winter, maybe sooner, Clarice, who had filled in everything I had left blank with a story of her own, would know the truth. It was inevitable, unless God came through with the miracle I still prayed for fervently.

I was safe only until someone smelled something rotten up on Lipsmack Hill. Even then they would probably think skunk or maybe dead deer. The smell might work for me, keeping kids off the top of Lipsmack, and no one ever went up there but kids.

But even if no one went looking for the source of the smell, I knew my days of safety were numbered. The heaps covering Jim Beverly would find him just another thing to climb. They would wrap threads of themselves around his limbs, lift him, and pose him to their liking. As winter came, the heaps would begin to lose their thick shield of waxy leaves. By November they would all have gone to bones. The heaps hiding him would become nothing more than a net of brown lace, holding up what was left of him for anyone to see.

# CHAPTER

# 13

AFTER WE bought the camera, Burr and I headed back to Aunt Florence's house. I was still steaming. Burr parked in the gravel drive.

"Maybe you should go gas up the car. Or something," I said.

"So you can attempt to kick your aunt's ass? Because frankly, baby, if you and Florence get into it, it's an even-odds bet."

I said, "She wanted to talk to me alone, fine. She's going to get her conversation."

We sat looking at the little white frame house with the green shutters. It looked very cheerful and bright in the afternoon sunlight. I couldn't quite force myself to get out of the car and go in yet.

"Who said that he couldn't go home again? Maybe he was lucky," said Burr.

"It was Thomas Wolfe," I said. "And he died of brain tuberculosis."

"Sometimes you scare me," Burr said.

I unfastened my seat belt. "Aunt Flo has left me no choice. She called around to every one of my relatives and warned them that I had Oh-God-No married a black man. You know she did. And I bet you anything several of my relatives have threatened to pitch all manner of ugly fits if I dare show my face with you at this party. That's fine, and I could walk away from that, but Florence took their side. No matter what she thinks to herself, she should have backed me."

Burr ran his hand over his buzz cut and shook his head. Up at the house, Aunt Florence came out on the porch and stood, shielding her eyes against the sun, looking down the drive at us. She waved.

I waved back through the windshield, feeling silly because I wasn't sure if she could see us through the glass with the sun setting behind us. Burr lifted his hand, too, and said, "There's another way to look at it. If we go, a bunch of ignorant racists may ruin your uncle's retirement party. That would be our fault. We know what they are."

"Yeah, there's that," I said. "But she still should have backed me." Aunt Florence came down the steps and stood on the sidewalk, still looking down the drive at us. She waved her hand again, this time impatiently, in a "come up here" motion. I said, "Let me go talk to her."

I hopped out and headed up the gravel drive, and Burr backed up and headed down Route 19 towards Possett.

"Where's he going?" called Florence, but she didn't wait for an answer. "Could you get a fire under your butt there, Arlene? I need you inside."

"Oh no," I said. "Mama?"

"Yes. I was glad to see you pull up. I can't tell if she's breathing."

I was swamped with a rush of mingled nerves and the ghost of an old anger. I picked up the pace and jogged to the porch. "You don't know what she took?"

"No," said Florence. "Who knows what all she squirreled away yesterday."

"Where is she?"

Florence led me through the house to the den, where Mama was lying still and waxy in her favorite chair. She did not look like she was breathing. I put my hand on her cold arm but could not find a pulse.

"Mama?" I said. I could feel a curl of panic beginning to rise low in my belly.

"Is she breathing?" asked Florence. "I can't tell."

"I don't know," I said. "Maybe you better call 911."

"Arlene, if I called 911 every time your mama looked dead, Bruster and I would be in the poorhouse by Tuesday. It's five hundred dollars for an ambulance ride if they don't admit."

"Mama?" I said again. No response. Her arm was cold but pliant. This seemed to me like a good sign. I put my hand to her throat and, after a moment, felt the lazy thump of blood moving through her pulse point.

"Her heart is working," I told Florence.

"But is she breathing?"

"How would I know?" I asked irritably. I couldn't see any discernible movement of her chest.

"Gladys," Florence said, pinching Mama's arm hard. "Gladys, you answer me."

I rummaged in my purse for my compact and then flipped it

open and held the mirror up to Mama's lips. A faint fog clouded
it.

"There she blows," said Florence. "You think she's just sleeping hard? Or do we need to ipecac her or make her take milk?"

I sighed. "Let's watch her for a minute. I had forgotten this
part."

We squatted on the floor on either side of Mama, looking at
each other across her legs.

"Why'd you send him off?" Florence asked. "Because I had a
hissy at breakfast yesterday morning?"

"I guess I thought if you wanted to talk to me alone so bad that
you'd come creeping into my room at night, I ought to let you."

Florence said, "You came up the walk as ticky as a cat. Something else decided you."

Before I could answer, Mama's mouth opened, and she let out
a short, sharp burp, loud as a gunshot.

"Crap!" said Florence. She reached around the back of Mama's
chair and pulled out a bucket. "Get her sitting up, Arlene. Get
her head up!"

I grabbed Mama by the shoulders and flopped her forward.
She was heavy with sleep, and her head lolled sideways and then
rolled forward. One of her legs fell off the ottoman, and I was
suddenly fighting two hundred pounds of deadweight, trying to
keep her in the chair. Florence stuck the bucket between Mama's
knees and grabbed her other shoulder, and together we got her
butt shoved back into the depths of the chair and bent her at the
waist over the bucket. Once I had a grip on her, Florence used
one hand to hold the bucket and the other to gather Mama's hair
backwards, off her face.

"You keep that behind her chair?" I said, looking at the bucket.

"I got tired of paying for Stanley Steemer," Florence said. "Your mama is going to kill herself, Arlene. It's just taking her longer than I think she planned on. Now, don't look so hangdog guilty. She wouldn't stop for you when you were little and needed a mama every minute, she sure isn't going to do it now that you're twenty-seven and don't need a damn thing from any of us."

I didn't know how to answer that. Mama jerked in my hands and released two more of those barking burps, and then she threw up thin green juice into the bucket Florence was holding. The smell was abysmal, like something evil you would meet in passing on the highway.

"Lordy my, oh crap," said Florence, turning her face away.

"You have the foulest mouth of any Baptist Women's League president in America," I said.

"Oh, get off your horse, Arlene. Everybody craps."

Mama answered her by throwing up again and then choking. She fought us weakly then, trying to rear back. I had to grab her head and push it down to keep her over the bucket. Florence let go of Mama's hair and banged her hard on the back, sharp blows between her shoulder blades. Mama hawked and spit and then pulled a long, shuddering in-breath.

"I think that's all she's got," said Florence. We eased her back into the chair.

"Arleney?" Mama said in a creaky voice. " 'S that you, sugar?"

"Yeah, Mama, I'm here," I said. Her head sagged sideways onto her shoulder, and she was out again, but her breathing was better. I could see the steady rise and fall of her chest. I picked up her foot and propped it back on the ottoman. The bare flesh of her ankle was smooth, and my fingers sank into it too easily. It felt like she had an inch-thick layer of Vaseline under the skin, and if I pressed too hard, the imprints of my fingers would remain, denting her.

Aunt Florence took the bucket into the kitchen. I followed her. "Your uncle Bruster put in a garbage disposal last year." She dumped the bucket into the sink and ran the disposal, then scrubbed the bucket's insides. I sat at the kitchen table and watched her. She had a can of orange-scented air freshener by the sink, and after the bucket was clean, she sprayed it all around until the air was so spiced with citrus and ammonia that it stung my throat and put a tickle in my lungs. She turned and faced me, leaning against the sink.

I said, "You shouldn't have to do this. I should be the one taking care of her."

Florence shook her head at me. "I don't know why you would. You don't owe her. She didn't take much care of you when you were little, and that's what makes kids think to turn it around when a person gets older. She's good here with me. I know her ways, and I can be home with her."

We couldn't quite meet each other's eyes. "Where is Uncle Bruster?" I said. "I thought he'd beat us home."

"He went for beers and wings with his working folks. The party tomorrow is going to be mostly family, so he's having a last hurrah with his boys tonight."

"So here we are, just the two of us. Why did you want to get me alone so badly, Aunt Flo? I'm all ears," I said. I had intended to sound belligerent about it, but Mama had taken the wind out of my sails. Florence didn't answer. She turned away from me and stared out the window over the sink. The kitchen faced the backyard, and when Clarice and I were children, we had played on the tire swing and the picnic table while Flo washed dishes and kept an eye on us through the window.

"Clarice said you didn't want Burr and me to come to the party for Uncle Bruster. She said you were worried some of our folks would make a scene and ruin his day."

Aunt Florence hunched her shoulders in what might have been a shrug. She said, "I thought about it. You know your aunt Sukie is in a snit. And all her boys. Her youngest one, Dale, is wild. He's threatening an ass beating at the Quincy's. All her boys blame him, that Burr, saying he's got you hypnotized with black sex. Your uncle Justice and aunt Caroline are going to walk out if you show up, even if you show up all by your lonesome, just because they know he exists somewhere. That Caroline, she can't resist having a drama."

"What do *you* want, though?" I said. "I was going to go to the mat on this, but now you tell me what to do, because I quit caring five minutes ago. If you don't want us to come, we won't."

She turned back around and met my eyes. Her mouth was turned fiercely down, and her eyes were narrowed, searching me. She clasped her big hands in front of her, worrying at her wedding ring. "Arlene, why are you pussyfooting around with this Quincy's crap? Come or don't. Do what you want, you always do. You know that's not what I want to talk to you about."

I was surprised to hear her dismissing Bruster's party so easily. I said, "You told Clarice that you wanted to talk to me about it, that you were really upset."

Aunt Florence said, "I had to tell Clarice something, didn't I?"

"If that's not it, Aunt Florence, then I do not have a clue."

"Yes, you do," said Florence. "You know." She ducked her head at me, a fierce sharp bob of a nod. "You know, and I know you know," she said. Her hands turned her ring around and around, almost violently. "I need to know if you told him."

I looked at her blankly. "Told who what?" I asked. "Burr?"

"Yes, Burr."

I hated the way she said his name. Every time she said it, it was like she had quotation marks around it. She said it the way you would say someone's alias once his real identity had been exposed.

"Aunt Florence, I am telling you for the last time, I have no idea what you are talking about."

Her eyes were piercing, searching me, and I could see anger welling up, filling them to the brim. "Excuse me, I forgot again how stupid you think I am," she said, her voice low and trembling with an icy rage. "I forgot you been up there in your big city getting all them degrees, and you think I'm ignorant and don't see nothing. But you got your smarts somewhere, girl, and it wasn't from those Fleets who don't have three brain cells to rub together between every one of them. Fleets are sweet-natured but dim as pre-dawn rocks. You may look like one of them, but inside, you are purely Bent, Arlene. You don't have a sweet bone in your body, nor a stupid one. You're smart as a whip and devious with it. Don't you forget, I'm a Bent, too. And I know, I *know*, why you left home. And I know why you haven't been back in ten years. I know. Do you hear me? And what I need to know now is, did you tell him. Did you tell your husband why you left here and didn't come back."

My mouth had gone dry. I was terrified that she really did know, but it didn't seem possible. No one knew but God, no one. I shook my head at her.

"Don't you doubt me, girl. Do I need to say his name?"

I stared at her, hard, and then nodded.

213

Aunt Florence swallowed, and it sounded like her throat had gone as dry as mine. When she spoke, it came out in a hoarse, husky whisper. "Jim Beverly," she said. "There, it's said. I was there. I came after you, as you damn well know, so quit your lying. Between us, at least."

I struggled to breathe. The air was acidic with the smell of oranges, sweet and cloying, and yet it scraped like razors down my throat.

"Did you tell that husband of yours? Did you tell him?"

I shook my head no.

A bit of the tension ebbed out of Florence then, and she nodded at me, twice, my sudden co-conspirator. "Don't you get stupid and tell him," she said. "Don't you trust him thataway."

"I do trust him," I said.

She snorted. Before I could answer, the front door opened, and I heard Burr calling, "Lena?"

I couldn't look away from Aunt Florence. "You came after me?" I said. I was studying the strength in her tall, spare frame. Even now, past fifty, she had a lean hardness to her. She could have pulled his body out of there, pushed away the clinging fingers of the kudzu, dragged it straight up to the top of the hill, and taken it away somewhere. She was capable of it. She was capable of anything. "I thought it was God. I thought God took him out of there," I whispered.

"Maybe it was," hissed Florence. "You don't know how God works. Maybe I was His instrument."

"Lena?" Burr called. He was in the hallway, checking the bedroom.

I whispered back, half panicking, "That winter I went up on

Lipsmack Hill all by myself. I had prayed and prayed, and he was just gone. I thought it was a miracle."

We could hear Burr crossing the den, so she could not answer me. In another moment the swinging door opened, and he entered. It seemed odd to see him so himself, easy and unchanged, when my whole world had gone sliding sideways.

"Hey, baby," he said. "Look what they had at the Shell station." He held up a three-pack of York peppermint patties, a favorite of mine, and then said, "Heads up," and tossed them to me. They sailed over my shoulder and smacked into the back door, falling to the floor.

Burr seemed to take in the scene then. I saw him register how stiff and still Aunt Florence was standing. He looked at my hands, gripping the table so hard they had gone dead white.

"Okay," he said. "Do I need to go get more gas?"

"Get me out of here," I said. I stood up. I had been clutching the edge of the table so tightly that it was physically painful to let go.

"Arlene," said Florence in a warning tone.

"No," I said. I held up one hand to silence her and was surprised to see how steady it was. "Burr, you get me out of here." I started walking, fast, sure he was following me, and halfway through the house, I was running. I passed Mama without a glance, ran out the door of the den into the entryway, and burst free into the yard, where the air had oxygen in it and I could finally get a breath. I ran to the Blazer and was in and buckled before Burr caught up. He climbed into the driver's seat and started the Blazer. As he was backing out, he said, "Where are we going?"

"Away," I said. He took a left out of the drive and that seemed to me to be the right way to go. After a mile or so, I told him to take another left, and after I gave the direction, I realized where I was taking him. We were heading towards Lipsmack Hill.

I couldn't get my head around what Florence had told me. Where had she taken the body? And why? Why had she done it? You don't cover up murders for people, even relatives. The only person you might take that kind of risk for would be your husband or your wife, or of course your own child. But maybe that made sense, then. Maybe, like me, she had done it for Clarice.

"Where are we going, Lena?" Burr asked again.

"I'm taking you somewhere I used to go when I was a kid," I said.

"What happened with you and Florence?"

I didn't answer. I was staring out the passenger-side window, looking for the turn. The side road that led to Lipsmack was dirt and hard to see. We almost hurtled right past it, but at the last moment I saw it and yelled, "There. Turn right!" Somehow Burr made the turn.

The whining drag of the branches against the Blazer made my teeth grind, and Burr was wincing for his paint job. It seemed to me the road had shrunk from the overgrowth quite a bit since I was a girl, but then I thought maybe it was because most of the boys who had brought me here drove smaller cars.

I wondered if kids still made out back there. These things seemed to be handed down from generation to generation, but to me, Lipsmack felt haunted. I wondered if that reverberated beyond my own imaginings, if the kids could feel the cold eyes of Jim Beverly's ghost on them as they grappled and mated in the backseats of their daddies' cars.

As we pulled into the clearing in front of Lipsmack, I could see in the waning light that the ground was littered with a few soda cans, a few beer cans, chip wrappers, and a sad, deflated condom. There was an ancient VW Beetle parked there, too, but it was empty. Probably some kid's car had died, and he had left it until he could come back with jumper cables or get a tow. Sunset on a Thursday, and we had the place to ourselves. No white T-shirt adorned the low branch by the path up the hillside. The tree itself had ten years of growth on it. If the T-shirt rule was still in effect, the kids must have been forced to use the scrub bush that surrounded the tree. The grass was still flattened and the undergrowth dead from being driven over by herds of cars.

Burr parked the Blazer at the foot of the hill, by the path that led up the side of Lipsmack.

"What are we doing here, Lena?" said Burr. Night was coming on fast, and I could not read the expression in his eyes. Burr had beautiful eyes, small and square but so sweet, a warm brown toast color, two shades lighter than his skin. A legacy from his mama. "This looks like a make-out spot. I don't think you brought me here to make out."

"Maybe I did," I said. I had left a dead man on top of that hill once, and my aunt Florence had dragged him away. I knew he was gone, but I could still feel him up there, cold and still. I was cold, too, so cold I was shaking with it. "Nothing good ever happened here, Burr. Maybe I brought you here to make something good happen."

I clambered off my seat and swung one leg over his legs, resting myself on his lap. I was tucked in front of the steering wheel, straddling him and facing him. He was so alive; I had a strange, almost clinical interest in the quicksilver heat of him. I started undoing the buttons on his shirt and slipped my hands inside, trying to warm myself with his skin.

"Lena," he said to me, and he caught my hands and held them fast between us. "Look at me."

I wouldn't meet his eyes, even in the safety of the growing night. In that moment, I was not interested in seeing him. All at once I was back in a place I hadn't been in years, up in the driver's seat of my brain, chilled to my core, dissociated from whatever my body might want to do. He still held my hands, so I couldn't touch him, and he was strong. I knew there was no fighting him, so I did not.

I was the driver, and my body was only my instrument, my tool. I forgot my hands, let them go limp in his, closed my eyes, and dropped my head back, exposing my throat to him. I gave him the top half of me, helpless, relaxing at the waist so only his grip kept me from toppling sideways. I felt the steering wheel behind me, pressing my back, holding me close as I straddled him. Below my waist, I was alive. My body ground its hips against Burr and rejoiced in the helpless physical response the movement pulled from him. My ownership of him and of the moment was complete and dizzying and ugly.

"What is this?" he said.

I pressed into him again, hips grinding, my upper body slack and helpless so he couldn't release me unless he was willing to let me fall. "Lena," he said, angry now, and as his grip loosened on my hands, I pulled them free and twined them around his neck, leaning forward so my long hair swung around our faces in a curtain, hiding us. I kissed him hard, riding him.

"Shit," he said into my mouth, and his hand fumbled at the door. I felt the night air come in as he found the handle and swung it open. The dome light came on, hopelessly dim. Burr pulled himself sideways, trying to get out, but I was all over him, clinging, ruining his balance. He lost his innate grace, his legs tangled in mine, and we fell out. He recovered quickly and already was half rolling in midair, so he landed on his back, taking the brunt of the fall. We hit the dead grass, hard, my legs still locked around him. Our teeth banged together, and I felt the sharp tang of blood in my mouth, familiar and bracing. I caught his breath, sucking it into my lungs as it came out of him in a rush.

He was struggling to inhale. My hands were free and I used them on him, running them down his chest. I sat up, straddling him, crotch to crotch, and reached one hand behind my back, low, to cup his balls through his Levi's. My body was a million different pieces, all separate, moving on him, and meanwhile, I was sitting cold and quiet in my driver's seat. I watched the two of us fighting each other silently as Burr struggled to breathe.

"Stop!" he whispered as soon as he could inhale. "Shit, get off me." I was already leaning down to kiss him again, but he grabbed my shoulders to stop me, saying my name, trying to make me look at him. My hands were free, so I slapped his face then, hard, and that shocked him enough to loosen his grip on my shoulders. I bent and kissed him on his slack, surprised mouth. And then I trailed my mouth sideways to suckle the heat of the stinging flesh I had hit.

He caught my hands again, hard and bruising, and I felt some of the coiled strength in him escaping his control. "Lena, stop," he said, and his voice was soft but intense. "I don't want to hurt you. I don't want this."

"Then why is your cock so hard," I said, in a voice so low and dark I didn't recognize it.

"That's it," he said. He shoved himself up, bending at the waist to sit with me in his lap. My legs were still wrapped around him, and he grasped my wrists between us again. He was long in the torso, so I had to look up at him. For a moment I was afraid, afraid of him, of Burr, and my control trembled. He was so much stronger than me. It was like waking up. This was not some frightened boy I could own so easily with testosterone and dirty talk.

It was like falling a long way and landing in myself. I stared at him, and then I said, my voice as soft as his had been, "I'm sorry. I don't know what that was." We sat looking at each other. The night was quiet around us. Whatever it had been, he felt it leave me. We both did. His grip on me loosened, and I took my hands away from him. I reached up and touched my lip. It was bleeding from where his teeth had banged into it. I looked at my fingers, and the blood looked black in the faint light.

"Baby," he said. "Don't you think it's time to talk to me?"

I leaned over and gently shut the door to the Blazer. It clicked shut, and the dome light went out. The sun had gone all the way down, and the moon had not yet risen; we were blanketed in a darkness almost absolute. I shifted off of him and sat on the dead grass beside him. I leaned against his shoulder, and he put one arm around me.

Burr said, "If it helps, I think I know where you're going, baby. I want you to talk to me. I don't think you're going to surprise me."

My opening sentence was running through my head. I knew exactly what to say, but I could not begin because Burr, the man who had helped me invent What Have I Got in My Pocketses, was leaping pell-mell to the endgame.

"Baby, say it," he said. "It isn't so bad. I won't stop loving you. It's not your fault."

"It's so bad," I said.

"No, it isn't. It's not bad. You're not bad. It's not like you killed someone."

I felt my silence change then, as my body went so still that a single beat of my heart shook me like an earthquake. In the pause after that heartbeat, the world was without sound. Burr felt it, too, that everything around us was holding its breath. I felt light break in him in the absolute darkness, and then he knew. "Oh. Shit," he said quietly. "Yeah, you should talk to me."

And finally I found that I could. "There are gods," I said. "There are gods in Alabama." And I told him almost everything.

It came spilling out of me in a great wash, breathy and fast. I talked and talked until my voice was cracking with the strain of constant use. I took him up Lipsmack Hill with me to be my witness. He saw me heft the bottle. Swing. Connect. Then I told him about Clarice, how she rescued me when I came to Alabama with the burnt shell of my mother.

I could not stop after that, could not let him take over. I told him about Rose-Pop. About Jim Beverly's kindness to me. I told him how I had loved Jim Beverly with a secret, hopeless love. I told him about the aftermath, when Clarice found me in the hydrangea bushes. I spilled out my fears and prayers as I begged God to hide me like He had hidden Cain, to mark me as safe from the repercussions of the world.

I told him everything but why I did it. And the why of it was crafted so deep into the story that I did not have to say it. The story itself was designed to make him say it for me.

But when I wound down, he sat silent for a long time. I waited for him to speak for me, but he did not. He sat digesting, and then he asked the wrong question. "What happened in the winter when the kudzu went to bones?"

"Nothing," I said.

"Something had to happen," he said.

I did not want to lie to him, would not lie, but while I could confess my own sins to him, I had no right to give him Florence's. I said, "Nothing happened. All fall no one complained about any smell. No one went looking. Everyone assumed he had run away. And in winter I went back up there and looked. The body was gone."

"How is that possible?" Burr said.

"I think—or I should say I thought, at the time, that God had moved him."

Burr stirred against me in the dark. "God moved him?"

"Yes," I said. "That's what I thought. It was what I had prayed for, after all. I thought it was a miracle. Like maybe God had sent a bear to drag him off, or—"

"God sent a bear? God sent a bear to lower Alabama," Burr said.

"Will you stop repeating everything I say in that skeptical tone! I told you what I saw. I thought God took it, or a bear took it. I didn't know. That's not the point. That was never the point. The point is that I killed a man. I killed Jim Beverly. And you have to hate me now or you have to forgive me, and how can you decide?" I had talked for so long, my voice was a raw whisper.

Burr seemed distracted by his own thoughts. I could almost hear his brain charging up, humming and whirring as it ticked over into lawyer mode, picking through facts.

I said, "How can you decide what to do if you don't even know why I did it? If you won't even say why?"

"I'm not done with the bear yet, Lena. You say you killed a man. And God took the body. I can't get it processed." He stood up abruptly, and I was instantly chilled.

"Burr," I said.

"Just wait." He was pacing up and down a few steps in front of the Blazer. "I have to think it through. Wait. Did you say? Oh Christ Almighty. Did you say you killed him? You killed this boy, this Jim Beverly?"

"Yes," I said miserably.

"With a bottle?" he said.

"Yes," I said.

"Did you ask me a minute ago how I could decide what to do if I didn't say why you killed him?"

"I think so," I said.

"If I, Wilson Burroughs, didn't say why?" he said. His voice was rising, angry in the darkness. "If I didn't? Oh, Christ, you have to be kidding me."

He pushed past where I was huddled on the ground, and opened the driver's-side door. He leaned in, and I heard a click, and then the path up the hill was flooded with light. He had turned on the headlights. He came to me, grabbed me by the arm, and hauled me to my feet. I stumbled after him as he dragged me into the light, staring down at me so he could see my face.

"I'm supposed to tell you why? This is What Have I Got in My Pocketses, isn't it? And now I'm supposed to say why? I have to tell you the motive? What are you pulling, Lena? What's true here? Look me in my eye, because I know you never lie. Tell me. Did you do it?"

I thought I was crying, but I couldn't tell. I stared up at him. "Yes," I said.

"Why?" he said, practically yelling.

"You're hurting my arm," I said miserably.

"Why?" he said, undeterred.

"Burr, please," I said. "Please. Let me go, you're hurting me."

But he did not move or release me. "Why, Lena?" he said.

I said, "It happened, I swear it happened. But then I stole it."

"Stop dancing," he said. "Tell me. Tell me why."

I opened my mouth to tell him, and Rose Mae Lolley came pounding down the last few steps of the path up Lipsmack Hill. Burr still had my arm, but he half turned towards her when he heard her coming. She grabbed his shoulders and jerked her leg up. Her knee rammed into him between his legs. Burr let go of me and doubled over. Rose twisted at the waist and brought her elbow down hard on Burr's head, and he fell to the ground.

"Run like hell! Run like hell!" Rose screeched at me and took off like a deer.

I dropped to my knees beside Burr. "Oh, honey," I said. "Oh, baby, are you okay?" He groaned in answer, curled up on the ground.

I glanced over my shoulder. Rose had stopped a few yards away, her white T-shirt glowing in the darkness. "Arlene," she said urgently. "You have to run while he's down."

"Shut up, you head case," I said. "He's not going to hurt me." Burr managed to sit up, and I put an arm around him, supporting him. "He would never hurt me."

"Shit, shit," said Burr, still bent at the waist, hunched over himself.

"What the hell are you doing here?" I yelled at Rose.

Rose took a hesitant step back towards us. "Meditating. Until I heard him bellowing at you. I came creeping down, and I heard you say he was hurting you. I saw you in the headlights. He was shaking you."

I rubbed Burr's shoulder. "He was just angry, Rose."

She took another step towards us. "That's what they all say. They're all angry, and being sorry later doesn't mean shit, Arlene."

"Not every man hits girls," I said. "Burr, baby, are you okay?"

He nodded. "I think I'm going to live," he rasped out and got a deep breath in.

I said to Rose, "What the fuck were you doing meditating up on Lipsmack?"

Rose crossed her arms and said, "What are you doing in Alabama?"

"I came down here to meet you," I said. "I've called the hotel over and over."

"I haven't checked in yet," said Rose. "I came here first. This was a special place for us. It was . . . Let's just say it was very special for me and Jim."

I rolled my eyes. "This was a 'special place' for everyone, you numb fuck." I was rubbing Burr's shoulders. "I think you owe him an apology."

Rose shrugged defensively. She came a step or two closer. "I'm sorry if I misinterpreted what was happening. But it sure as hell looked to me like you were hurting her," she said to Burr.

"There is such a thing as a good man, Rose," I said.

Burr had his head down, taking in long slow breaths.

"I know that," she said. "I had one once. I told my therapist, and that's why I'm looking for him. That's what I came here to prove."

Burr shook his head, and I said, "If you're trying to use Jim Beverly to prove you know how to pick a good boyfriend, you're barking up the wrong tree."

"What does that mean?" said Rose. "You don't know anything about him."

"Tell her," said Burr. "Tell both of us. Finish this."

He nodded at me, and I realized there had never been a need to craft a lie for Rose Mae. The truth would do everything I had wanted the lie to do. I could stop Rose and send her home, away from Clarice, but only if I at last told the entire truth. I stood up and walked a few paces away from Burr, into the darkness. "Sit down, Rose, and don't look at me."

She hesitated, and then she sidled over and joined Burr on the dead grass, sitting with him next to the spill of light from the Blazer's headlights. Burr was sitting up straight now, breathing normally.

I said, "The Jim Beverly you are looking for, Rose? He doesn't exist. Your therapist is right. It isn't men. It's you. You pick bad men. You can't even see a good one when he's right in front of you and you're beating the crap out of him. Jim Beverly wasn't any good. He was a rapist, Rose."

To Burr I said, "I think you figured out it wasn't me. That's why you wouldn't say it for me. And you're right, Jim Beverly never touched me. It happened, though, Burr. It did happen. But it wasn't ever mine. I stole it from her. I stole it from Clarice, and I never knew how to give it back."

# CHAPTER

## 14

S INCE CLARICE AND I could date only if we doubled with each other, Jim Beverly's friend Rob Shay was coming along. I knew Rob was about as interested in me as he was in macramé. He was a baseball boy, tall and cleanly handsome with dark hair and an all-American jawline. He had his pick of cheer-leaders, but he was Jim Beverly's wingman. He swung by my lunch table one day after Jim Beverly had officially asked out Clarice and said, "Hey, Arlene, you and me Friday, with Jim and your sister, okay?"

"Cousin," I said.

"Whatever. You in?"

I shrugged, and he took it for a yes. He made a gun out of his fingers and tipped me a wink as he shot me with it. "Great, see ya then." He cruised on past to his regular table.

That was fine with me. I was, if possible, even less interested in Rob than he was in me. Even though I knew the score, I kept catching myself accidentally thinking of the evening as "our" date with Jim Beverly, mine and Clarice's.

Getting ready on Friday afternoon, I had herds of jungle cats prowling through my stomach, and even Clarice seemed uncharacteristically jittery. We fussed our way through our pre-date preparations in a round-robin of nerve-racked primping. I started at my dresser drawer, wishing I needed a bra or at least owned a bra that made me look like I needed one, while Clarice chastised her hair. After I had dressed in a T-shirt and a pair of jeans that mercifully hid my skinny legs, I moved into the "yelling at my hair" slot, while Clarice shifted to rummaging through her makeup. Then we switched again, and she busied herself with hating all her clothes while I cursed my inability to understand eye shadow.

I foolishly got into Clarice's makeup bag and test-drove some robin's-egg blue. I ended up looking like a disco raccoon. Clarice had put on a short flippy skirt, pale pink with darker pink tulips growing up from the hem. She had on a short-sleeved sweater the same color as the tulips. The sweater clung to her curves. The skirt came down almost to her knees but was so light and full-cut that it swirled and floated as she walked, showing off her long legs. She put on a pair of flat strappy sandals, and I noticed her toenails were painted a pale pink, like the insides of seashells. Even Clarice's feet were pretty.

I took one look at her and felt my heart drop out of my chest and roll across the floor, collecting grit. She looked like Ken's Dream Date Barbie. She took one look at me and said, "Oh, wow. Arlene, what were you trying to do with the, um . . ." She pointed at her eyes.

I shrugged and drooped pathetically in the chair. "I don't want to go," I said.

"Don't be silly. We still have twenty minutes, and you know they'll be late. Boys think girls can't be ready on time."

She grabbed her makeup bag and pulled me to my feet, dragging me down the hall to the bathroom. We passed Aunt Florence coming the other way. Florence stopped dead when she saw me, her eyes widening. Clarice held up a hand to stop her before she could speak. "She's washing her face right now, Mama."

In the bathroom, Clarice handed me some cold cream and said, "Take everything off and let's start fresh."

I did as she asked, scrubbing my face clean, soaking my T-shirt and dampening the front pieces of my hair in the process. Then I slumped in despair on the closed toilet. With my long damp hair stringing around my bare face, I looked about ten years old.

"Perk up," said Clarice. "It's all fixable. I swear, Arlene, I have never seen you fuss around so much before a date. Close your eyes and tilt your face up thisaway." She turned my face from side to side, and I kept my eyes closed while she messed around putting things on with sponges and Q-tips and all her makeup brushes. "What's with all the nerves and the eye shadow, anyway?" she asked. "Arlene? Do you kinda like Rob Shay?"

"No!" I said. "It would be dumb if I did like Rob Shay. Or any boy like that, a sports boy who's all-popular and every other girl in school goes to mush when he walks past. You know he's only taking me tonight because of your mama's rule. No boy has ever asked me out except ones who have friends that want to date you."

"Stop talking. I want to do your lips," said Clarice. I felt the cool tip of a liner tracing the outline of my mouth, and then one of her brushes painting inside the lines. "You're too hard on yourself. I think boys just don't ask you out because you don't flirt. You have to talk to them like you think they're the very best one. They won't ask you unless you practically send up a big firework that will explode right over their heads saying, 'Yes, yes, I totally like you!' Boys live every second scared to death a girl is going to say no when they ask her out."

"No, boys live scared that *you'll* say no when they ask you out," I said when the brush left my mouth.

But Clarice only said, "Turn sideways on the toilet, and I'll French-braid your hair."

After she braided it, she picked fronds out of the front and left them to wisp around my face. Then she dragged me back to our room and re-dressed me from the skin out. She pulled a long black knit skirt out of the back of my closet. It had been part of an outfit I wore to church the year before. It was tighter this year, and Clarice gave a nod of satisfaction. She handed me a cranberry-red tank top that Aunt Florence had told me suited my coloring, and made me put that on with my black flats. When I looked in the mirror, I was surprised to see I didn't look ten years old anymore. I looked like a teenager.

The tight skirt showed off the dipped-in waist I had recently acquired, giving me the illusion of hips. The tank top would have been risky on a bustier girl, but on me it looked nice, showing off my pretty collarbones. Clarice had not done much to my eyes at all, just mascara and liner. But she'd put blush lower than I usually put it, and all of a sudden I had noticeable cheekbones. She'd also done my mouth darker than I ever would, a red as deep as the color of the tank top. I was surprised to see I had a pretty mouth, full and heart-shaped like my mother's in pictures I had seen of her when she was younger. I had a girl mouth. A kissing mouth. I couldn't help but smile at myself. Clarice hadn't transformed me into some sort of teen school beauty queen, but I looked nice.

Clarice and I headed into the den where Aunt Florence and Uncle Bruster were watching TV. Mama was in her recliner at the back of the room, holding her hands up flat and stiff, about six inches apart. She was staring intently at the space between her hands.

Uncle Bruster smiled at us and said, "My girlies are looking real pretty." He dug into his pockets and pulled out two quarters and two ten-dollar bills. This was a standard pre-date ritual. He handed us each a ten-dollar bill and said, "If something happens with your date, and he gets fresh or takes to drinking or runs off, you go someplace public and get yourself a Coke while you wait for me to come get you."

"Yes, sir," we said. Mama banged her hands together, hard and sudden, and Clarice and I both jumped. Florence and Bruster didn't even blink. Mama opened her hands like a book and stared at her palms, then held them up again, six inches apart.

Uncle Bruster handed each of us a quarter and said, "If your date starts asking you to do things you don't feel comfortable about, you give him this quarter. You tell him he can call me and ask me the question he's asking you. If I say okay, then you'll go along with it."

"Yes, sir," we said, and Mama banged her hands together again. Clarice and I watched her studying her palms.

"There's a fly in the room," Aunt Florence explained impatiently. "You listen up to Daddy."

Clarice looked around. "I don't see any fly."

231

"That's because there's not really a fly," I said, and Clarice flushed faintly pink. Mama had her hands up six inches apart again. "Can we maybe wait in the living room, Aunt Florence?"

Aunt Florence cocked a suspicious eyebrow and said, "Yes, you may, but no scooting out the door like dogs coming to a whistle if those boys sit out there and honk at you. You will wait until the doorbell rings, and Bruster and I will come in the living room and meet them before you even think you'll head off into the night with them."

"Yes, ma'am," said Clarice as Mama banged her hands together in another emphatic clap.

In the living room, Clarice and I perched on the orange sofa. We could hear the muted burble of the TV, punctuated by my mother's sporadic applause, coming from the den.

"I hope he doesn't honk," whispered Clarice. "I hope he thinks to come up to the door, or Mama might march out there and get him by the ear and give him her 'never underestimate the power of good manners' speech." Clarice shivered her shoulders in a horror that was only half mocking. Florence might actually do it.

Luckily, either Rob or Jim Beverly had been raised right, or they had heard locker-room tales about Clarice's strict parents. They came up to the door to collect us. Clarice and I stayed sitting on the sofa in the living room while Bruster and Florence went to let them in. We listened to introductions going all around.

When the boys came through the doorway, I saw immediately that Jim Beverly had misread the situation. He was smiling and chatting easily with Bruster. Usually the girl's father is a safe bet, but he'd missed seeing the actual danger. Florence watched him with cowboy eyes, cool and level, a deadly shot from fifty paces.

"Where are you taking our girls this evening?" Bruster inquired.

Jim Beverly outlined our plans, telling him we would see a movie at the Dupe in Fruiton and then head to Mr. Gatti's for Cokes and slices with some other kids from school. Jim Beverly was using lots of eye contact and pushing his eyebrows up sincerely, but the real interview was going on in the living room doorway.

"I know that name, Shay," Aunt Florence said to Rob. "Where do you boys get your preaching?"

"Jim and me, our folks all go to Mount Olive," said Rob, and I saw Florence relax a notch. Mount Olive was a Southern Baptist church in Fruiton.

"You're Caroline Shay's boy?" Aunt Florence said.

"No, Caroline is my aunt. You're thinking of my cousin Ronny," said Rob. "I'm Darcy and Pam Shay's oldest."

Florence gave a curt nod. "I know Pam Shay. You have yourself a good mama."

"Thank you, ma'am. I know," said Rob. Clarice and I exchanged glances. Mount Olive and the "ma'am" meant our dates had just been approved.

"You have them home by eleven sharp," Bruster was saying to Jim.

"Daddy," said Clarice, protesting. "Eleven-thirty?"

I saw Bruster and Florence's eyes meet, and she tipped him an almost imperceptible nod. "I tell you what," said Bruster. "You leave the pizza place by eleven. It's what, about a twenty-minute drive? But you act like Cinderella. When the clock is bonging eleven, you girlies better be climbing in the carriage."

"Thanks, Daddy," said Clarice. She hopped up, and I followed as if on a string attached to her. "But you know Cinderella got to stay out till midnight."

"Cinderella was a sophomore," said Bruster.

The movie was some underwater special-effects thing with a sea monster and bikini-clad skin-diving scientists getting eaten all over the place. It was what Clarice's borderline-slutty friend Janey called a clutch film. Things kept popping up from the shadowy depths. I had managed to slip into the row of seats before Rob could, and we were sitting in a line with Clarice on the end next to Jim Beverly, and then me in between the two boys. I clutched nothing but my own hands in my lap, happy to be sitting next to Jim.

When the bikini-eating went on hold while some plot points and conversations happened, Jim Beverly shifted in his chair and whispered to Clarice, "I'm gonna go get me a Coke. You want a Coke? Or Milk Duds or something?"

Clarice said no, but Rob overheard him and said, "Get me a popcorn, bro." He passed a bill to Jim, who took it and said, "Arlene?"

I shook my head, but then I whispered, "I'll come with you. I need to go to the ladies'."

I let him go past me and then stood up and followed him out of our row and up the aisle. I liked it, the two of us heading to the concession stand, as if he were my date. He nudged my arm and said, "Girl, I better not get you a Coke, if you already need to hit the loo twenty minutes into the movie."

We slipped out the double doors. The Dupe had only two theaters, and the doors led directly out onto the lighted lobby. I flipped my long braid over my shoulder and smiled up at him the way Clarice would have. I tried to emulate the teasing tone I had heard her use so often to fuss at boys. She could complain about something they'd done as if she secretly thought it was adorable or naughty or both. "I would have gone before, but you boys were late coming for us. I didn't want to miss the previews."

Jim Beverly grinned back at me and said, "Blame Rob for that. He had to blow-dry his pretty—"

He stopped talking abruptly and came to a dead stop so fast I was two steps beyond him before I realized he was no longer beside me. I looked back. He was staring ahead at the concession stand. He was no longer smiling, and his eyes were no longer kind. I followed his line of sight.

At the head of the line, standing with a boy who could only be her date, was Rose Mae Lolley. She had not seen Jim Beverly yet. Her hand was moving with its customary slow grace to pull her mink-brown braid around. She draped it over her shoulder and was musingly stroking its smooth length as she waited for the senior she was with to pay for their drinks. She was wearing a long-sleeved shirt, cranberry red, so sheer that a hint of her pale belly glinted through. She was obviously wearing a black bra. Her knit skirt was long and black, like mine, but tighter, with a slit on the side that came to about mid-thigh. She had on knee-high boots, and I could see a sliver of her thigh, framed in a triangle formed by the slit and the top of her boot.

As if she felt my gaze, her head turned languorously and our eyes met. Her eyebrows went up in astonishment as she took in my outfit. In another moment, she noticed Jim Beverly standing beside me. Her mouth opened, and then she gave her head a tiny shake. She lifted one shoulder in a slow half-shrug of disbelief, then turned away from us, sticking her hand in her date's back pocket and worming up under his arm, showing us her elegant back.

We both stood silently, and then Jim Beverly said, "I thought you had to pee?" without looking at me and with no inflection.

I scurried obediently to the ladies' room, where I bolted myself into a stall and leaned against the door, trying not to cry and ruin the pretty makeup job Clarice had done. I pulled the band out of my hair so savagely that I broke it. I threw it on the floor and combed my braid out with my fingers. When I had myself together, I went back out into the lobby. Neither Jim Beverly nor Rose-Pop and her date were there.

I went back into the theater, and made my way to our row. On the screen, a pretty girl who looked much too young to be a scientist was holding up a test tube and saying, "The light! It's like poison to them!" in a wonder-filled tone. Jim Beverly's seat was empty. Becky Spivey from school was sitting on the other side of Rob, whispering to him. I said, "Excuse me," and made my way past both of them. I sat down in my chair. Clarice leaned across Jim Beverly's empty one and said, "Where did he go?"

I shrugged. "I went to the bathroom."

I wasn't sure how much I should say, especially since Rob and Becky Spivey might overhear. Clarice looked over her shoulder worriedly.

Rob was tapping at me from the other side. "Where's Jim?" he whispered.

"I went to the bathroom," I said again.

A guy behind us made a shushing noise.

I folded my arms around myself and put my eyes on the screen. Rob was still in whispered consult with Becky Spivey. He turned to me again and whispered, "Hey, a bunch of people are already down at the gulch, so do you want to maybe skip out of here? This movie blows."

"You go ahead," I said quietly.

"C'mon, it'll be fun. Becky'll take us in her car, and we can meet up with Jim and Clarice later at Mr. Gatti's."

Becky Spivey leaned over. "Come on, Rob, she doesn't care." I could smell butter on her breath. She was wearing a tank top, too, a peach one. She was spilling out the top of it as she leaned over. Between my insistence that he go, Becky's cleavage, and the person a few rows behind us releasing louder and more enraged shushing noises, we finally got Rob unglued from his seat.

"Are you sure you don't care, Arlene?" he asked.

"She said she doesn't mind four times now, go already," said the shushing guy loudly. And Rob went.

Clarice watched them leave and then leaned across Jim Beverly's empty seat again. "What on earth's going on?"

I whispered, "Rose-Pop," to Clarice. She pointed back towards the concession area and whispered, "Out there?" I nodded.

Clarice sat up straight in her chair, looking back at the screen. I looked behind me up the aisle and realized she had looked over my shoulder and seen Jim Beverly returning. He had a huge tub of popcorn and two Cokes balanced in his hands. He sat down between us and said, "Where'd Rob go?"

As quietly as possible, I tried to give him a brief explanation, but three words into it, the guy a couple of rows behind us piped up again. "Do you mind?"

Jim Beverly whipped around so quickly that some of the popcorn came spilling out of the tub and scattered at his feet. "Yeah, I do fucking mind. Do I need to come up there and explain why?" he said loudly.

When the guy did not answer him, he turned back to me and said, "So. Where's Rob?" in a casual, conversational tone.

Clarice was looking at him with round, surprised eyes.

I explained about the gulch party and Becky Spivey and meeting up later. He handed me the popcorn tub and said, "Well, this is his." Then he handed one Coke to Clarice and stared morosely at the screen, gulping at his own Coke. He sucked about a fourth of it up through the straw in thirty seconds.

Clarice and I were watching him now instead of the movie. He reached into the pocket of his baggy Levi's and pulled out a flat pint bottle of vodka. "Sorry I was gone so long," he said to Clarice. "I had to make a run out to the Jeep."

He peeled the plastic lid off his Coke and spiked the hell out of it, pouring about a third of the pint into it. He tilted the pint bottle towards Clarice, indicating her Coke. She shook her head and set her Coke down on the floor, whispering, "I didn't even want the Coke, remember?" He capped the bottle and put it away.

We sat in silence through the second half of the movie. Jim Beverly was brooding. He glared at the screen with malevolent eyes, gulping down his spiked Coke so fast that I developed a sympathy ice headache. I could sense Clarice's discomfort. She sat stiffly on the other side of him. When his Coke was gone, he got hers off the floor and poured another third of the pint into it. He gulped that one down, too.

At last the credits rolled and the lights came up. We filed out with the few other people who had been in our theater. The guy who had been sitting a few rows behind us was gone. He must have slipped out quickly to avoid us.

As we made our way up the aisle, I noticed Jim Beverly was

listing a tiny bit to starboard. Clarice had noticed it, too. By the time we made it out to the Jeep, neither of us had any doubts that he was halfway to stinking drunk.

"So, what? We meet up with them over at Mr. Gatti's? Or go down to the gulch?" Jim asked.

Clarice smiled up at him as he fumbled around with his keys. She said, "Hey, Jim, why don't you let me drive. I always wanted to drive a Jeep."

He looked back at her, incredulous. "You aren't driving my Jeep. What, do you even know how to drive?"

"Yes, I know how to drive," she said, laughing. "I got my learner's last month."

"Oh, your learner's," he said. "Yeah, great, whatever. Get in." He managed to get the passenger door open.

I clambered into the backseat, but Clarice stayed right where she was. "You might as well give her the keys," I said. "Clarice won't ride with anyone who's been drinking." I buckled myself in.

Clarice shot me an exasperated look as Jim Beverly drew himself up and looked down at her. "I'm not drunk," he said belligerently.

She lifted one shoulder and said, "Right. You're just scared to let me drive your car. What do you think is going to happen? I'll run it into a chicken truck and get you in trouble with your daddy?" Her voice was half sassy, half mocking.

"I'm not scared," he said, slurring the *s*.

"Whatever," she said, looking away.

"Fine. You want to drive so bad, here." He looped his index finger through the ring on his keys and dangled them in front of her. "Take the keys."

She reached for them, but he snatched them out of her reach.

As soon as she put her hand down, he dangled them in front of her again. She reached for them, and he snatched them away. She folded her arms across her chest. He dangled the keys in front of her again. She just stood there with her arms crossed, shaking her head at him. He said, "Come on, puppy. Jump for it. Jump for it, puppy. Bounce a little." He was laughing.

She thumped him in the chest with the back of one hand. "You're such a jerk," she said.

"I know, I know," he said. "Sorry. Come on. Get in."

"No," said Clarice. "I'm not riding with you when you've been drinking. Give me the keys, and we'll go to Mr. Gatti's. You can have a couple of slices of pizza, we'll hang out with everybody, and you'll be totally fine to drive us home. Come on, I'm a good driver. I do this for my friends all the time. I learned how to drive because Missy Carver's older sister was so drunk once she couldn't get the car out of reverse. And it was an automatic. Just give me the keys."

She was smiling up at him, sweetly reasonable, and for a moment I thought he was going to do it. But then he closed his fist around the key ring and said, "No. Bad puppy. Get in the Jeep."

"No."

They stayed in a Mexican standoff for a few seconds, and then Jim Beverly climbed in through the open passenger door. He pulled it shut behind him and crab-walked across into the driver's seat, steadying himself with the roll bar. He sat down and jammed the key into the ignition.

"Get out, Arlene," said Clarice.

I rolled my eyes and unbuckled myself obediently, slipping between the front seats. I rested my butt on the passenger seat, reaching to open the door, but Jim Beverly snaked one long arm across me and caught my wrist, stopping me. "You're not the boss of her," he said to Clarice, laughing again.

"Get out, Arlene," Clarice repeated. She was deadly serious.

I hesitated. I couldn't help liking where I was, sitting in the front seat of Jim Beverly's Jeep, with his warm, callused hand holding my wrist.

Jim Beverly felt my hesitation, and he let go of my arm and turned the key. The Jeep's engine came to life. "We're going to Mr. Gatti's," he said. "You coming or not?"

"Arlene," said Clarice.

"Going once!" he said, and tapped the gas and hit the brakes. The Jeep lurched forward a foot and then stopped.

"Going twice!" he said, and lurched us forward again.

Clarice took two running steps to catch up to us, used the back bumper as a step, and grabbed the roll bar, vaulting herself into the backseat just as he took off for real. He was laughing like crazy, and I was a little, too. Clarice reached into the front seat and gave me a hard pinch as we rocketed out of the parking lot onto Firestone Drive.

"This is so not funny," she said.

"It's a little bit funny," Jim Beverly said.

Clarice buckled herself into the back. "I think you better just take us home."

He leaned towards me sideways and said in a stage whisper, "I think Mom's pissed."

The Jeep listed to the side as he leaned, and we bumped briefly up onto the curb. Jim Beverly jerked the steering wheel hard, and we thumped down. He got us centered on the road, laughing and cussing under his breath.

Clarice had grabbed my arm as the Jeep bumped up and down. "You better stop this car and let me drive, you asshole," she said.

"Too late," said Jim Beverly and got on the entrance to the highway. "I'm taking you candy-asses on home."

Rocketing along on the highway in the dark, I lost the brief fear that had surged when he ran us up on the curb. I was instead exhilarated to be beside him, and the nastiest inside bit of me couldn't help but enjoy the reversal, having Clarice for once in her life take the backseat while I rode shotgun. My long hair was whipping around my face, getting in my eyes, and I gathered it up into a wad and held it against my head with one hand.

Next to me, Jim Beverly got the flat pint bottle out of his pocket again. It was less than a third full. I tried to hold the irritating pieces of my hair flat as Clarice and I watched him unscrew the cap and take a healthy swig, steering with one knee pressed up against the bottom of the wheel. I glanced back at Clarice. She was holding her breath. As soon as he had capped the bottle and had one hand back on the wheel, she started yelling at him.

"You better exit and let us out right now. I mean it. Right now. You asshole. You total asshole."

Her color was high. I had never seen her so angry.

"You want out?" he said. "Fine. Jump out." The Jeep was doing over sixty.

Clarice shut up and did not speak again for the rest of the long ride down the highway. Jim Beverly polished off the bottle.

Finally we saw the exit to Route 19 coming up, and he took it smoothly, rocketing off the lit highway into the darkness of the access road. Nobody spoke until we had gone through Possett and were heading down the solitude of Route 19, soybean fields on either side of us.

"Damn, but I have to pee," Jim Beverly said.

"You're not coming in my house drunk like this to use the bathroom," said Clarice. "My daddy would kill me for getting in a car with you, and my mama would kill you for making me."

"I don't need no toilet," said Jim Beverly, and he cut the lights on the Jeep. The road disappeared in front of us, and he banked hard right. I grabbed the sides of my seat, and Clarice let out a short, sharp scream. The Jeep ran off the road onto the shoulder, bumping us up hard and then landing us with a jarring crunch, leveling as we hit the plowed field.

"Stop. Stop. What is wrong with you?" Clarice was almost screaming.

"Gotta piss!" said Jim Beverly, in a voice that was a perfect marriage of cheerful and hateful.

I clung to the seat as we thumped our way over the plowed rows, tearing a swath through some farmer's crops with nothing but a thin patina of moonlight to guide us. About 250 feet into the field, Jim Beverly braked and we skidded sideways before coming to rest in the soft soil. He hopped out and walked a few feet away from the Jeep. We heard the metallic slide of his zipper going down and then a pattering noise as he urinated on a young soybean plant. He released a long, loud sigh of relief.

"Get out of the car, Arlene," said Clarice.

I did not move. She kicked the back of my seat three times, hard, each kick punctuating a word as she said, "Get. Out. Now."

I unfastened my seat belt and hopped down. My feet sank in the loam, and I felt a trickle of dark soil entering my shoe. Clarice was climbing out after me, fast. She grabbed my arm and pulled me along in her wake.

"We're walking home. It's not even a mile," she said before I could get the question out.

Jim Beverly had finished peeing and came after us before we had gotten even ten feet. He ran around us and loomed up in front of Clarice, surprising us in the near-dark.

"Get your ass back in the Jeep, Clarice," he said.

"No," she said. She tried to step around him, but he blocked her easily. I was behind her, uncertain what to do.

"I said, get your little ass back in the car."

She tried to step around him again, and he put his hands on her shoulders and pushed her. She fell back a step, and so did I. "Now," he said. She tried to move forward, and he shoved her again, this time placing his hands deliberately just above her breasts and pushing her.

"Arlene, take off," she said, suddenly uncertain.

"Yeah, Arlene, why don't you do that," Jim Beverly said without looking away from Clarice.

"Quit it, Jim," I said. My breathing quickened and my pupils dilated as a trickle of adrenaline fed into my blood. It was as if the night was brightening around me, the thin moonlight bouncing silver and surreal off his teeth and his cheekbones as he flashed us a nasty grin.

"Why don't you run too, puppy," Jim Beverly said to Clarice conversationally. "I want them to bounce."

He put his hands out, directly onto her breasts this time, pushing her backwards, and her hands came up trying to knock his away.

"Arlene, go," she said. Even as she was saying it, she was turning and running, propelled by the momentum from his latest shove, so I ran, too. We ran directly away from him, which meant we were heading for the Jeep.

Clarice was very fast on her long legs. She caught up with me easily, and we ran side by side for three long strides. Then I saw his hand reaching for her head. He grabbed her by her long hair, catching a huge handful close to the scalp and jerking her off her feet. She screamed as she went over, and I stopped so fast I almost fell.

Jim Beverly had her off balance, and he kept her that way, jerking her along towards the Jeep by her hair while she yelled and her hands scrabbled at his wrist. She couldn't get her feet underneath her as she stumbled helplessly along behind him. They were almost to the Jeep.

"Arlene, run for home," she yelled. "Get Daddy, get my mama."

"Shut up, puppy," said Jim Beverly, and he jerked her so hard she fell to her knees. Before I knew what I was doing, I was running at him with my hands out in front of me like claws and my teeth bared. He watched me coming with cool eyes. He had one hand tangled deep in Clarice's hair, pulling her along, but one arm was free. He sidestepped as I came, bringing his free arm up to meet me, shoving at me. He used my own momentum against me, and I went hurtling sideways. I felt both my feet leave the soil. Then the back of my head slammed into the side of the Jeep, and I was falling.

I fell for a long time. I fell for so long that I realized I wasn't falling at all. I was floating. I was floating down in a black sea that smelled like the sad sunbaked worms you always find right after a summer rain.

I heard someone singing, but I couldn't move my head. I

seemed frozen in a single position, floating endlessly down through the warm black waters. My mother floated into my view, shiny and pale in the dark water. She had on a bathing suit like Esther Williams always wore in those old movies, and a flowery rubber swim cap. Mama held out one hand, and I could see she had a little black starfish sitting in the middle of her palm.

She said something, but it was hard to understand her around the bubbles that came out of her mouth. She sounded a little bit like Clarice. Every summer Uncle Bruster took us to Pensacola Beach for vacation, and when we were small, we used to play mermaids in the hotel pool. We would sink to the bottom and scream things, trying to make the other understand. The water would dampen the sound and distort our words, but if I watched her lips and listened close, I could sometimes understand what she was saying.

I tried it now, listening hard to my mother. She seemed to be saying my name. "Arlene," she said. "Arlene, don't be dead."

"Okay," I agreed. "I won't, then." But I could not hear myself.

I noticed my mother had no legs. She had traded them in for a long white tail, and it was churning powerfully around in the black water, sending bubbles up.

"You killed her," my mother said through the rising bubbles. "Arlene, Arlene."

"I didn't kill anyone," I tried to tell her, but I still couldn't hear myself. I wondered, with no heat or rancor, why I should bother trying to explain. It seemed complicated, and why shouldn't she just think whatever it was she needed to be thinking? The dead white churning of her tail, all that motion in the middle of this black floating sea, was making me sick. I thought with mild irritation that if she would stop churning that tail, I wouldn't feel so sick. But I couldn't stop looking at it.

I tried to close my eyes, but they wouldn't close. They were stuck. So I tried to look up at her face, and she had no face. She wasn't my mother at all. She wasn't anything but a long paleness grinding around in the darkness of the moving black sea. I was sick from the motion and wishing that I could stop falling, and then once I had stopped falling, I could perhaps ask the tail to stop its winding around. If everything would only be still and quiet, I could sleep.

One by one, other colors began to paint themselves into the moving picture. The tail grew two pink bands, one dark, one light. I came to rest on the black-sanded bottom of the sea, and once I had stopped moving, the things around me came slowly into focus. I realized that the tail was actually Clarice.

The dark pink band was her top, shoved up around her shoulders. Her arms were over her head, and Jim Beverly was holding then down with one of his big hands. I was surprised to see both her breasts were out of their bra. Jim Beverly's other hand was clutching at one of them.

Clarice and Jim together made a shape like a capital Y lying on its side. Her pale leg was the white stalk of the Y; his legs, still in blue jeans, were camouflaged against the black earth. His white ass was in the juncture where I thought the mermaid's tail had forked, and it was from this point that the movement, the rhythmic churning, had come. Her skirt was rucked around her waist. His belly slapped into hers with a meaty bounce as he churned against her, and that was where the Y forked, as his torso arched up away from hers. The dark sea was the waves of plowed earth that stretched around us in all directions.

"Everything interesting always happens to Clarice," I thought idly. I wanted to look away, but I couldn't seem to move my eyes or even close them. I noticed then that Clarice's face was filthy, and she'd cried silver tracks through the dirt on her face. Her eyes were red and swollen, and her mouth was bent into an ugly braying shape, and she was yelling something. She was calling my name, and she wouldn't leave me alone, and together they were making the churning motion that was making me so sick when what I needed was for everything to be only still and quiet so I could sleep.

But they did not stop, and I watched them, seeing how they were joined into the shape of the letter Y. A dull red anger began to spread slowly through me. I could see what was happening now. He was picking Clarice. Everyone always picked Clarice. And she was yelling at me about it, yelling my name, "Arlene, Arlene, don't be dead." She wanted me to be alive so I would be forced to see that it was always her he liked. Like I had not known that.

Clarice pulled one of her hands out from under his, and then her hand was moving so fast it made me dizzy to see it. She was flailing at him with it. He reared back, higher than she was, and took his hand off her breast to slam his fist into her stomach. I heard her breath whoosh out in a rush, and her hand fell back, down beside her. She was fighting hard to breathe, and when she caught a breath, it came back out again as a sob. She said, "You're hurting me, please, please no." She said my name again and turned her face away from him, back to me.

She sounded so pitiful that some of my anger went washing away. I blinked, and Clarice must have seen the movement. She said, "Arlene? Arlene? Are you alive?" Her limp hand came back up again to shove at him. He reared back, hitting her stomach to make her stop.

I was lying on my side by the Jeep. I pushed myself on my arms, and the effort made pain bloom in searing waves inside my head. As I raised myself up, my long hair swung down, strands covering my face, so it was like I was seeing the two of them churning together from behind black bars.

He drove his fist into the soft part of her belly again, and I said, "You don't hit girls."

He looked over at me and froze, staring at me, tiny and slim in my black and red outfit, with the long dark strands of my hair covering my face. He was completely still, and then he said, "Rose?"

I got onto my hands and knees somehow and said, "You don't ever hit girls."

"Shit, fuck," said Jim Beverly, and he propelled himself backwards, coming up off of my cousin and rising to his feet in the moonlight. He jerked up his jeans, stuffing his bloodied cock back into his underwear. It was still hard. He took two steps towards me but lost his balance and staggered sideways away. Clarice rolled onto her side and curled into a ball.

"Fuck," yelled Jim Beverly. He caught himself on the hood of his Jeep and then bent, draping the top half of his body over it.

Clarice was sitting up, pulling her sweater down, and already crawling towards me. I was resting, up on my hands and knees, before trying to stand. "Arlene, we have to go, we have to go. Get up, Arlene," she was whispering.

Bracing against each other, we somehow got to our feet. Clarice slung one arm around me, holding me up, and together we began limping away, slipping on the soft earth, clinging to each other. Every step drove a serrated blade of pain into the back of my head while we crept away from him as fast as we could go. Behind us, I heard the unmistakable sound of Jim Beverly puking his guts out.

I couldn't turn my head without almost passing out from the pain, so Clarice kept looking over her shoulder. Any second we expected him to come after us, but he didn't. Long after the darkness had swallowed him, and Clarice said she could no longer see him when she looked over her shoulder, we could hear him hacking and puking in the black behind us.

I barely remember the long hike home through the soybean fields. When the fields ended, Clarice led us through the large back gardens and pastures of our neighbors. It was all gray to me, a death march in a haze of pain. Clarice kept asking me questions. What my name was. The date. About what time I thought it was. It was getting on my nerves.

At last we reached our own backyard, and Clarice leaned me against the back wall of Aunt Florence's gardening shed. She let go of me and squatted down on the ground and burst into a flurry of short, racking sobs, her head cradled in her hands.

I leaned on the wall. After a few minutes she stopped. The back wall of the shed had a spigot with a garden hose on it. Clarice turned on the water and began washing, scrubbing hard at herself in the icy spray.

I wanted to tell her how sorry I was, so awfully sorry. Both for what had happened to her and for what I had thought. The worst part was that disinterested jealousy was still there. An ugly small piece at the very core of me still wanted him to have picked me. In my heart, the moment was mine. I couldn't hate myself enough for feeling it, and I couldn't stop feeling it.

"How did I let this happen?" Clarice cried, scrubbing and scrubbing at herself with her hands. "My brother is dead, Arlene. Wayne's dead. I shouldn't have let this happen."

I slid down the wall of the shed and sat, leaning my aching head back. I wanted to be asleep somewhere quiet, somewhere where none of this was true.

"I can't get hurt like this," she said. "This will kill my mama. I have to be all right. I have to be all right all the time."

"I wish it never happened," I said, meaning everything, meaning Jim Beverly and my need.

She stared at me, her eyes wide and gleaming in her filthy face, and then she nodded. "That's what I want, too. Let's make that true. We can't let it have happened. We'll just get as clean as we can out here. And we'll wait here until it's at least eleven-fifteen, so they won't think anything, and so they're sure to be in bed. And then we'll go on in like normal. We'll do everything like normal. We'll get in our pajamas. And in the morning, it will be just like you said. Mama can't know it ever happened. Can we do that?"

"Sure," I said. "We can do that." Later, when I failed, and flopped around the house in my tragic black layers, palpably suffering, it was a punishment. I was flogging myself for those moments when he was hurting her so badly and all I could do was wish it was me—not to spare her, but because I wanted so badly to be picked, to be chosen. I had stolen something from her then, in my bitter thoughts, and I never knew how to give it back.

That night Clarice was the one who washed us both down. She was the one who lay awake all night in my bed, waking me every few minutes to ask me my name and what year it was, until dawn came in the window and showed her both my pupils were the same size again. And she was the one who, when we came in the house, called in her normal voice down the hall to her parents, "Mama? We're home."

After a pause I heard Florence answer, her rough voice blurred by sleep, "All right, then, Clarice. Did you girls have a nice time?"

"Sure we did, Mama," Clarice said. "Sure we did."

# CHAPTER

⧞

# 15

"MAN, CAN I pick them," said Rose Mae Lolley. She stood up and brushed at the seat of her pants.

I stayed where I was, a few feet away from both of them in the darkness. My throat hurt from talking, and I was exhausted.

Rose said, "No wonder you didn't want me talking to your cousin." She walked along the side of the Blazer. "You know what gets me? You know what really gets me in all this? My fucking therapist was right." She kicked the Blazer's front tire savagely with her scuffed yellow boot.

"I'm sorry," I said. I wanted her gone. Burr was quiet, and I didn't know what he was thinking.

"He was always nice to me," Rose said. She tucked the sharp points of her bob behind her ears. "Maybe he's changed."

"He hasn't changed," I said. "People don't change."

Burr got up abruptly and said, "Yes, they do. I'm tired of that."

"Fuck it," said Rose. "It doesn't matter. What matters is what he was when I picked him. Man, can I pick them." She stood tense by the Blazer, vibrating with energy and anger. Maybe Burr had a point. I couldn't see a trace of the languid, passive Rose who had drifted carefully down the halls ten years ago. She fished around in her pocket and pulled out her keys and headed for the VW Bug.

Burr put a hand out and I took it, moving in close beside him.

"I hope your car starts. You've left the headlights on forever," said Rose. But she didn't wait for us to check. She scrunched down in her car, and the engine roared to life. It sounded like she'd left her muffler back in Texas. She reversed violently and swung the car around. Her lights came on, and she drove away from us, disappearing down the dirt road.

"What do you think she'll do?" I said.

"I have no idea," said Burr. "But I don't think she'll bother Clarice."

I nodded. "You don't think she heard us, do you? I mean the earlier parts. She can't have heard me say I killed him. She was all the way up the hill." Burr shook his head, and I swayed where I stood. "I'm so tired," I said.

"All right, baby," said Burr. He put one arm over my shoulder and bundled me into the Blazer as if I were an overwrought toddler. The engine mercifully started, and he turned off the lights and let it run for a bit. We sat together in the darkness, looking at Lipsmack Hill.

"I wish you would say something," I said.

"Like what?" said Burr.

"Anything," I said. "Like you should say if you still want to marry me. Or if you love me. I told you I killed someone. You have to say something."

Burr turned towards me in the darkness and looked at me for a long time. Then he said, "Of course I still love you. That's not even an issue. But you didn't kill anyone, Lena. I think you know that."

"I told you. I did," I said.

He was shaking his head. "You took on the idea that you killed him because you already felt guilty. You believed you'd stolen something from your cousin. But you have to know better. An underweight teenage girl can't beat a man to death with a bottle. Especially not with one blow."

When I didn't answer, he sighed and rubbed one hand over his eyes. I knew what he was doing. He was crafting a closing argument. He began laying out his case, point by point, fact by fact.

"Drunken teenage girls don't get away with murder. Period. But you weren't caught. You know why. He must have been alive when you left him."

"Burr, I saw him, and his body was an absolutely dead body," I said.

"And as a teenager, exactly how much time had you spent with freshly dead corpses?" Burr asked, cocking an eyebrow at me. "Had you ever seen a dead body?"

"I'd been to my aunt Niner's funeral," I said. Burr gave me a patient look, raising his eyebrows, waiting. I looked away and grudgingly added, "When I was ten."

"There you are," he said and started laying out his case. Now, when it was too late, and I'd spilled the truth out onto the dead grass at his feet, he was doing what I had always wanted him to do. He was being my advocate, keeping me from lying by forging a truth of his own. He was defending me. And he spun a pretty good tale.

The freshman girl, according to Burr, must have had her own keys out as a weapon, to fend off Jim Beverly. She didn't steal his car. Jim Beverly, alive, dragged himself out of the kudzu and took it. He wrecked it himself, driving drunk and with a head injury.

Then, in the aftermath of the crash, Jim Beverly must have stopped pushing heedlessly forward as truth came to him like a blinding light, painful as it illuminated his ugly, ugly life. His scholarship, his girlfriend, and his godhood were all gone. He'd served himself a pretty slice of consolation pie in the form of the freshman girl. He'd been expecting a rush, a surge of power, whatever payoff rape gave him. But this girl, no bigger than a napkin, fended him off with a set of house keys and stomped away huffily with no clue how dead serious he'd been about fucking her into the ground. He probably thought the angry freshman came back and brained him from behind and kicked his sorry ass down a hill. She might as well have clipped his balls with pink nail scissors and taken them with her. And then he had dead-drunk totaled his Jeep, and if he waited for the cops, they'd pop him for DUI on top of everything else. So, in Burr's version, the police got it right. Jim Beverly left. He ran away.

And the truth was, if Burr had said all this to me yesterday, I would have believed him. Ten years ago, when the weather got cold, I had gone up on Lipsmack Hill and stared down into the kudzu. It had gone to bones, become nothing but the brown lace frame of itself, and I could see the shapes of dead trees and ground cover clearly within its outlines. I could see all the way down through it to the ground. Jim Beverly wasn't there.

Half of me believed that maybe God had moved him, but of course a piece of me wondered if he hadn't moved himself. It was easier, almost, to think of him as dead. The truth was, I would rather be Lena, his killer, than Arlene, a girl so desperate-hungry she had wanted to be his victim.

Still, up until today, it might have been a huge relief for Burr to absolve me. I had put paid to the rape. I had given it back when I told the truth to Burr and Rose Mae. And in the middle of giving it back, I had realized it was easy because I did not need it anymore. If I could give up the murder, too, it would be like I was starting fresh. No deals with God, no desperation. I could learn to tell the whole truth when it was right, and to lie when a lie was needed. I could learn to make love with Burr. I could maybe come home. But Aunt Florence had tipped her hand in the kitchen, telling me how Jim Beverly's body had been mag-icked out of the kudzu. He wasn't anywhere in the world, and he hadn't run away. I'd killed him.

I said, "So you know what happened. You weren't there or anything, but you have it all figured out because you're a tax at-torney who's read enough John Grisham to get how these things work."

He straightened and looked down at me. "Yeah," he said. "Pretty much. You didn't kill anyone. Look at the facts. My ver-sion makes a hell of a lot more sense. Yours won't play. His car was moved. A boy who matched his description was seen hitch-hiking after you killed him. If you had killed him, you would have been caught."

I looked up at him, mute, because I had told Burr my secrets, but I could not tell him Florence's. He was right when he said a teenage girl had no chance of covering up a murder. But Florence could have come in behind me and done it without break-ing a sweat. I thought of Wayne's dog, Buddy. Mrs. Weedy's chicken. Florence was ruthless enough for anything.

There were loose ends. I didn't know, for example, how Flor-ence had known to come after me, or how she had known where the body was. Had Clarice woken her up, spilled the beans, told her I had gone up the hill after Jim Beverly? Even if she had, how would Aunt Florence know he was dead? How would she have known to search for his corpse in the heaps? Staring mutely at Burr, I tried to do what he had done, to build a story that fit the facts. He was right when he said mine did not, but neither did his, mostly because he did not have them all.

He was better at this sort of thing than I was. I had no doubt that if he knew everything, he could figure it out. He was talk-ing again, and I half listened while I racked my brain, trying to see how Florence could have possibly known to come up Lip-smack.

"It's easy enough to check," Burr said. "The guy was a serial rapist. You say he was a good guy. You say you were in love with the real him, but a monster got out when he drank. Okay. That lets you beat yourself up. But the good guy knew the monster was there. He chose to drink. He chose to let it out. He liked it. And I doubt he quit liking it. I am willing to bet he has a crim-inal record. You know his MO. A good private detective could find him by checking the prison systems. We can put the money in it and find him, if you need that to let it go. But you're going to have to let it go. You didn't kill Jim Beverly."

Burr was still talking after that, but I could not hear him, be-cause all at once I saw how it must have happened. In a heart-beat I had it in front of me, adding up perfectly, and it all fit and

it all made sense. Burr saw something in my face, an idea growing, and put his hand on my leg in its habitual place, just above
my knee.

"The girl sees reason," he said.

I looked up at him, clear-eyed, absolutely earnest, and I lied
to him. The lie came tripping lightly off my tongue, and my
gaze did not dim or waver. "You're right. He has to be alive
somewhere. He must have run away." I smiled as I said it. I felt
the lie as something giving in my chest, expanding and unfolding like a rosebud, blooming. "Jim Beverly is alive," I said, lying
through my teeth, and it felt utterly beautiful.

He leaned over between the seats and kissed me then, and I
kissed him back.

"Let's get out of here," he said.

"Yeah. Let's go home. I think I must have really freaked out
my aunt Florence. And I am so tired."

Burr turned the lights back on and backed up the Blazer. We
drove back to the white frame house quietly, Burr's hand resting
peacefully on my leg. We pulled up the gravel drive and parked,
heading in the back door through the kitchen.

My mother was sitting up in her chair in the den, looking
alert and cheerful. She was wearing a cotton nightgown with
sprigs of flowers, and her feet were bare. The den was covered
with Mama's scrapbooks. They were lying open and scattered all
over the coffee table and the sofa and the floor. Mama had one
in her lap and was looking down at it, bright-eyed. "It's my wedding," she said as I entered.

"Mama, do you know what time it is?" I said.

"Late?" she answered, and then her voice became petulant.
"Bruster went to bed, but Florence won't come and tuck me in."

At my feet was another scrapbook, opened to a picture of us all in Florida, on vacation. Mama was off to the side, staring vacantly at something that wasn't in the frame. Clarice and I stood together in front of Aunt Flo and Uncle Bruster. We were grinning like monkeys, Clarice leaning back against her dad. Aunt Florence had one bony hand clamped on my shoulder.

Burr knelt down and closed it. Underneath, another scrapbook was open to a picture of a pretty blonde. At first glance I thought it was Clarice. The girl in the picture was leaning on a rail fence by a pasture, wearing a pair of shorts and a cutoff T-shirt that said I ♥ THE BRAVES. She was a pretty girl, with the Lukey blue eyes and the same kind of tall, willowy figure as Clarice, but the smile was different, and this girl had a longer nose.

"Who is this, Mama?" I said, holding the book up.

"It's your cousin Fat Agnes," said Mama. "That was last year, at the family reunion up at Swit Bee Park."

"Holy God!" I said.

Mama said, "Don't take the Lord's name in vain, sugar."

"That's Fat Agnes?" said Burr, taking the album for a closer look.

I said, "She must have dropped two hundred pounds."

"Oh yes, she did that Weight Watchers," Mama said, yawning.

"I never would have recognized her," I said. "Mama, where is Aunt Florence?"

"Florence went on up to the attic, I think," Mama said.

"Are you sure?" I said. The clock in the den said it was after midnight. The attic was a low cramped space under the eaves of the house. The only entrance was a trapdoor that pulled out of the ceiling in the hallway. It had a rickety folding ladder attached. I went through the den and stuck my head into the hallway, and sure enough, the ladder was down.

"Hey, Burr?" I said. "I need to go apologize to Flo. We had that blowout while you were getting gas. Do you think you can walk Mama back to her bed? And then you can hit the sack if you're tired. I'll join you as soon as I get Florence down."

"Sure, baby," he said, looking at me carefully. "Are you okay?"

"I don't know," I said. "Are we okay?"

"Of course we are," he said.

"Then I am, too."

Burr set the scrapbook down atop a pile on the sofa. He held his hand out to Mama and said, "Mrs. Fleet? You want to go to bed?"

Mama nodded and boosted herself up. He walked her down the hall. They negotiated their way around the ladder, Mama squeezing against the wall. I followed them that far, and then as they continued down the hall to Mama's room, I climbed up the spindly ladder to the attic. I could feel the heat oozing out of the trapdoor and pushing at me.

I poked my head through the rectangular hole in the ceiling. The attic was exactly as I remembered it. The floor was nothing but beams with heaps of pink insulation between them. Many pieces of plywood in various sizes had been placed from beam to beam, and bits of insulation tufted up between the plywood scraps. All around the entry hole was a veritable wall of boxes sitting on the plywood slats. Some were labeled with the names of family members who had died. I saw a few with Aunt Niner's name, and others with my asshole grampa and Saint Granny's names. Some were just labeled CLOTHES or KITCHEN, and some were not labeled at all.

Behind the boxes was a light source, and I could see by that light a narrow path made of two-by-fours leading through the wall of boxes. I boosted myself up through the hole into the oppressive heat of the attic, resting my butt gingerly on a bit of plywood. I got to my feet and followed the path around the boxes, touching the wall to balance myself on the narrow boards.

The box wall was six or eight rows deep. Behind it, a huge sheet of thick planking had been placed over the beams and insulation, and more boxes and fat black Hefty bags rested on it. One of the boxes was open, and behind that box, in a folding chair, sat Aunt Florence.

An apple-green lamp was sitting on a box next to her, illuminating the cramped space. It was plugged into a fat orange extension cord that looped away across the planking. Aunt Florence had been unpacking the box, and bits and pieces were scattered all about. She glanced up at me as I came into the light, and then she looked back down at a toy person she had in her hands.

"I thought you'd gone back to Chicago and left your suitcases," she said, staring down at the toy. "I wasn't going to stuff them up here. I was going to ship them."

With a jolt I realized she was holding Mr. Minkus, the daddy of my dollhouse family. The apple-green lamp on the box matched Clarice's, except it had no daisy stickers. It was mine. And now the things she had strewn out on the plank floor came into focus. My old Narnia books and my stuffed animals, the hot-pink throw pillows from my bed. My postcard of a kitten at the end of a rope beneath the words HANG IN THERE was still in its cheap frame, lying on the floor at her feet. Beside it was a cross-stitch sampler Aunt Niner had made for me. It had the "Footprints" story of Jesus on the beach and had hung on the wall over my desk.

"These are all my things," I said wonderingly. I walked around Florence, behind her to a stack of three large cardboard boxes that said ARLENE: CLOTHES and ARLENE: BOOKS/ALBUMS and ARLENE: GAMES/TOYS/MISC. The flaps of the top box were open, and I could see my old dollhouse in there buried among loose game pieces from Scrabble and Operation and Mouse Trap. Mrs. Minkus and the Minkus baby floated on top. Under a tilted Monopoly board, wedged sideways in the jumble, the glass mouth of a bottle glinted in the light. I reached into the box and pulled it out.

It was tall and clear, with the thick, bubbled base I remembered. I'd never looked for it, because I had assumed Clarice had sneaked it out of the house. It must have stayed where she shoved it, under my bed, getting pushed farther and farther back until it came to rest behind the storage boxes where my winter sweaters and shoes were kept.

By the time Aunt Florence had come across it while eradicating my room, it would have been scentless, and it had never had a label. She'd packed it away with all my other things. It seemed smaller, so much lighter in my hands than I remembered. I dropped it back into the box and said, "I thought you threw my things out."

"Why would I do that?" Aunt Florence said tonelessly.

Next to the boxes was a black Hefty bag, stuffed full and closed with a twist tie. I opened it up and looked in it. At first it seemed to be full of crumpled paper, trash, but when I touched it, the mass was crackly and stiff like papier-mâché. I tried to pull a piece of it out and realized it was all attached, congealed into a single huge lump. In the dim light, I could make out words or drawings on the paper, but it was so crumpled that I could not resolve it. Then I started picking out tiny recognizable bits: a cowboy hat, a coiled rope, the leg of a horse.

"This is Wayne's wallpaper?" I said. "You peeled off all Wayne's wallpaper and kept it?" There was another Hefty bag behind it, smaller, and when I touched it, I could feel more of the same crackly stuff in it. I was willing to bet that if I opened it up, I would find the leavings of the dinosaur paper she had put up in the bathroom when Wayne was a baby.

Aunt Florence, her back to me, hunched her shoulders up in a shrug. "I couldn't look at it every day. Those grinning cowboys, and my boy dead. But I couldn't throw it out, either."

I walked back around the chair and shoved the box of my things out of the way. I sat down on the floor in front of her. "Why are my things up here with Wayne's things, and Aunt Niner's, and Granny and Grampa's? I'm not dead, Aunt Flo."

"Same reason," said Florence. "I couldn't throw them out, but I couldn't stand to look at them every day, either." At last she stopped twisting Mr. Minkus's head around and around and met my eyes. "You never came home, Arlene. Maybe I'm dumb like you think, and it took me a few years to get it, but once I did, I couldn't look at your things, and you somewhere in the world judging me, and never coming home."

I dropped to my knees and put my hands on her legs, one on either side. She was stiff and unyielding under my fingers, but that was how Florence always felt. "I never judged you," I said. "You misunderstood. You thought I knew stuff I didn't. There was all this space between us, and you put whatever you wanted in there. But you got it wrong. I wasn't judging you, and you are not the reason I didn't come home. Up until yesterday, when you said what you said in the kitchen, I had no idea you even knew Jim Beverly was dead. And until this morning, when Burr pointed out a few things I had wrong, I had no idea that you killed him."

There was a moment of silence, and we let that settle between us for a moment.

Aunt Florence shook her head at me, disbelieving. "But that day Mrs. Weedy came over. You asked about the car. You had to have known. I figured you had been in the car when he crashed it. I thought you'd hit him in the head while he was driving you off to somewhere, and that had run him off the road. I thought that's how you got away."

"No," I said. "I was never in the car with him, Aunt Florence. I thought there was a chance that he had run away. But mostly I thought I'd left him dead up on Lipsmack Hill, and that's why I never came home. But now I need to know, Aunt Florence. What did you do?"

"This is how it happened," Aunt Flo said. She began talking, and between what she knew and what I knew, I was able to put it all together. The truth this time, undiluted. As she spoke, as we talked it through, it was happening again. It was like time travel. It was like putting something ugly and exhausted to bed at last.

The night Jim Beverly dies, Aunt Florence hears Clarice come in the front door and pad, alone, down the hall. It's just before midnight. Clarice has made curfew. Bruster is sleeping solid beside her. My mama is in Wayne's old room, dead to the world.

"We're home, Mama," Clarice calls.

Aunt Florence is not fooled. She has known this trick ever since it began. She always stays awake until she hears the second girl come in safe. She knows better than to tip her hand. You squeeze girls too tight, they go wild. This is a harmless thing, she thinks. We are good girls. We are not out drinking or letting some boy get us pregnant. We are somewhere with our friends, giggling a little longer. Or maybe we are with a boy, whispering and kissing, feeling like hot stuff for getting away with it. The second girl always creeps in half an hour or at most an hour later. We do not do it often. She gives us this room so we won't rebel in bigger ways and get ourselves in trouble.

But this night she hears Clarice up in our room fluttering around. And I do not come in. An hour passes, and Florence's blood is moving faster, heating as it speeds through her veins. She is wide awake. Another half hour crawls by. She is about to go and confront Clarice when she hears her daughter creep down to the kitchen. After a moment, Florence stealthily lifts the receiver on her bedside phone, holding the button down until the phone is to her ear. She breathes silently and covers the mouthpiece with her hand in case Bruster stirs, and then she lifts the button.

"—went up on Lipsmack Hill. Jim Beverly was up there with some girl," Clarice is saying.

That's all Florence needs to hear, but she doesn't hang up lest Clarice hear the click. Clarice wants Bud to go and find me. Bud reminds her that she has his car. He wants to know why I would be chasing after Jim Beverly, but Clarice blows him off. The main thing, she tells him, is that I have not come home and I was last seen heading up Lipsmack. They make a plan. If I am not home by dawn, Clarice will leave a note for her parents, something about a breakfast picnic and football practice, and she will go pick up Bud and they will find me. Aunt Florence waits until Clarice has hung up before she hangs up herself. She listens to Clarice sneak back to her room and take up her vigil by the window, watching for me.

By three, Clarice has fallen asleep with her head down on her desk. I am still not home. Aunt Florence gets out of bed, moving slowly so she doesn't wake up Bruster. She is seriously worried now, angry and single-minded. She does not think. She acts. She slips into yesterday's clothes, leaving her nightgown by the bed. As she leaves the house, she peeks in on Clarice. Clarice is beautiful in the lamplight, ethereal and fragile. Clarice is alive; there is satisfaction in watching the breath move in and out of her, but it is not enough. Clarice is not enough. The world is not a safe place, and Wayne's room down the hall is stark and ample proof. Aunt Florence marches out into the world to find me and bring me home. She wants me beside Clarice, filling and completing the room that is apple green and pink and the living heart of the house.

Florence heads first to Lipsmack. She knows the way. The make-out spots have not changed since she was a girl; she once walked up that hill holding hands with Bruster. It's deserted. Jim Beverly's red Jeep is gone. All the cars are gone. She walks up anyway. She has a flashlight in the trunk of her car and knows the path. The top is deserted.

She gets in her car and heads for the highway. Jim Beverly, she knows, lives in Fruiton. On the access road, she sees his red Jeep, crumpled against the pole. She slows down and pulls off. She rolls down her window to look, but the driver's-side door is open, and the Jeep is empty. She calls for me, yelling my name into the night, but I do not come. She takes her foot off the brake and leaves the Jeep behind, continuing on to the highway. She thinks perhaps I have gone there to flag down help.

She heads for the on-ramp, but as she gets on to drive to Fruiton, she sees a hitchhiker on the other side, heading the other way. He is illuminated briefly in the lights of a passing car. He is blond, the right size. He has his thumb out.

She exits as soon as she can and loops around, getting back on the highway heading the other way. She is relieved to see that no one has picked up the hitchhiker. She slows beside him, pulls over. It's Jim Beverly. He is alone. When she stops her car, he climbs in without looking at her.

"Hey, thanks," he says. "I wrecked my Jeep, and I need to get home." She doesn't answer.

He seems disoriented. His clothes are dirty, and his speech is slurred. She pulls back onto the highway and gets her speed up before she speaks to him, and then she says, "Where is she? Where's my girl?"

Jim Beverly has no recollection who Aunt Florence is. "What girl?" he says. "Girl?"

"She was up on Lipsmack Hill with you. You tell me, where is she."

"The little bitch?" he says. "Little bitch hit me." He is probably talking about the freshman, but Aunt Florence thinks he is talking about me.

"Good," she says viciously. "Then what. What did you do with her?"

Jim Beverly shrugs at her, insolent, uncaring. "Take me home," he slurs. "I don't care where your bitch is."

gods in Alabama

Florence steers hard right, taking the first exit she sees. It shunts them out of the streetlights, leading them into the wilds of Alabama. They pass a gas station and a fireworks stand, both closed. Then they are alone, speeding down a dark country road, with heaps on either side of them rising up black and mountainous in the moonlight.

"This isn't right," says Jim Beverly. "I said take me home." He sounds petulant, and his words are so slurred that it is hard for Florence to understand him. He stinks of tequila. He keeps rubbing the back of his head. Florence brakes and pulls onto the shoulder, killing her headlights. "Where are we," says Jim Beverly. He is utterly unafraid. He is at most peeved.

He faces Florence in the moonlight, and she can see one of his pupils is huge and the other is a pinpoint. "She hit you hard," Florence says. "What did you do?"

He shrugs at her again, that insolent roll of his shoulders, and she knows in her heart that I am dead somewhere. She has no illusions about what this boy is capable of. I am dead somewhere and the world is a black place, and in that moment she believes, bleakly, that everything will eventually be taken from her. Her blood surges, and she hates God and this wild boy He has let run loose upon the earth. It is pounding through her, hot and unforgiving. Her vision narrows to a tunnel, and all she can see is this floppy boy with his careless shrugs and his insolent smile. In this moment she is stronger than he is. She is stronger than anyone alive. The adrenaline rush is a black high wave surging upward, lifting her. She rides with it, her blood on fire, rising, and as it crests, she moves.

She reaches out with her big hands. It seems a calm slow movement to her, endless, because here at the peak, time has slowed. She is in a place that I know. I have been there, too, earlier this same night, when I was standing behind Jim Beverly with a bottle. She has a moment to choose, and she chooses. She takes his neck in her huge hands, and he is so surprised or drunk or hurt that in the endless fraction of a second it takes her to grasp him, he is yielding in her hands. He does not fight her at first, as she tightens her massive grip.

At first he cannot process what is happening. Then he begins to struggle, weakly, or it seems weak to her. She is in a place where she could move a mountain with her bare hands. His fists beat at her chest harmlessly. Later, her chest will be black-and-blue from his blows, but now his fists feel as insubstantial as trapped birds, fluttering weightlessly against her.

The blood is coursing through her strong arms like liquid fire, and she feels him yielding to her. His feet drum against the floorboards of the car, a desperate lunging tattoo. The drumming slows and stops, and she remains where she is, holding his throat closed in her grip. Making sure. When she is sure, she releases him and turns his head, so she cannot see his eyes, but she knows the light has gone out of them and he can't see anything and he never will again. And then she sits quiet. There is nothing else to do.

After a little while, she wrestles the deadweight of him out of the car and heaves him into the trunk. At that point she is thinking not so much of hiding him as of not wanting to drive around looking for me with him dead beside her in the car. Beyond that, she does not think.

No cars pass. No one sees her. By the time she gets him loaded and closes the trunk, she is shaking and weak as a kitten.

She heads back to where he wrecked his Jeep, but sees the state police hooking it up to a tow truck. She cruises past without slowing. Dawn is coming. She drives the route from the wreck to our house. She drives slowly, as if she believes she might catch me trekking home, but in her heart, she has no doubt that I am dead. She feels the same emptiness in the world that she felt when she saw Wayne lying in the yard, tangled in his dog's leash and with his eyes puffed closed, features swollen, unrecognizable as Wayne to anyone but his mother. She feels me the same way people sometimes feel silence. She feels me as the absence of a heartbeat that, like your own, you hear so constantly you do not notice it until it's gone.

As she comes over the hill to the house, the sun is rising, and she sees Clarice. She stops as her heart gutters and spits, catching at the sight of her living child. Clarice is bending down, facing away from Aunt Florence, digging in the hydrangea bushes. Clarice is helping me up. I am filthy, and I lean heavily on Clarice, but I am alive. Florence can't breathe, watching Clarice load me into the window. Clarice puts the screen back on once I am through, and then she creeps to the front door and slips inside.

Florence watches the silent house with both her girls safe in it, and the world begins to turn again. She hears birds, and it's like the first sound she has ever heard. It's beautiful, and there is a dead boy in her trunk. She realizes that she isn't afraid or sorry. There isn't room for anything in her but a fierce ripping joy and the loveliness of the birdsong.

Bruster will be up any second, and she knows better than to lie or try to explain. She simply parks the car and walks straight into her garden and squats down in it, weeding in the dawn, and of course this is the first place Bruster looks.

"You forgot to start the coffee," he says reproachfully. He is rumpled with sleep, disgruntled and blinking. She shrugs an apology. After he heads back to the house, she realizes she is gutting her vegetable garden, taking out her young tomato plants and setting them aside. She immediately knows why. Behind the shelter of a high bushy clump of lemon balm and in the shadow of the shed beside the garden, she is going to dig a pit.

When she heads in to make breakfast, she absolves us all of yard work. She will need the yard to herself. The house will shield her from the road. Her shed will hide her from Mrs. Weedy. She can back her car down the concrete drive to the garden.

She can see I am so hungover that I can barely function, so she sends me back to bed, where I sleep like a corpse. She sends Bruster off with a huge errand list, and Clarice drives off in Bud's car to meet him at his Saturday practice. While they are gone, she plants Jim Beverly deep in the corner of her garden, dumping a twenty-pound bag of lye from the shed over him to keep the neighborhood dogs out. Then she repairs and replants her tomatoes, and the lye makes them grow like crap, and for the first time in three years she doesn't get a ribbon on them at the county fair, and that's just fine with her. That's just fine.

After Florence finished talking, I sat with her for a long time, my hands still resting on the unyielding flesh of her legs.

"Why would you think he had killed me?" I said at last.

"That boy was capable of anything. I knew what he did the year before."

"You knew?" I said. "Clarice told you?"

Aunt Florence shook her head at me. "No, Arlene, you know Clarice better than that. She kept your secret."

"My secret?" I said.

"But I knew," Florence said. "When you changed so much, I backtracked it to the night you and Clarice went out on that double date with him. You weren't ever right after that, wearing all those black clothes and not leaving the house. Never taking a bath. Clarice did a pretty good dance, trying to keep your secret, but I guessed the why of it. At first I thought it had been that Rob Shay, but then we ran into him one day at the Wal-Mart, and you were sweet as pie with him. You didn't even blink. I figured it was the other one. A football boy like that, you didn't think anyone would believe you. But I would have. I knew what he was."

"What have I got in my pocketses," I said softly, and Aunt Florence looked at me, questioning. I shook my head at her. I didn't have any of my own secrets left, but I could keep Clarice's. I could keep Aunt Florence's, too.

I turned around and leaned my back on her hard shins, dropping my head to rest on her knees. We sat there together for a long time, baking in the dry, dark heat of the attic. Aunt Flo's fingers rambled in my hair. I suppose there was a lot for us to talk about, but in the silence I think we were both deciding not to. I was done with deal-making and telling secrets. I had told the truth to Rose Mae Lolley, and I had lied to Burr, and I was fine with it. Everything could rest right where it was, even Jim Beverly, in his back corner of Aunt Florence's garden. We would never say his name to each other, to anyone, again.

"What if I came back down for Christmas?" I said at last. "I've spent the last nine by myself or with Burr's mama, so I figure it's about y'all's turn."

Aunt Florence's hands stilled, and she said, "That'd be real good, Arlene. I'd like it if that happened."

"Then that's what we'll do. But you know, Aunt Florence, if you want me back here, you get Burr, too."

Her fingers began drifting gently through my hair again. "You know I don't hold with it. These mixed marriages," she said, but softly, almost musingly, as if her mind was somewhere else. I smiled, knowing she couldn't see my face. I was more like her than I had thought; I knew at last how much she loved me, and I was ruthless enough to immediately use it against her, even while I was basking in it.

"We're a package deal. Love me, love my Burr. And I mean that. You don't get to be all stiff and barely tolerating. I don't care how you feel about it, Aunt Florence, as long as you're a good enough liar. And I guess I know you are. You lie to both of us. Him and me. Every minute. You take care of him like he was me, and you make him welcome. And you make Uncle Bruster be good to him, too. Or I won't come," I said.

After another long pause, she said, "I can do that, Arlene." Then she got a hunk of my hair and gave it a jerking yank that hurt down to the roots. "Ow!" I said and tried to sit up, but she pulled my head back down gently onto her bony knee and rubbed the hurt place. "And you don't leave me anymore. You bring your little butt home when you have vacation time without me having to fight you near to death over it."

"Yes, ma'am," I said.

After that we were quiet again for a long time. I suppose I felt too peaceful to move, with Aunt Flo's hands moving soft in my hair, soothing me. I knew that on Friday we would all go to Uncle Bruster's party, and nothing bad would happen. Florence wouldn't let it. There wasn't a Bent or Lukey alive she couldn't bend.

I do not know how long we sat there, both of us pouring sweat, but eventually we had to get up and go downstairs. I walked Florence to her bedroom door and kissed her dry cheek. I waited until she had disappeared inside, and then I crept into my old room. Burr was sleeping hard with his face to the wall. I climbed into Clarice's little bed and molded myself to his back. I fell asleep almost instantly, beside him with my family surrounding us, right where I belonged.

# READING GROUP GUIDE

# NOTHING SAYS LOVE STORY LIKE A TEQUILA BOTTLE UPSIDE THE HEAD OR WHAT'S A NICE GIRL LIKE YOU DOING WITH A STORY LIKE *THIS*?

———— ∞ ————

When you write a book, people are always asking you what kind of book it is. I am tempted to say something like, "It's a *good* book, a well-written book. Look, just read a sentence or two. I think you'll really like it." It's hard for me to put a label on this book because it's such an odd blend of humor and violence. When pressed, I'll say something like, "It's Southern fiction seasoned with a dash of literary murder mystery." That's probably accurate, but in my head, GODS IN ALABAMA has always been a love story. I don't mean that in the traditional sense of boy meets girl, music swells, cue the naked fat babies with heart-tipped projectile weaponry. I'm talking about a mother-daughter love story, about the relationship that grows between the narrator Arlene and her estranged aunt, Florence.

Now, I should mention that the second most common question you're asked when you write a book is "Which character is most like you?" And once people have read this book, they always think they know the answer: Arlene. I can see where they get the idea; Arlene and I are both Southern women who moved to Chicago for school, and we're both a little bit high-strung. Yet, strangely enough, Florence is the character I identify with most strongly. I hesitate to admit this: She's two decades and change older than I am. She's a virulent racist. She's tough and bloody-minded: a steel magnolia with *zero* magnolia. More like a steel lump of steel. She's made up entirely of corners and brickle burrs and bile. None of that is me. But I can't help but feel close to her because of the relationship she and I share with motherhood.

Florence, long before the book began, lost her son, and that's why she's such a dried husk of a woman. She loved her son so deeply, so fiercely, with a love that was ferociously all-consuming. Like Florence, and like every other mother under the sun, I am held hostage to the world in the form of my children. Sam and Maisy Jane are the sum total of my heart. And sum total of my heart is even now, even as I type this, out in the world wandering around, probably in traffic. It's unendurable. How do we go through every day with them out there on their bikes, among snakes and lightning and mean kids and rabid squirrels and chaos theory and predators? Florence did, and she lost one of them, and the world changed for her.

I remember when I was pregnant with my daughter Maisy I almost never wanted it to end, even though I hate pregnancy and would never, never do it if I didn't get a baby at the end. Even if I got, say, my own tropical island at the end, I wouldn't do it. But with Maisy, I wished I could stay miserable and sick and pregnant forever. My son Sam was already five and bounding around like a goat, leaping carelessly up the sides of mountains, running like a joyful lemming straight into the wide, wet sea. I knew, even as Maisy kicked viciously at my bladder, that this was the last time I would ever feel I could adequately protect her. It was the only time in her life when, at every moment, something would literally have to go *through* me to harm her. I didn't understand that when I was pregnant with Sam. I didn't understand how he would be so immediately separate from me, so perfectly himself, and so absolutely vulnerable.

But now I can see that the idea of Florence, her character, was conceived in my brain on the morning I first felt Sam quicken inside me, felt that almost imperceptible flutter, the suggestion of a shadow of movement. Long after my babies left my body and became independent creatures, busy and fearless, the idea of Florence remained. The idea that I could become her, that the world is not safe and yet my children are out running around in it, is never far away from me. Florence will be with me as long as I am living.

I came awfully close to not writing GODS IN ALABAMA at all. As I worked on it, I kept thinking, "I can't seriously want to write the love story of a pathological liar who isn't quite an orphan and a pet-killing, borderline sociopath who isn't quite her mother." But Arlene and Florence's storyline was the one thing I couldn't change. The parent-child relationship that blooms between them is the heart of the book.

And yes, in some ways, it is a cold, small, awful heart. It is at least two sizes too small and made of flint to boot. But once I had chipped my way inside, I found it to be rich and sweet, five times a normal heart's density. I realized then that I had I brought the two of them together as a talisman against my own fears, against every parent's fears. It's terrifying to have your soul walking around on earth separate from you, on unsteady legs, absolutely convinced it is immortal. Florence knows that in ways Arlene and I cannot imagine, and yet she chooses to love anyway. That choice makes me proud to identify with Florence, in spite of her flaws. And that choice means that, to me, this book will always be a love story, no matter where it ends up being filed on the bookstore shelves.

# DISCUSSION QUESTIONS

1. Who or what are the gods that the title refers to? Who are the gods in your hometown, workplace, or culture?

2. Arlene finds an imperfect but workable way to live around her family's deeply ingrained racism while maintaining the two most important relationships in her life. How satisfying is this compromise? Is it fair to Burr? To Florence? Should Arlene have asked for and expected more?

3. In what ways does Arlene's "deal with God" allow her to protect herself? How much of it is true penance and how much is a defense mechanism?

4. Arlene has painted a picture of Clarice as beautiful, pure, passive, and wholesome. How does idealizing Clarice influence Arlene's own behavior and sexuality?

5. Arlene's biological mother is almost a nonperson in the book, and Arlene has surrounded herself with replacement mothers. Who are these replacements, and what aspects of mothering does she get from each of them?

6. The women in this novel generally tend to overpower the men, whether in conversation, romance, or physical altercations. Is this indicative of Southern society in general? What point might the author be making about gender relations in an outwardly traditional society?

7. The main character in this book is alternately known as Arlene and Lena. What are the distinguishing characteristics of Arlene? Of Lena? How do you think she would identify herself? By the end of the book, had she changed in your mind from one to the other, or had the two been integrated?

8. Arlene has clearly rehearsed a confession for years and years. How do you think her commitment to this retelling of the events of the past has shaped her current course of action?

9. Who is Jim Beverly? How do you reconcile the "pure-hearted, sole good man" Rose Mae Lolley has ever known with the scoundrel on Lipsmack Hill that fateful night?

10. What role does the Southern locale play in the novel? Could such a story take place in another region? Why or why not?

11. Forgiveness and atonement are two of the major themes in this novel. Who do you believe has done the most genuine atoning in this story? Who has the biggest sin to forgive?

12. Arlene baldly states that she is a game player, and she plays both literal and metaphorical games with Burr and the other characters throughout the novel. She is also, on some level, playing a game with the reader. How did you react to this? Do you think she played "fair"?

Please turn this page
for a preview of
Joshilyn Jackson's
new novel

# Between, Georgia

Available Now

# CHAPTER

## 1

THE WAR BEGAN thirty years, nine months, and seven days ago, when I was deaf and blind, floating silent and serene inside Hazel Crabtree. I was secreted in Hazel's womb, which was cloaked in her pale and freckled skin, which was in turn hidden by the baggy sweatsuits she adopted so she would look fat instead of pregnant. Which was ridiculous, because who ever heard of a fat Crabtree? They were all tall and weedy, slouching around like wilting stems, red hair blooming out the top.

Hazel Crabtree was fifteen years old, and no one thought twice about her expanding waistline as she crept around the edges of rooms, watching her mother ignore her and ignoring me in turn as I kicked at her and spun and grew myself some lungs.

I never heard Hazel's side of the story. She birthed me but was never in any sense my mother. I heard an expurgated version from my aunt Genny; to hear Genny tell it, I frolicked bloodlessly into the world attended by singing rabbits. From Aunt

Bernese, I got raw medical data and a flat recitation of events in the order they occurred.

But my mother, Stacia Frett, told it to me as a love story, hers and mine. It wasn't a declaration of war to her, it was simply the tale of how we found each other. My mother's version, with every nuance communicated by her expressive face and flashing hands, dominated my imagination. Over the years, I interwove her story with what I had gleaned from Genny and Bernese, until I had an interpretation that felt like truth. It was as if my soul had been floating above the scene, watching, waiting to be sucked into my body with the air of my first breath.

I don't know why Hazel Crabtree went to Bernese for help the night I was born, and Bernese did not think to ask her. The why of things did not often trouble Aunt Bernese, but she was a master at discovering the how. Before agenting my mother's art became a full-time job, Bernese had worked in labor and delivery over at Loganville General. I like to think Hazel came to the Fretts because she knew Bernese was a former nurse and pragmatist savant who, beneath her bluster, had a kind heart. This was a distinct possibility: At that time Between, Georgia, had a population of about ninety people. Everybody knew everything about everyone.

But more likely, she was being practical. Bernese and her husband and their boys lived on the lot at the dead end of Grace Street. Her sisters, Stacia and Genny, lived together in the house next door. There wasn't another house on the block, and Bernese's backyard overlooked empty miles of Georgia pine trees. The only other nurse in town lived on one of Between's more populated streets; she had close neighbors. The last (although perhaps the most important) factor was that Hazel had to know going to the Fretts for help was a surefire way to piss off her family.

Bernese woke to the sound of someone banging on her front door a few minutes past four in the morning. She came down the stairs pulling on her robe, getting her gun hand stuck in the sleeve. Her husband, Lou, trailed behind her, saying nervously, "Is the safety on? Is the safety on? Hand the gun to me and then put your robe on, Bernese. Is the safety on?"

Bernese got herself untangled and tucked the gun into her armpit, barrel down, while she tied her robe belt.

"Is that the thirty-eight?" asked Lou. "Lord-a-mercy, why didn't you get your little purse gun?"

Bernese opened the door and there was Hazel Crabtree, holding a wad of her mucous plug cupped in both hands and saying, "This came out. Is this a piece of baby? I hurt."

Bernese said, "Holy monkeys! You're pregnant? Lou, call for an ambulance." Tiny towns like Between didn't have 911 service in 1976, so Lou went to get Bernese's emergency-numbers card from the drawer. But Hazel shoved past Bernese and grabbed at him, falling to her knees as she yowled, "No, no, you can't call anyone. My mother can't know."

Then she let go of Lou and said in a high, panicked voice, "Something's coming. Something else. Something bad is coming." Hazel scrabbled at her belly and crotch, frantic. Her sweatpants were soggy, and she shoved them down to mid-thigh. She wasn't wearing any panties. Then she tilted and tipped over, writhing on the foyer carpet.

Bernese looked up and saw all three of her young sons huddled in a clot on the stairs. They were clutching one another on the second-floor landing, staring down through the banisters with wide, horrified eyes.

"Never you mind," Bernese said to Lou. He was tugging at his earlobe as he watched Hazel flail and howl on the floor. He set the phone back down in its cradle on the hall table. Bernese said, "Get up there with the boys. Tell them something. I will fix this." Lou trotted obediently upstairs and picked up the toddler, herding the two older boys back toward their bedroom. Hazel's contraction subsided, and she rose up on her hands and knees, panting.

Bernese's front door opened into a carpeted entryway. A wide doorway on the right led to the den, and straight ahead was a long hallway to the kitchen. On the left, the stairs went up to a landing that overlooked the foyer. There was a heavy table, almost a sideboard, that ran the length of the staircase. The phone was on the edge of the table, close to the front door, and the rest of it was taken up by the huge glass terrarium that housed Bernese's beloved luna moths. The adult moths were awake, some fanning their wings as they posed on the perches and twigs. Others had paired off, attaching end to end to make the kind of desperate love that comes with an extremely short life span.

Bernese tried to step around Hazel, heading for the table so she could set down her gun and pick up the phone, but Hazel reared up on her knees in front of Bernese, crying, "No, you can't! No one knows I'm this way. No one can find out!"

She was grabbing for Bernese's arm, but she fell short and jerked at her hand, squeezing. The gun went off. The bullet whizzed past Hazel's head, smashing through the glass of the terrarium and burying itself in the staircase. Glass showered down, pattering onto the carpet and sprinkling Hazel's wild red hair.

Hazel and Bernese froze in the sudden silence, their eyes locked on the smoking hole in Bernese's stairs. From upstairs, Lou yelled, "Bernese? Bernese?" They heard his footsteps clattering across the upstairs hall, the little boys running in a panicked herd behind him.

"Stop!" screeched Bernese, and the footsteps stopped dead. "No one is hit, Lou. Stay with the boys."

"I asked you was the safety on," Lou called down, aggrieved.

Bernese hollered back, "Maybe you better put the safety on your mouth."

Next door, the gunshot woke up Bernese's sister Genny. Genny bolted upright, clutching the covers to her bosom. Her bedroom window overlooked Bernese's front lawn, and she saw the downstairs lights blazing and Bernese's front door standing open. Genny got up and ran on tiptoe down the hall to Stacia's room. She flipped the light switch and sat on the bed, shaking Stacia awake. Stacia sat up, her gray eyes opening wide, immediately alert. She held her fist up to her chin, thumb and pinky spread wide, asking by sign and her expressive face what was wrong.

Genny shook her head and signed back, *Heard gun.* She cut her eyes to the left to indicate Bernese's house, then signed, *Lights on, door open. What do we do?*

As soon as she finished signing, she moved her right hand to pluck at the fine dark hairs on her left forearm, tugging hard enough to lift her skin in points. One of the hairs popped out, torn root and all from the follicle.

*Don't pick,* Stacia signed. She gently peeled Genny's fingers away and gave her a bracing pat, then signed, *I'll handle it.* Stacia climbed out of bed and pulled on her robe. She tied the belt with savage efficiency, then spun on one heel and took off for the front door at a dead run. Her long black hair was unbound, and it unfurled behind her like a banner.

Genny stared openmouthed for a moment and then said, "Goodness grief!" She ran after Stacia, waving frantically in a futile attempt to catch her eye, signing, *Wait! Wait! Call police! Help! Wait!* at Stacia's implacable back.

She chased Stacia in this manner all the way across the lawn to Bernese's front porch. She stopped short of the stairs and leaned down and grabbed up a pinecone, ripping up a chunk of sod with it. She threw it as hard as she could past Stacia, through her line of sight. It thunked against Bernese's siding, and dust puffed out of it all the way around, like a firework going off. It left a black smudge on the porch, like an outsize thumbprint on the wood. Stacia paused to give Genny an irked look over her shoulder before she disappeared through Bernese's front door.

Genny stood a few steps outside the glow of the porch lights, tugging at her long black braid. Her nervous fingers climbed up, following the weave of her braid, all the way until she touched the fine hairs at her nape. She gathered two or three in a pinch and ripped them out, twiddling her fingers together to shake off the loose hairs and then immediately seeking out another pinch. A luna moth came fluttering drunkenly out the front door and wafted up, disappearing into the night. Genny watched it go, and then she scuttled up onto the porch. She peeked inside.

Bernese and Stacia were helping Hazel to the other side of the foyer, picking their way through shattered glass from the terrarium. Hazel was moaning and naked from the waist down. Her sweatshirt had hiked up over her grossly distended abdomen. The rest of her body was so skinny that Genny could see her ribs. Hazel's thighs were streaked with blood. Glass fragments sparkled

in her hair, inappropriately festive. Three or four of the luna
moths were dancing up around the light fixture, and one wa
fluttering in Hazel's wake, as if drawn by her bright hair. Genny
saw the gun sitting by the phone on the sideboard.

"What's happening?" Genny squawked, jerking out anothe
pinch of hair at her nape. "Is she shot? Was she shot in her pants?"

"No one is shot," said Bernese. "It's a baby coming, and it
coming now, very fast. Help me here."

Bernese and Stacia lowered Hazel back down to the carpet i
the doorway to the den. They tried to get her to squat, but sh
flopped onto her back and lay there, thrashing back and forth
another contraction took her. Stacia signed rapidly, and Genn
said, "Stacia wants to know, what do you need?"

"Boiled string. Scissors. Clean towels," said Bernese as Genn
repeated her words in sign. "Hot water. A doctor, but that's n
going to happen. I think this baby is coming now."

Stacia nodded curtly and ran down the long hallway into t
kitchen. Bernese knelt by Hazel until the contraction subsid
and she was still again. She was sobbing quietly on the floor:
has to stop. Make it stop."

"It will stop," said Bernese. "We have to get this baby out is
Genny, come sit by her head."

"Me?" Genny squeaked.

"Unless you want the naked end," said Bernese, staying bes
Hazel. "Breathe," she said.

"Oh, oh, oh, oh," said Genny. She stayed right where she
in the doorway, rocking back and forth, her gaze flicking arou
the room, glancing off the moths and Bernese and the blood
the gun on the table, unable to light on anything. Her busy
gers sought hairs to pull as she rocked herself faster.

"Another one is coming," said Hazel. "Make it not come."

"You want it to come," said Bernese. "It will get this baby out, and then it will all stop. So let it come."

"No, no, no, I don't want it to come," Hazel moaned, but it came anyway. It came relentlessly, and she was helpless in it, with Bernese roaring at her to push.

Genny was weaving harder, panting, tugging at her hair. Bernese glared at her. "Quit that picking and get by this girl's head. Now. And quit panting. I don't have time to drag your big butt out of the way if you faint."

Hazel shook her head wildly back and forth, twisting her body as she fought the contraction. Genny, watching, dug her finger-nails into her forearm hard enough to draw blood and then stared down at her arm for half a beat. The pain cleared her head, and she accessed the thread of Frett resilience buried in her, deep under her nerves. She stilled her hands and scurried over to kneel beside Hazel's head.

"There you go. You and her breathe together," instructed Bernese. Once Genny was in place, Bernese braced herself against the doorway and put the heel of her hand at the top of Hazel's belly. She leaned in to it, bearing down and saying, "And you, girl. Push hard from here."

Hazel shoved at Bernese's hand, weeping. She slumped again as the contraction ended, and Bernese said, "Next time you push like that at the start."

Hazel said, "I don't want a next time."

Genny reached out and patted ineffectually at Hazel's shoulder. Hazel grabbed Genny's wrist, looking up at her, beseeching, "Please tell her to quit it."

"Oh, honey," said Genny, pity softening her horror. "No one can make Bernese quit anything."

"I hate you," said Hazel to Bernese. "I hate you, you dumb whore."

"Why, this is Ona Crabtree's girl!" said Genny. "This is little Hazel Crabtree!"

"Course it is," said Bernese, a world of Frett contempt ripe in her voice. The two families had nothing in common and had long regarded each other with animosity. The Fretts were a proudly emotional bunch. No Frett lips ever touched liquor (they even sipped grape juice at communion), but their moods could sweep through them as fierce and fast as any drug. Their decisions came from the gut, and they didn't care one fig for what outsiders thought of their actions.

The Crabtrees, on the other hand, almost universally had the deadeye, and their emotional range ran from sullen right on up to enraged. Wary and canny, they felt nothing more keenly than the gaze of the disapproving world, a world that was out to get them. Their responses to feeling judged were shrugs and sneers followed by lashings of great, cold violence.

The Fretts were meticulous, order incarnate. The Crabtrees lived in unimaginable squalor. The Fretts lived within convention and tradition, while the Crabtrees spread like kudzu, generating chaos and more Crabtrees, generally without benefit of marriage. The Fretts had both money and the respect of the town. They were the royal fish in this tiniest of ponds, and the Crabtrees fed along the bottom.

This defied what the Crabtrees felt should be the natural order of things, because the Crabtrees, like everyone else in Between, were white. They were paper-white, pure Irish, most of them, maybe a little French or English or German blood in some of the branches. It was merely annoying when morally solvent white folks looked down on them, but it was maddening to take it from the Fretts, the children of a white father and a mother who was, as Ona put it, "half a damn squaw-Indian."

Hazel had closed her eyes for a moment, resting. Genny looked down at Hazel's pale eyelids, so smooth and dewy, and said, "Goodness grief, honey, how old are you? Bernese, you be sweet. She's a baby herself!"

Bernese said, "Apples don't fall off trees and land all the way downtown. She's almost sixteen, and I think her mama is my age."

"I hate you," said Hazel to Bernese, and then her eyes opened wide again. "Oh no, it's coming."

"This time you push," said Bernese.

"I don't know how to push," said Hazel, looking desperately to Genny. "Oh no, please do something. Do anything."

"Push like you're going number two," said Bernese, and Genny said, "Bernese! Really!"

"How many babies have you had?" Bernese barked, and Genny dropped her eyes. "So shut up and let me help this girl."

"Do something," said Hazel to Genny. "Talk to me. Anything. Sing."

Genny shook her head, but she opened her mouth and started to sing in her quavering soprano. "'There's not a friend like the lowly Jesus . . .'"

Hazel lashed up at Bernese with one foot and screamed, "Oh fuck, please not Jesus." Bernese caught her thrashing leg at the knee and bent it back toward her abdomen. "Get ready," said

Bernese, anchoring the heel of her other hand at the top of Hazel's swollen belly.

"I'm not ready. Help me," Hazel wailed to Genny, and twisted on the floor while Bernese wrestled with her leg. "Help me. Sing. But not about Jesus."

Genny patted frantically at Hazel with her free hand and sang the first thing that came into her head. "'Sigh no more, ladies, sigh no more, / Men were deceivers ever . . .'"

Hazel thrashed and writhed. "It's here! It's here!"

Bernese bore down, saying, "Push, you hear me? You better push."

Genny kept singing. "'One foot in sea and one on shore, / To one thing constant never . . .'"

Hazel was shaking her head but pushing anyway. Genny saw my head coming out, slick with blood and slime, and she paled and felt her head getting light. Hazel's death grip on her arm was the only thing keeping her upright. She closed her eyes, weaving herself back and forth, and sang, "'Then sigh not so, / But let them go, / And be you blithe and bonny; / Converting all your sounds of woe / Into hey nonny, nonny.'"

"It's crowning. Where is Stacia?" said Bernese. "Genny, get between her legs and catch this baby."

But Genny had reached her limit. "'Hey nonny, nonny,'" she sang with her eyes squinched tight.

Stacia came in from the kitchen with a pan of hot water and clean dish towels, scissors, and string. She set them down and knelt between Hazel's legs as the next contraction hit.

Hazel pushed as Bernese bore down on her abdomen, and my head came out of her. I arrived faceup, staring into the light with my eyes open and angry. It seemed to Stacia that I was staring up at her. My eyes were puffed almost shut, slitted, but she thought my gaze was meeting hers. I looked aware to her, so angry and alive. My face was framed by the darkness that was eating the edges of her vision, and in that moment there were only the two of us. Not even Hazel existed.

Stacia dipped a finger into my mouth to clear it. As she did so, my eyebrows lowered and my lips opened wider. I looked like I was squalling, but it was airless and silent, my body still compressed inside Hazel. As Stacia stared at me, I spun slowly in the birth canal, rotating, turning facedown. Stacia cradled my forehead in her rough palm as another contraction hit. I came slithering out, slick as a fish into her waiting arms.

"Is it done? Is it done?" Hazel said.

"I think so, honey," said Genny, peeking. The skin around her eyes and mouth had turned green. "Oh please, please, I think it's over." Stacia looked across Hazel's prone body, and her eyes met Genny's. Genny signed one-handed, *Boy? Girl?*

Stacia slid her thumb down the side of her right cheek.

"A girl," said Genny, rocking herself and nodding. "That's good. That's not scary. Look, you have a sweet little girl."

"My cooter hurts," said Hazel.

Stacia stayed where she was, holding me with the cord trailing down into Hazel.

"Is it out?" asked Hazel. "Why is it coming again?"

"Again?" Genny squawked.

"It won't be half so hard this time," said Bernese to both of them, and she leaned down and grasped the cord, easing out the afterbirth as Hazel contracted. Genny shut her eyes and started singing again, "'Hey nonny, nonny, so weep no more, my ladies.'" Hazel relaxed, snuffling, and Stacia busied herself cleaning me up and tying off the cord.

"Genny, shut up that caterwauling," said Bernese.

"'Hey nonny,'" Genny sang, trailing off. "Please, is it over?" Hazel released her, and when Genny opened her eyes and looked down, she saw perfect red handprints braceleting her wrist.

"Who is Nonny?" asked Hazel in a puny voice.

"What?" said Bernese.

"She was singing 'Hey, Nonny.' Who is Nonny? Is that the baby?"

Stacia stood up, holding me wrapped in a towel. I was wide awake, staring up into her cloud-gray eyes, solemn and interested. Bernese had moved between Hazel's legs.

"You look good. No tearing. You want to hold your baby?" said Bernese to Hazel.

"No," said Hazel, and she turned her face away, looking at the shattered terrarium. A caterpillar had negotiated its way out over the glass and rubble and was oozing down the sideboard.

"It's a nice little girl, and she is looking much cleaner," said Genny. She sat slumped and exhausted, flat on her bottom on the floor by Hazel's head, faintly rocking herself.

Stacia looked up from me at last, and Genny signed that she should hand me to Hazel, but Stacia did not move. She looked at Hazel as Hazel said, "I don't want it," shaking her head petulantly. Stacia curled her lip and held me tighter.

"Maybe later," said Bernese.

Stacia stamped her foot to get Genny's attention and signed one-handed, cradling me in her other arm.

"Stacia says it's her baby," said Genny.

"Obviously," said Bernese. "Give the girl a minute. She'll take it."

Genny shook her head. "No, I mean Stacia's saying, 'This is my baby. I want her.' Stacia wants the baby."

There was a long silence as everyone digested this. Bernese looked from Stacia to Genny and back again and then snorted. "Don't be ridiculous." She tilted her face and bellowed up the stairs, "Lou, leave the boys for a sec and throw me down some sheets. The oldest ones we have. And any old towels you see in that linen closet."

"Stacia says, 'I am not being ridiculous. She came to me. She's mine.' I think she really wants this baby, Bernese."

"Oh good," said Hazel to Genny. "Take it. It can be y'all's Nonny."

"Let's get you to the hospital," said Bernese.

Hazel immediately said, "No hospital. They'll call Mama, and I'll never get away. She'll keep me. And she'll make me keep it." Her eyes filled up with tears. "Please, I'm fine. Just let me sleep a little and then I'll go away. Y'all can have that Nonny."

"You need to see a doctor," said Bernese. "You could have a complication and bleed out on my floor."

"I won't do that. I promise," said Hazel, and the tears spilled down her cheeks. "You said I looked good. And if you make me go to the hospital, I'll throw myself under a truck. I really will. I'll throw Nonny, too."

Stacia stamped her foot again, signing, and Genny said, "Stacia's insisting. She says, 'This baby is my baby. I know it. I don't know how to do it, how to keep her, but Bernese does. Bernese, you do it.'"

Genny got up and walked over, folding back the towel to look at me. "Oh, goodness grief, look at all that red hair. And the teeny feet."

"This is not like a hamster, Genny," snapped Bernese. "This is a person. A little Crabtree person."

Lou's pale face appeared at the top of the stairs. His brown hair, thin and gingery, was rumpled, and his comb-over was hanging down past his ear on one side. He had wrapped the sheets and towels into a bundle, and he tossed it over the banister to Bernese.

"Get back with the boys," Bernese commanded, and he disappeared. Bernese began gently packing the towels under Hazel's bottom to catch the fluids that were oozing out of her and soaking into the carpet.

Stacia was signing again, rapid and angry, her free hand flashing. Genny interpreted, and as she spoke, she got the roller-coaster look that she always got when she had to say things out loud for Stacia that she would not have said for a million dollars on her own account. Her eyelids lifted so high that the whites were visible all the way around.

"She says, 'Don't lecture me, and don't dare patronize me. I am telling you something real here, if you aren't too stupid to hear it. So shut up and help me.' "

Bernese ignored Stacia; she was still carefully arranging the old sheets and talking to Hazel. "Are you comfortable? You want some water?"

"Please don't tell," begged Hazel.

"Your mama's Ona Crabtree?" Bernese said.

"No," said Hazel.

But Genny said, "Yes, that's her mama." Over Hazel's head,

Genny's eyes met Bernese's, and Genny mouthed, "Drinks," then bobbed her head in a wise nod.

Bernese wrapped the afterbirth in the nastiest towel. She noticed Genny's hands creeping back up her braid and said, "Genny, for the love of Baby Jesus, get your hands off yourself. Don't start picking now when it's all over but steam-cleaning the carpet. Do you need a pill?"

Genny shook her head and rubbed at her forearm for a second, then went back to signing what Bernese was saying for Stacia. Bernese said, "Good, then make yourself useful. See if that girl won't nurse her baby. She should nurse it while it's awake. I am going to go get some trash bags, and I will call for an ambulance from the kitchen."

Bernese headed up the long hall, her arms full of filthy towels. Hazel watched her go, panting, and then she rolled over painfully and got to her hands and knees.

Genny said, "Honey, you should be still." Stacia, holding me, hesitated. She tried to hand me to Genny, but Genny, still dizzy and faintly green, did not take me. Stacia walked toward Hazel, holding me, and Genny followed, saying, "Honey, you need to lie down on this pad, you are . . . Oh my. You are leaking things."

Hazel crawled miserably across the foyer. She left the doorway to the den and crept back into the glass. It bit into her knees as she headed for the long table. Stacia followed, with Genny clucking and tutting along behind her. Hazel reared up suddenly on her bleeding knees and grabbed the gun off the sideboard. Stacia froze, and Genny almost ran into her.

Bernese was at the end of the hall when Hazel called, "If you go one step more, I will shoot you."

Bernese stopped and turned around. Hazel was so weak she

was swaying drunkenly from side to side, trying to hold up the heavy gun so she could aim down the hall. "I will shoot you if you tell my mama."

"Put that down, you idiot. I don't need more holes in my woodwork," Bernese said.

"I mean it," said Hazel.

"Spare me," said Bernese contemptuously. Blood was trickling out of Hazel, oozing in rivulets down her thighs. "You can barely stay erect. You couldn't hit me if I stood dead still and gave you all six tries."

"Fine," said Hazel. She twisted at the waist, bringing the gun around. Stacia was close behind her, and Hazel pressed the barrel into Stacia's belly, under me.

"Bet I can hit *her*," Hazel said.

Bernese became very still, and it was silent for a long, ugly moment.

"Jesus, help us," whispered Genny, barely above a breath.

"Will you stop with that Jesus? I told you!" Hazel's voice was shrill.

Stacia moved her free hand up very slowly to sign, making no sudden movements, and Genny managed to look away from the gun and focus on the familiar sight of Stacia speaking. "Hazel, Stacia wants to know where your sweetheart is," said Genny. Her voice was tinny and high.

Hazel looked in confusion from Stacia's slowly signing hand to her face and said, "My sweetheart?"

Genny was so afraid that all she could do was watch Stacia's hand and repeat after it, saying what Stacia's hand was saying, not looking at anything else. "You have a baby. You must have had a sweetheart."

Hazel sucked air in through her nostrils, loud. "I had a lot of sweethearts," she said. She shrugged. Bernese knelt down silently and set her armful of towels on the floor.

"I had a sweetheart," said Genny for Stacia, her eyes locked on Stacia's fingers. "Just the one." Stacia signed, her movements gentle and slow, as the luna moths fluttered up around the light and the barrel of the gun pressed into her soft belly. "His name was Frank. I don't have him anymore. He did something stupid, and I'm done with him. I thought I'd marry him and we'd live with Genny. Me and Frank and my sister, and I would have my own babies. But that's not going to happen now." Stacia kept signing, but her gaze lifted, and she looked over Hazel, meeting Bernese's eyes as Bernese stood and began creeping up the hall toward them, step by silent step. Stacia glanced back down at Hazel, at her trembling hand on the gun, and then back at Bernese. "Do you know what Usher's syndrome is?" Genny said for her.

"No," said Hazel. Her thin arms were trembling with effort, and Genny was terrified that she'd inadvertently pull the trigger. Genny kept her eyes on Stacia's hand and interpreted, hardly aware of what she was saying. The gun pressing into Stacia's belly was a black beast in her peripheral vision.

"It means I'm deaf," Genny interpreted. "I was born deaf. And it means my eyes are going. I'll be blind in another ten years, fifteen if I am lucky. The edges are closing in already. It's dark beside me, like shutters are being drawn. At some point my depth perception will go, and I won't be able to work anymore. I'm a sculptor; I make molds and cast dolls in porcelain. That's my work. So I've lost my sweetheart. And I'm losing my work. And here's this baby.

"This baby is mine. You brought her to this house, and she slid into my arms. No one is going to call your mama, because no one is going to take this baby from me. Frank is gone, my work is going, and I've been asking God, 'Why does my heart keep beating?' And you brought me the answer. Don't worry about Bernese. She won't do a thing to take this baby out of my arms. She's going to help me keep this baby. Once she sees my side— and she's seeing it now—she won't worry about what's practical or legal or even what's right. She'll make it happen. I'll take this baby, and you can go home. Home or anywhere you like."

Stacia looked hard into Hazel's eyes and signed, and Genny said, "But if you shoot me, Bernese is going to have to call your mama."

After a long moment, Hazel's arms dropped, pointing the gun down into the carpet. She sagged, and Bernese ran the last few steps up the hall and caught her before she slumped into the glass. Bernese peeled the gun out of her limp hand, flipped the safety on, then set it carefully back on the table.

"Help me," said Bernese, and Genny darted forward, panting, and together they lifted Hazel out of the glass and half carried her back to her pad of old sheets and towels.

"All right, then," said Bernese. "Let's make sure you haven't ruptured anything. What a mess."

Hazel closed her eyes. The sun was rising, spilling pale light across the lawn. Stacia turned and shut the front door. After a few minutes, Bernese got up from between Hazel's legs.

"You look okay," Bernese said. Her gardening shoes were sitting by the front door, and she slipped them on and crunched into the glass. She picked up the phone.

"Bernese!" said Genny. Hazel's eyes flew open and she started crying again, making piteous mewling noises deep in her throat.

But Stacia smiled and shook her head, meeting Bernese's eyes with a cool and level gaze.

"Don't get your pants in a bunch, Genny," said Bernese. "I'm calling Isaac." She added to Hazel, "That's my lawyer, so stop with that fuss. You sound like a kicked cat."

Bernese dialed from memory and stood waiting for the phone to wake up Isaac Davids.

"It's me," she said when he answered. "Yes, I know what time it is, but this is an emergency. You need to walk down here, quick as you can . . . I know, but pull some pants on and hurry down. Stacia needs us to help her steal Ona Crabtree's grandbaby."

# ABOUT THE AUTHOR

JOSHILYN JACKSON is a native of the Deep South, a former actor and award-winning teacher, and now a full-time writer and mother of two. Her work has previously appeared in *TriQuarterly* and *Calyx*, as well as the anthology *ChickLit II*. She is currently at work on her second novel. She lives with her family outside of Atlanta, Georgia. You can visit her Web site at www.joshilynjackson.com.